SHATTERED
ROSE

TAMMY L. GRAY

ACKNOWLEDGMENTS

A special thanks to Kristina Krause of Redzenradish Photography for allowing me to use her beautiful rose photograph for the cover art.

To my brother, Josh Webb, of Root Radius, thank you so much for giving me the courage to self publish and for designing the amazing cover for my book, along with providing all the media marketing I needed. You are a true friend and constant inspiration for me.

To Brandon Hixson for my book trailer video, thank you so much. Your talent and professionalism is remarkable.

To my friends and family who helped make my dream become a reality, especially my sister, Angel, my aunt, Nancy and cousin, Katy who all painstakingly edited each word, offering guidance along the way

To my favorite cheerleaders, Angie and Tonya, thanks so much for all your encouragement and belief in me; it made all the difference in the world.

To my wonderful husband and children, thanks for suffering through the fast food dinners and lack of laundry so I could pour my heart and soul into this book.

Finally, to my best friend, Sara, who has taken this journey with me for nineteen years and whose steadfast faith in me gave me the courage to overcome.

For my best friend, Sara, whose love and support
encouraged me to accomplish the impossible

PREFACE

Nothing made sense; nothing was in focus.

I sat down, hoping to end the crushing pain. I didn't know who I was anymore. Everything I once valued and held true, I had discarded without any regard for the consequences.

Numbness stretched over my shaking body, leaving me cold and empty. If only it would reach my mind, consumed still with thoughts of him. Thoughts frozen in permanent rewind, reminding me over and over again of how much I had failed.

How did I get here? How did I let the chains get so tight they were crippling every part of my body, dragging me further and further into this pit?

I heard screaming in my head, begging for me to let out its fury, but I just sat there, unable to move, trapped in a silent prison of my own making.

The truth glared at me, mocking me for denying it for so long.

I had become nothing…and he knew it.

The bench shifted slightly and a warm hand covered mine. Looking up through my tears, I saw warmth and compassion in the eyes of a stranger.

A distant voice became audible, drifting slowly in the air, and penetrated the depth of my heart.

"Even the darkness will not be dark to you; the night will shine like the day, for darkness is as light to you. For you created my inmost being; you knit me together in my mother's womb. I praise you because I am fearfully and wonderfully made."

The words rolled around in my head and suddenly, deep down, I felt a spark. I had forgotten the feeling as it had been so long since I'd felt anything other than despair, but it was there… hope, just a glimmer, but hope all the same.

"Dear Lord, I may not know who she is yet, but until that day, I pray Your hand never leaves her side. I pray that You sustain her when she is in the transitions of her life and guide her on the path You've chosen for her…"

1. APARTMENT 204

Four Months Earlier…

I hated change. Totally detested it usually, but not today. Even though change meant I hauled all my meager belongings—currently packed floor to ceiling in my Toyota Corolla—to yet another residence in less than two weeks.

But I refused to complain. Truth was, I would have moved for days if it meant the same end result… my first apartment.

The housing office had placed me with two girls I didn't know. Kaitlyn Summers and Naomi Bennett, who was currently on exchange to Portugal.

I knocked lightly, my nervousness blending with excitement.

No answer.

My lungs deflated. I wasn't expecting a welcome party or anything, but I did feel a little disappointed no one was home.

Opening the door, I was pleased to see that the apartment was fairly clean, dishes in the sink and in the living room, but nothing unbearable.

I walked through the room, running my hand along the large brown and tan sectional sofa, and set my bag down on the end table.

It would have felt much like a waiting room if not for the outrageous loveseat sticking out like an eyesore. It was fuzzy, bright red and in the shape of lips.

My laughter echoed in the room as I wondered which roommate purchased that thing.

I unlocked my bedroom door and noted the room was identical to those in the dorm, cold and sterile. The loneliness of freshman year threatened to resurface, but I pushed it down, choosing instead to focus on the positive—a small, private bathroom.

I inched to the window. In front of me were two large trees, parted just enough to expose the sun glistening off the campus lake.

Pulling up the blinds, I let the rays warm my face. I felt happy and healthy for the first time in years.

Grabbing my cell phone, I plopped on the bare mattress and dialed my best friend. I had known Cara since middle school, and she was one of the few people in the world I trusted.

"Hello?"

"Guess where I am?" I asked, my voice gushing with excitement.

"Um, could it be your new apartment? Or did our

amazing summer together convince you to transfer to Georgia and go to school near your hometown?"

"I wish. Tell the administration to give me an alumni scholarship, and I'm there." That wasn't entirely true. I loved that Winsor was in Ashville, North Carolina, putting nine glorious hours between me and my family.

"Have you met any hot neighbors who are just dying to help you move all your stuff in… without shirts on of course?"

"You are officially boy crazy. I haven't met anyone yet, not even my new roommate."

She must have sensed my unease. "Are you nervous? I mean, are you feeling anything we should talk about?"

I wasn't surprised Cara asked me that question. I had had struggles peak last year and let the pressure of maintaining my grades get the best of me. In a moment of full disclosure, I opted to tell Cara about my issues, but had since wondered if sharing had been a mistake.

"Cara, I'm fine. I haven't thought about it. You don't need to worry." I was lying, but I didn't want to start a long conversation about decisions that weren't a factor today. Today was all about the future, not the past.

"Okay, but I do worry, and I want you to know I'm here for you if it becomes a temptation again. You got it?" She was stern, but I knew it was because she cared.

"I got it. I promise. Okay, I have to go. I left all my things in the car. I'll call you later." I pressed END on my cell phone and headed back out the door.

Seven trips later, I was pulling the last box out of my car, the heaviest one, of course. My legs burned like wood under an acid wash. It seemed crazy that something like stairs could wind me so much when I ran at least three miles a day.

Even the thought relaxed me. I loved to run. It was my retreat. A place where I could clear the chaos. I was my own worst enemy, analyzing and re-analyzing everything around me, but when I ran, I felt invincible.

Unfortunately, I wasn't invincible climbing the stairs.

I missed the first step and went sprawling forward. The box slammed into the staircase. In my attempt to recover, my exposed shin slid across the concrete step making me wince in pain. I got to my feet and watched the box bounce down the stairs, hitting the ground with a thud.

Footsteps approached from behind. "Hey there, need some help?"

I turned. Cara must have seen the future because there stood two attractive men in running shorts, sweat glistening on their bare, muscular chests.

Heat filled my cheeks. "I'm okay." My awkwardness around guys was annoyingly obvious.

The one with light brown hair and matching eyes

grabbed the box easily off the ground while the other, the more attractive one of the two, eyed me like a lion stalking his next meal. He was the first one to notice I was now bleeding.

"I think you may need to put something on that," he noted, walking up to me. "I'm Aaron. This here is Danny. You must be new here." He said the words as if he knew every woman that lived in the building, but then again, he was looking at me as if he already knew me too… in the biblical sense.

My skin crawled as if tiny little ants were marching through my veins.

Danny adjusted the box in his arms. "Don't mind my roommate; he has no manners. What apartment are you in?"

His words allowed me to break Aaron's eye hold. "204. You don't have to. I can get it."

"Nonsense." Danny navigated up the stairs with ease despite his heavy load. I followed behind him, trying not to fidget.

I felt Aaron's gaze on my backside.

The ants returned and with greater numbers. My shorts weren't that short, but I still wondered if the back of my legs looked grotesque. With each step, my insecurity got more and more extreme. I hated when anyone looked at my body.

The door was propped open, so Danny strolled in casually and set down the box on the coffee table.

"Are you new to Winsor?"

"No. I'm a Sophomore, but I was in the dorms

last year."

"That's cool." He looked around the apartment as if searching for someone. "Is your roommate home?"

"No. Do you know her?"

Aaron snorted. "He wishes."

Danny hit his friend and hissed something under his breath. A second of strained silence followed.

"Well, thanks for helping me." I walked them back out to the hall, a silent encouragement to leave.

Danny hesitated, his voice soft and unsure. "We're in apartment 315. Y'all are welcome to come by tonight. We're having some friends over."

Aaron leaned his hand against the frame and moved closer than was natural between two relative strangers. The scent of sweat and raw masculinity assaulted my nose. His gaze drifted from the top of my head down the length of my body.

I didn't know how it was possible to feel so violated without even a touch, but I did.

"You should definitely come... um?" He raised his eyebrows as a way to ask my name.

"Avery." I hugged myself, wishing I had something to cover my tank top. Maybe a full sheet or oversized lab coat. Anything that would stop his perusal of my body. A body I couldn't look at in the mirror without flinching.

He winked at me one more time before Danny pushed him along. "See you around, Avery. Hopefully tonight."

I shut the door with a sigh and then scolded

myself. I couldn't be a recluse forever. New apartment. New me.

Oh, who was I kidding, I wasn't going anywhere near those guys.

"Dear Lord, Your way is in the sea and in the mighty waters. Your footprints may not be known, but I pray You guide each one of her steps…"

2. NEW ROOMMATES

I sat in my room trying to conjure up any excuse to procrastinate unpacking until I heard laughter fill the apartment. The light giggle was contagious, one that made a person want to laugh even when he or she had no idea what was funny.

I was drawn to the sound as if it held some kind of promise.

Peeking out of my room, I saw the source. She was talking on the phone and laying on the hideous lip love seat with her head hanging over the edge. Her hair was long and dark, with alternating streaks of blue and purple at the ends. She had it pulled to the side with a sparkly black hair comb and wore tight red pants with black converses.

I waited until she got off the phone and then knocked on the doorframe so I wouldn't startle her.

"Hi, I'm Avery, your new roommate. Are you Kaitlyn?"

She stood up from the lips, looking at me with a mix of interest and horror.

I immediately noticed her body, a habit I'd been trying to break for years. It was perfect. Thin and petite, yet curvy where it mattered.

The girl was a classic beauty… the kind artists of old would use as their muse to create stunning portraits. Her skin was like porcelain ivory, not pale, just delicate.

"I am certainly not Kaitlyn. That is a name my mother gave me. I go by Issy, which is short for Isadora, my middle name. It was originally my grandma's, who was totally cool." Her stare remained intense, a complete contrast to her animated style. "We were wondering when you'd get here."

"We? I thought Naomi was in Portugal."

"Oh, she is. I'm talking about my cousin, Jake. He crashes here a lot, especially since I've been alone these last few weeks. He's a little protective of me, to put it mildly. He has a key to the apartment, so don't be freaked out if he just walks in." She said all this flippantly, as if it were a normal thing that a guy I didn't know had a key to my apartment.

Unease settled over me. My comfort zone was already stretched, and I had a feeling Issy planned to rip it to shreds.

She crossed her arms and examined me. "What's your story? Are you wild and crazy, totally annoying, or a kleptomaniac?"

I laughed shyly and joined her in the living room. "No, I'm afraid I'm boring, somewhat clean, very private, and not at all annoying, I hope."

"Fantastic! Then you and I will get along fine. I was worried when the University said they were giving away Betsy's room. The three of us have known each other since high school, and well, you've seen the crazies around here."

I had to hold in a laugh, thinking of how most people who met Issy for the first time would probably use that same descriptor.

"Having hot roommates is kind of an essential part of the guy magnet thing." She looked me up and down as if to check my credentials. "You'll do just fine. You've got that hot Midwestern look."

"I'm sorry?" *Was that a compliment?*

"You know, blond hair, blue eyes, sweet face." She shrugged. "It's a good package. By the way, we're heading to Caesars tonight to catch the *Wild Cats* play. They totally rock. You wanna come?"

"Um, thanks." I had been to Caesars one time last year when I first met my old roommate. She was hooked up in a matter of minutes and left me to make conversation with complete strangers until I finally dragged her home. Remembering what a colossal disappointment that night was made it pretty easy to decline. "You know what? I'll take a rain check. I have a ton to do tonight."

"Suit yourself, but if you change your mind, you know where to find us."

As I watched Issy frolic and sing around the apartment as if in her own Disney movie, I almost changed my mind out of sheer curiosity.

I envied her lightheartedness. She was so dynamic and free, whereas I felt like I was constantly contained in a box. Ironically, I had spent my life running in different directions just trying to escape but realized last year I was my own jailer. I had put these expectations and standards in my life that I just had to achieve, making perfection my unending pursuit.

I looked in the mirror and I pulled back my hair. "What is wrong with you?" I scolded myself. "This is a great day, and you are a strong, self-sufficient woman."

With my perspective back on track, I put my headset on and headed out the door. At least for the next thirty minutes or so, I would feel free.

My run was amazing. I wasn't sure if it was from the adrenalin of moving or my own frustration with my shyness.

Either way, I felt great. This was a fresh start, a chance to have it all.

With new determination, I put on my favorite tank and pajama shorts, set my iPod to blaring, and started unpacking my mess.

My room was finally finished after what felt like hours. The closet was just big enough for my scarce wardrobe, and each one of my enormous engineering books fit nicely on the bookshelf over my desk.

The two blank walls were now covered in my favorite photographic art pieces.

Hands on my hips, I looked at my final product. One word—inspirational.

I started brushing my teeth, fully enjoying every beat coming from my Pandora dance station.

Next thing I knew, I was in full rock star mode, using my toothbrush as a microphone and my bed as a stage. It was only after the song ended and I heard the applause die down in my head that I opened my eyes and saw him standing there.

He leaned casually against the door frame with his arms folded, sporting a smile that said he had seen more than a few seconds of my *High School Musical* reenactment.

My startled scream echoed off the walls.

I jumped off the bed and slammed my door shut, allowing him only a second to jump out of the way.

Oh my gosh, that did not just happen!

My heart raced faster than a cheetah on speed, knowing how ridiculous I must have looked. Maybe he would be the type to blow off embarrassing situations and make you feel like nothing happened.

I slowly regained composure and cracked open my door. He was still standing there chuckling. Nope, he wasn't that type at all.

My cheeks flushed a crimson red. "You must be Jake. Um, sorry I slammed the door on you like that. You startled me." I fumbled over my words, sure this guy must think I was not only a nutcase but also an idiot.

"And you must be Avery, although Issy didn't

mention you were a performer." He drew out the words and paused, giving me an opportunity to respond.

I didn't take it.

"Where is she, by the way?"

Relief at the change in subject filled my voice. "She left hours ago. Said she was heading to Caesars to watch a band play."

"Caesars. Ugh. I hate that place. Total meat market." He walked past me and started looking around my room, stopping at one of my art pieces. It was a black-and-white photograph of a high swinging bridge completely engulfed in dense fog.

"Why didn't you go?"

"With that glowing review? Go figure." I felt exposed and vulnerable, so naturally I resorted to sarcastic wit.

He continued to examine the photo. He was tall; definitely over six feet, and I immediately noticed the resemblance to Issy. They both had the same intense eyes—iridescent lime with brown specks. His hair was dark as well, almost black, but Jake didn't seem to have the same need to add in multiple colors.

"Besides, I wanted to get settled in," I continued.

"Yeah, I can see that." He looked around my room and then back to the photo. "This print is amazing. Where did you get it?"

"They had an art fair downtown last spring. I picked it up there. I have the photographer's card if you want it."

"Sure, I'd like that." He smiled, confident and charismatic, and electricity bounced around the room and washed over me in a wave.

Old insecurities returned, leaving my mouth ashy and my movements awkward.

I didn't have much experience with boys and less with ones who looked like they belonged modeling Calvin Klein underwear. To make matters worse, he had an intoxicating smell that fully matched his self-assured demeanor.

My feet were having a hard time functioning, but I managed to pick up the card and hand it to him without tripping over myself. "I can tell her you came by?"

"No need, I'll probably see her before you do anyway."

He walked of out my room and then glanced back at me, full of swagger and charm. "Nice to meet you, Avery."

"You too, Jake."

He left the apartment, but his memory and scent lingered, leaving me restless long after I settled into bed for the night.

A loud bang shot me straight up at two in the morning. The room was completely dark except for light peeking under my bedroom door.

The next bang, followed by laughter, sent me opening my door a crack.

My eyes took a second to adjust to the bright light, but eventually I could see the cause of the commotion. Issy had her arm wrapped around Jake's neck and was singing what I was sure were lyrics from the band they watched tonight. It took her only a second to notice me.

"Roomie! We missed you tonight. Didn't we, Jake?" She attempted to walk over to my room but stumbled over the boots she had just kicked off. Jake was luckily strong enough to keep her vertical, but she was fighting off his hands. I quickly walked over to her and put her other arm around my neck.

"Aren't you sweet? Jake, she's sweet, isn't she?"

I secretly wondered if he agreed, but his eyes were vacant, fully absent from anything going on around him.

"Did you have fun tonight?" I asked, trying to keep my eyes off Jake—a restraint as difficult as turning down gooey chocolate cake.

"Yes. It was amazing. The lead singer totally hit on me. He is so cute. He pulled me on stage, and I got to sing with the band." She threw her arms in the air and spun around, almost falling again. "I was supposed to meet him after the show, but Jake here totally got in the way, like he always does, and here I am." She glared at Jake. "Did I tell you how much I don't like you?"

He appeared to snap back to reality. "Only about twenty times on the way home. Now, lets get you to bed or you won't like *anyone* in the morning."

We laid her down, and while Jake was pulling the covers up, I went to the sink and got her a glass of water and aspirin. I set them on her nightstand under Jake's watchful eye and left the room.

She cursed at him and then she must have passed out. He quietly shut her door and fell onto the sofa.

"Is she going to be okay?"

"She'll be fine. We ran into her ex at the bar, and then it all seemed to go downhill." His voice matched the exhaustion on his face. Jake ran his hands through his thick, dark hair and started rubbing his temples.

"You look tired. I'll let you get some sleep." I started to head back to my room. I'd never been one to linger when I felt uncomfortable.

"Don't go. Stay and talk to me. I'm too wired to sleep right now anyway." He shot me pleading puppy eyes that could only be described as irresistible, and for the first time since I woke up, I realized I probably looked like Medusa.

I ran my fingers through my hair to try and settle the waves and slipped into the kitchen to snatch a mint. "Would you like something to drink?"

"Sure, thanks."

I handed a water bottle to Jake and sat down on the opposite side of the couch, keeping a safe distance.

After a slow, deliberate gulp, he set down the water and fell back on the cushions. "I love Issy to death, but I hate when she gets like this."

"Does she always drink that much?"

"No, not really. I mean, she's a drinker, don't get me wrong, but it's usually for fun. Tonight felt a little more forced." He stretched out his arms, his long limbs settling on the back of the couch. His fingers were mere inches from my shoulder.

The anticipation of his touch sent a shiver through my body, and I prayed he didn't notice.

I tried my best to relax as he continued, "Ben did a number on her. She dated the guy two years in high school and then he came here while she finished her senior year. They seemed like the perfect long-distance couple until I ran into him at the Varsity, and he was definitely not acting like he was in any sort of relationship. It seriously took all the willpower I had not to hurt the guy."

"Ohhh," I said, fully understanding her need to escape.

"Yeah, when I told her she was livid. She broke three of her mom's favorite vases before I could calm her down." An affectionate laugh came in response to the memory. "Ironically, I think she was madder at the fact she didn't date anyone else her senior year than she was that he cheated."

Jake suddenly shifted, folding his arms across his chest, and turned his attention to me. "How about you? Any ex-boyfriends lurking around that we need to avoid?"

A shy grin took over my features. "Nope, no current or ex-boyfriends. I haven't had much luck dating." I caught myself before I rambled on further and turned my attention to the lines in my palms, uncomfortable looking at Jake right in the eyes. He was incredibly handsome and seemed to get more so each time I looked at him.

"Yeah, men are jerks." The statement wasn't made with much conviction, but then again, he looked ready to drop.

"It was nice of you to take care of Issy like that," I said, trying to fill the silence.

"That's what I do. I'm a perpetual caretaker." He closed his eyes and rested his head on the back of the couch.

He appeared to be comfortable with me, like we were old friends, but his presence made me jittery. I was acutely aware of him and had to keep reminding myself not to watch him shamelessly.

The silence lingered, and I wondered if he had fallen asleep.

I pushed off from the couch, ready to make my silent exit, when I heard him say, "It started with my mom, the caretaking that is." His eyes were still closed.

"I've always been the man of the house, but when I was fourteen, she got sick and I was the only one around to take care of her. She was able to work for a while longer but then had to go on disability.

"About a year later, my teachers were starting to suspect something was off because of the amount of school I was missing. I deflected as long as I could, but finally, one of the teachers called the state and Child Protective Services showed up at my door."

One of his eyes popped open to meet mine and

then closed again. I was riveted, hanging on to every word.

"At that point, my mom was having a hard time even standing on her own, and she needed more care than I could give her. We were living off her disability, which barely covered her meds, so things were pretty rough. They called my Aunt Diana, Issy's mom, and within a week we moved in with them. Things got better at that point, and Issy and I have been best friends ever since…" His voice trailed off at the end, but he didn't move.

My heart swelled with compassion. I had no idea why Jake would tell me his story when he'd known me for all of twenty minutes, but I felt honored. I also saw him differently. This was a guy who was handsome and caring…a true anomaly.

"I'm sorry," I whispered, not knowing what else to say. "Thank you for trusting me."

He didn't say anything else, and I realized he had fallen asleep. I grabbed a blanket from the closet, draped it over him, and headed to my room.

My body wouldn't let me leave without getting one more glance. His head lay relaxed on the back of the couch, and his chest rose and fell in peaceful rhythm.

My stomach started to flutter, sending waves of excitement through my whole body. I had heard about crushes from Cara but never experienced one myself. However, as I watched him sleep for far longer than was natural, I knew I was in trouble.

Dear Lord, I know You will place people in her path, people who may love her or hurt her. I pray those people bring her to know You either for the first time or as a rekindling of the relationship You already share…"

3. JAKE

The next morning I jumped out of bed, far too eager to see Jake again. I ran to the bathroom, brushed my teeth and hair, and put on a light sheen of makeup. I was going for the I-look-this-gorgeous-every-time-I-get-out-bed look.

I opened my door and let out all my breath when I saw the empty sofa. My disappointment concerned me. I hardly knew this guy.

Issy sat hunched over the bar, slowly sipping what looked like a disgusting green drink. She looked awful. She still wore her clothes from the night before, and her makeup was smeared down her cheeks.

"Don't say a word. I'm fully aware of how scary I look this morning, and I really don't care." She took a sip of her green concoction. "When did Jake leave?"

"I'm not sure. He fell asleep on the couch, and then I went to bed." I tried to sound nonchalant, but Issy's brow shot up.

"I was kind of brutal to him last night." She seemed genuinely remorseful until a moment later when her eyes became cold. "I'm so frustrated. I mean, I love him, don't get me wrong, but I'm in college, and I feel like I have my dad following me everywhere I go. It's not like he doesn't have his own demons. He spent the last two years in a frat house hooking up with anything in a skirt." She let out a dramatic sigh, reached her arm across the bar and laid her head on it. "Owww…my head hurts!"

I held in a laugh. I was starting to wonder if this girl ever had a thought that she didn't verbalize. I looked at her drink again and couldn't help but ask, "What on earth are you drinking?"

"It's my hangover juice. Does the trick every time." She sat back up and looked at me intensely, making me a little nervous. I swear her eyes could penetrate the soul. "So, what did you and my cousin talk about last night?"

I shifted uncomfortably and started pulling cereal out of the pantry. "What do you mean?"

"Oh, come on, that's Jake's MO—the tortured, brooding type. Girls love it."

I didn't know what to say. I wanted to believe her words had no effect on me. After all, I'd just met the guy, so who cared what his "MO" was. Yet, my neck tensed and my defenses shot up.

"He told me about his mom and how he came to live with you. That's all. We really didn't talk much. He did say you were his best friend, though." I was hoping she would take the bait and change the subject.

"I am his best friend, and that's why I know he's intrigued with you."

My immediate smile gave me away.

"Ah ha, I knew you liked him," she accused. "Yes, he's intrigued with you. I know this because he mentioned you more than twice last night. But don't be deceived. Jake is not the fall in love type. He's just not."

"Maybe I'm not the fall in love type either," I retorted, feeling annoyed by the conversation.

"Oh, please, you have hopeless romantic written all over you."

I rolled my eyes and continued to make my breakfast.

Not deterred, she continued, "Every once in a while a girl gets a glimpse of who he is, and they immediately fall head over heels. But a glimpse is all you get. He doesn't do more than that. Jake is complicated." She seemed careful in how she said those last words.

The hair on the back of my neck stood at attention while my ears tried to filter what her words implied. "What do you mean?"

"It doesn't matter. Just trust me. If I thought he would ever treat a girl the way he treats me, I would move out of the way, but he won't. You need to hear this before it goes too far."

I nodded and looked at her. "I hear you. I do. You don't have to worry; I'm not going to fall head over heels for Jake. I'm much too practical."

She looked at me skeptically but let the subject drop.

Searching for something else to talk about, I remembered Danny. "By the way, I met some guys from apartment 315. I think one of them likes you."

"Ugh, no thanks. I've already met Aaron and feel like I have to shower every time I see him." She shivered to make a point.

I laughed in agreement. "Not him. It was his roommate, Danny, that was asking about you."

"Huh? I haven't met him yet. Doesn't matter, I don't date guys from our apartment complex."

"Really, why not?"

"Because I only go out with guys once, maybe twice, and it's hard enough to make them go away. It would be impossible if they were living just up the stairs from me." She gave me another penetrating stare, almost a warning. "I have a short attention span… much like Jake."

Her words shot directly to my heart and squeezed, which is exactly what I think she wanted.

Issy slid off the stool. "I'm heading back to bed. Don't you dare wake me before two o'clock. It's Saturday, for crying out loud."

She slowly threw herself on her bed, arms and legs sprawled out across the entire thing.

Her words continued to gnaw at me. Jake was intrigued with me? I wasn't sure why. Jake could have any girl he wanted. He didn't have to settle for me.

Then again, Issy was probably reading into things.

Jake treated me like a friend, or at least someone he wanted to get to know. That was enough.

I admired him. He was fourteen when he had to become an adult and take care of his mom. Of course he would be emotionally guarded…who wouldn't be in the same situation? To his credit, he didn't seem bitter at all; just factual, almost nonchalant about what he went through.

I pulled out my statics book and settled in to read the first chapter. No luck. My mind kept going back to Jake on the couch, fully confident and relaxed, yet somehow exposed.

I shook my head, scolding myself, "This is ridiculous." I obviously needed to clear my brain before I could hope to get anything accomplished. Reading could wait; it was time for a run.

The breeze outside immediately cooled my flushed skin. The rain came earlier, and I could smell the scent of raindrops in the air. A haze fell just above the surface of the lake; it was eerie and breathtaking, full of mystery.

The ambience reminded me of Jake, and once again sent my stomach into a whirl.

I stood outside, stretching, when I saw Danny and Aaron descending the stairs. They looked ready to workout too, and I wondered if it was a coincidence.

"Hey, Avery," Danny called from the top of the stairs. "You going for a run?"

"Yep, too beautiful outside to waste the day." I

hoped my curt tone would imply I wanted to be left alone.

Danny seemed oblivious. "Want some company?" Aaron was right behind him, checking me out again.

No, I didn't, but unfortunately, I was one of those people who never said *no*. "Um, sure."

Danny scanned the parking lot. He was trying to be subtle, but I knew who he was looking for.

"Issy's not coming," I offered, hoping that meant they would change their mind about running with me.

Aaron started laughing and stepped around Danny. "Dude, give it up. All right, Avery, let's see what you've got."

We ran down fraternity row. The area was quiet and serene, a vast difference from the life it took on each night. Thankfully, I wasn't having any problems keeping up with the guys.

We passed one house that had plastic cups strung over the front yard and two empty beer kegs in the driveway. Five guys, who I assumed were pledges, were carrying around large trash bags to pick up the mess.

I wondered what house Jake was a part of and what he was doing at one o'clock on a Saturday afternoon.

"You didn't come by last night," Aaron said, pulling me from my thoughts.

"I had to unpack."

Danny's chuckle was lost under his hitched breathing. "That's pretty sad when unpacking is more appealing than hanging out with us. We really are fun, if you get to know us better."

He didn't act like he expected a response, so I just kept quiet and focused on my running stride.

We turned right to take the trail around the lake. The route would put us at six miles for the day, but I didn't care.

Every time Jake popped in my head, my stomach started to flutter, and then came an onset of nervous energy. I picked up the pace, and the boys matched my stride.

"I have to admit I'm impressed," Aaron said, starting to breathe a little heavier now. "Most girls just act like runners; they don't actually do it."

"Cross country in high school. Three years."

He nodded, his mouth puckering as if to show he was impressed. "That explains those rockin' legs of yours. Muscular and tan." He licked his lips. "I bet their smooth as silk, too."

My body almost came to a screeching halt. *Who says stuff like that?* I shook it off, glad that it was a compliment. In junior high, when a someone commented on my legs, they were brutal.

"Shut up, Aaron," Danny scolded. "I'm trying to convince her that we're nice guys."

"You just want to meet her roommate. Geez, dude, just go to Caesars. She's there every Thursday night."

"I'd be happy to introduce you." I cut in when Danny's ears turned red. "But I have to tell you that she doesn't date guys from our apartment complex. From what she said, I really don't think she dates at all."

Aaron snickered and gave me a yeah-right stare. "That's what all girls say. They act like they don't care, but deep down they are all dying to fall in love."

Issy was suddenly in my head. "Women get a glimpse of who he is and fall head over heels, but that's all they get, a glimpse."

The words were haunting. Was I going to be one of those girls? I was obviously headed in that direction. Jake had consumed my every thought since I went to bed last night.

Determined, I pushed the green-eyed boy out of my head and turned back to Aaron. "Well, I don't know her all that well, so I couldn't tell you."

We made our way back to the apartment and I checked my time. 52:25… by far my fastest in a while.

Aaron gripped his knees to catch a breath. "Girl, I don't think I'm running with you again."

I brushed off his compliment and started towards the stairs, ready to say goodbye. The guys followed, but I noticed they hung by the landing, not taking the stairs up to their apartment.

"Are you guys going out tonight?" Danny asked, looking shy again.

I felt bad for him. He obviously had a pretty severe crush on Issy and hadn't even met her yet.

"I'm pretty sure she's still asleep, but you're welcome to come grab a water from my fridge." I had no idea how Issy would feel about me bringing two guys back to the apartment, but I had a soft spot for people. Years of being teased and ridiculed had made me more sensitive to other's feelings.

Danny's face lit up, but Aaron just shook his head, declining my offer. I still couldn't figure out how they got along. Danny was kind and shy, while Aaron, well he was everything a girl should run from… and fast.

I ushered Danny into the apartment and went rigid when I heard Issy's agitated voice.

"Avery! Where have you been?"

The hung over monster from the morning had totally disappeared, and in her place was a stunning figure dressed for yet another night on the town.

"I invited some friends over before we head out to the club; you just have to come with us tonight."

I checked my watch…it was barely two in the afternoon. What club opened that early? Before I had the chance to ask, Issy noticed Danny standing behind me.

"Who's your friend?"

Danny stepped closer, and I didn't miss the appraisal Issy gave his bare chest. I also didn't miss that Jake was standing right next to her with his eyes narrowed.

"Issy, this is Danny. He's Aaron's roommate from apartment 315."

If she was irritated with me, I couldn't tell. She grabbed a towel out of the drawer and walked over towards Danny. She was the picture of beauty and grace, and he watched her with fascination.

She seductively draped the towel over his shoulder, touching him ever so slightly. "You're sweating on my rug." Her flat voice completely contradicted her body language.

Poor Danny was stricken and backed out of the apartment apologizing. Issy put her hand on her hip and smiled coyly at him. "I didn't say I minded."

Danny was lost, so out of his league that I felt sorry for him. He somehow managed a "nice to meet you," and a "goodbye" before running off.

Issy shut the door behind him and shot me an annoyed look. "I told you I don't date guys from our complex. Now you owe me. Go shower; we're going out."

I looked around at our guests. Jake was leaning against the bar talking to a shorter, stockier guy with a buzzed haircut. On the couch sat a guy and girl, who were practically wrapped around each other watching TV.

"I don't know, Issy, I'm already so behind, and class starts Monday." Two of my professors had posted the syllabus and expected three chapters read before the beginning of class.

I moved quickly to my bedroom, suddenly feeling out of place in my running tank and shorts. Not to mention, I was sweating buckets in front of the one person I wanted to impress.

Jake stopped talking and looked up at me. "You

should come. It'll be fun."

Tingles exploded everywhere, making me forget my own name. It was ridiculous how cute he was. "Okay, I'll think about it."

"Well don't think too long," Issy called from the kitchen. "Happy hour starts at four, and Jake here has agreed to back off tonight." I saw her slam her elbow into his ribs, and he retaliated by tickling her.

I shut my door and headed straight to the shower.

It dawned on me that I had seen Jake three times now. Once, dancing like a fool in my PJs, next, coming out of mid-sleep with wild hair, and now, sweating head to toe with a face the color of a tomato.

We were not in the same hemisphere, let alone the same dating class.

Yet, all the same, as if on auto pilot, I got dressed to go out with everyone. For some reason, I couldn't physically say no to him, even though my head was screaming at me, *Danger!*

I found my favorite pair of skinny jeans, the ones I could swear took off ten pounds, and a strapless blue shirt that fell right at my hips. I added a chunky necklace and hoop earrings and looked in the mirror.

I felt good. I felt pretty, which was rare.

With all the confidence I could muster, I came out of my room and said, "Okay, I'm in."

I'm not sure what I expected Jake's reaction to be, but the look on his face far exceeded anything I had hoped for. Jake was one of those guys who had subtle charisma, a vast difference from Aaron's obnoxious banter. I had his full attention, and when we locked eyes, I knew I was failing at the hard-to-get game.

Issy's cat call broke the trance. "Wow, girl. You clean up well. Now come over here so we can get the night started."

I walked over to the bar, not knowing what to expect, and found a spot open next to Jake.

His scent almost knocked me over. It was woody and inherently masculine, with a slight hint of cinnamon. The bottle should be labeled, *Perfection.*

All six of us were huddled around the bar staring at five shot glasses full of a clear liquid.

Personally, drinking was not really my thing. I tried it a couple of times my freshmen year and always hated how out of control I felt. In addition, anything so expensive that included a ridiculous amount of empty calories seemed like a waste. But this was my first impression with these guys, and I didn't want to seem boring.

Issy passed each one of us a shot, except for the guy with the buzzed haircut, who I assumed was the designated driver for the evening.

Jake moved his head closer to mine and whispered, "You look beautiful tonight."

My head went fuzzy without even a drop of alcohol. No one had ever told me I was beautiful, except maybe Cara, and she didn't count. I was the fat girl with bug eyes and booty lips. The outcast, the nerd, the freak.

Issy lifted her glass. "To being young and stupid."

Jake's words had put me in a dream world, and I eagerly drank the shot with the rest of the group.

Unfortunately, I was the only person in the group coughing and gagging on it. My throat felt like it was on fire, and my eyes immediately started to water.

"Oh my, Avery, I have a lot to teach you this year." She made a tsk sound and handed me a glass of water.

I was totally embarrassed, mumbling "sorry" while still trying to stop the hacking.

Jake wrapped his arm around me. "No worries, I'm the ultimate caretaker, remember?"

The gleam in his eyes told me he was flirting, and I wanted to capture every moment, decoupage it and keep it for all eternity.

"Dear Lord, I pray You will be there if her foot slips and catch her if she falls…"

4. THE VARSITY CLUB

The Varsity Club was in Asheville, which meant a thirty-minute drive with all of us crammed in a small SUV.

The mix of our perfumes was becoming stifling in the closed space, and I quietly wondered why in the world I had agreed to go.

The nausea in my stomach reminded me I hadn't eaten, but I didn't want to since I was wearing tight jeans and going out with Jake.

My head was already swimming from the shot, and I could tell by Issy's conversations that more were coming.

We finally got to the club and paid our cover. Issy and I got red stamps on our hands that said, "Under 21" and the rest of the crew got wristbands. Almost immediately after we got in the door, Issy pulled me into the bathroom, took nail polish remover out of her purse and wiped the ink off our hands. Next thing I knew, we both had on matching wristbands.

"Happy Birthday. You just turned twenty-one," she said.

Before I could respond, she pulled me out of the

bathroom and onto the dance floor.

It was eighties night at the Varsity, and Issy totally looked the part. She was wearing a short, lacy, black skirt and an Elvis tank top. On her right hand was a fingerless black glove. The blue and purple from the other day had been replaced with long pink streaks. They were striking in the light and looked amazing against her dark hair.

She danced with complete freedom, and I saw how others were drawn to her.

I glanced nervously around the room and wondered if people were looking at me while I bobbed next to Issy's erratic dancing.

Next thing I knew, we were surrounded by three guys, each rubbing themselves on us.

I tried to politely move, but they had me trapped.

Suddenly, strong hands wrapped around my waist, and I was pulled out of the group. I knew immediately who had me, because he had a smell I could pinpoint in a crowded room.

"I told you I'd take care of you." Jake eyes were smoldering. I stared at him, mesmerized, while we danced so close his lips were almost touching mine.

His hands were like live wires on my skin. I no longer cared who was looking at me, only that I was in his arms.

We stayed on the dance floor through two more songs. Sweat began to bead on my forehead, and I suddenly felt self-conscious.

"This isn't really your scene, is it?" Jake yelled,

trying to be heard over the music.

"No, it's not… but, I'm still glad I came."

"Let's get a drink." Jake held my hand and led me off the dance floor and over to the bar. He ordered a drink for himself and then gestured for my order.

"Oh, water please."

With water in hand, we made our way to the back of the club where there were couches and chairs. Jake found one empty seat, sat down, and pulled me onto his lap.

My body couldn't take much more stimulation. I had never felt such a physical reaction to a boy before. Sure, I had been kissed and I dated one guy for a month last semester, but none of them ever made every inch of me tingle. Even Aaron and Danny, who were both attractive, had nothing on the desire that raged through me whenever Jake glanced my way.

I felt guilty for all those times I judged girls who absorbed themselves in the guys they dated. For the first time ever, I truly understood pure, chemical attraction.

He rubbed his hand up and down my back and played with the nape of my neck, sending chills down my spine. He leaned in, his breath heavy on my neck. "Let's go outside."

I stood and blindly followed him out, as if we were connected by invisible handcuffs.

The outside breeze lifted my hair and my lungs begged for the freshness of it compared to the hot, stuffy club.

Jake led me around the corner and backed me up to the wall. He jammed his leg between mine and pressed against me. His chest was so close I could feel every breath he took.

I was shaking, from adrenaline, from fear, from lust. I felt it all.

He started kissing my neck with light, feathery touches and then moved up until he firmly covered my mouth.

My body raged with a fire that could demolish two counties.

I brought my hands to his face and then up around his neck. My inner voice screamed at me, *What are you doing? You are making out in public, outside a club. This is not you!* But my inner voice was a soft roar compared to my desire to be with Jake.

I'm not sure how long we stood there wrapped up in each other. It could have been seconds, minutes, or hours. Time was of no consequence to me.

Jake was the first to pull away, and I was left breathless, staring at him.

"We better get back in before Issy starts looking for us. I don't think she'd be that keen on us kissing." Surprise laced his husky voice, as if our intense chemistry was unexpected.

I looked down, trying to settle my trembling hands. "You're right, we should go."

Jake tilted my head back up, lightly kissing my lips before he led me back into the club.

The rest of the night was a blur, dancing and drinking, then more dancing.

I felt like I was swinging through the clouds, and Jake never left my side the entire evening.

At the end of the night, we all piled in the car. This time, Issy was in the front seat and Jake was in the back with me. I laid my head on his shoulder and closed my eyes. A perfect end to a perfect night.

When I woke the next morning, I thought it had all been a dream until I was slammed with an excruciating headache. My mouth felt like it was stuffed with cotton balls, and I could smell alcohol coming out of my pores.

I didn't remember drinking that much, but, honestly, I didn't think about much after *the kiss*. The last thing I remembered was getting in the car to come home.

I looked down at my clothes; everything was intact minus the shoes. Did Jake put me to bed? Did I act like Issy had the night before? I was horrified. How could I not remember?

My clothes smelled like smoke, and my eyes had large dark circles under them.

How in the world could Issy do this every night?

It was already after twelve, and I started to panic. There was no way I was going to get my chapters read in time, not when I couldn't get my face to focus in the mirror.

My body was full of toxins, and I couldn't stop sweating, even in the shower.

I threw my smelly clothes in the laundry bag and put on my running clothes. I had to get this stuff out of me.

In the kitchen I found a note on the fridge that said, "Hangover juice inside. You're welcome." I took the green juice and brought it up to my face.

My stomach lurched. It smelled like the produce department in a grocery store. Disgusting. But, I kept thinking of the transformation Issy had made and somehow managed to drink the thick liquid.

My head was swimming. Where was Jake? Did I embarrass him? Did I throw myself at him? Memories of his kiss flooded me, and my stomach lit up with tiny fireflies.

Confused and frustrated, I grabbed my headset and headed out the door.

I could only go a mile, and it was a slow one. Lots of walking. The heat of the day and the exercise were making me sweat profusely, allowing my body to rid itself of the alcohol. At least I felt really skinny. I had practically gone twenty-four hours without eating and was sure I'd dropped at least two pounds between the run and the dancing.

Issy's green juice helped my massive headache, and soon I could see the world wasn't coming to an end. I'd get dressed and head to the library. I still had time to get my work done if I focused.

Feeling better, I walked into my apartment ready

to tackle my assignments. Jake was lounging on the couch watching TV.

My insides went liquid.

"There you are," he said, sitting upright. "Here I was coming over to check on you, and you're already out running again. I'm impressed."

I had no idea how to act around him after last night. "Oh, don't be that impressed. You should have seen me an hour ago."

"It's the hangover juice," Issy called out from the kitchen. "We brought home lunch if you're hungry."

"Yes, thank you. Let me go shower first."

"Wow, you were hammered last night," Issy said, walking into the living room while she popped a grape in her mouth.

I stopped at my door and cringed.

"You totally passed out in the car, and Jake had to carry you up the stairs. If he wasn't here, you'd probably still be passed out in T.J's car."

She acted like it was the most amusing event ever, but I was mortified. Not just at the fact I'd passed out, but that Jake had to carry me.

My past returned like a punch in the face. I imagined him sweating and straining to climb the stairs under my massive weight.

I wanted to crawl into a huge hole and never come out. I shook my head and shut the door, tears streaming down my face the whole time I showered.

Lord, I know she will face temptation and disappointments. I pray You serve as her mighty deliverer. I pray You bring her peace in the midst of hardships and carry her when life's burdens are too much to bear..."

5. FAILURE

Paying attention in class was proving to be impossible.

I hadn't seen Jake in five days. He had stayed Sunday afternoon, watching the football game and acted like nothing had happened between us. He wasn't rude or anything, just indifferent.

I was supposed to leave to go study, but I stayed, hoping the Jake from Saturday night would return. He never did.

What did I expect? Who would be attracted to a girl who passes out and then makes you carry her to bed? No one!

I just felt so tired.

I had spent three excruciating afternoons in the engineering lab, taking samples every twenty minutes.

Work study was a requirement for my scholarship, and this year's lab assignment was especially painful. I should have studied, but I couldn't focus.

Thank goodness it was the weekend.

Issy was leaving this afternoon to go home for a

couple of days, so that meant my apartment would be free of people for more than two hours.

Issy was the social queen of our apartment complex, and everyone wanted to be around her. She had some place for us to go every night, and despite my growing "to do" list, I would tag along.

We had conveniently "run into" Danny and Aaron a few times, but Issy never gave them the time of day.

I started to see Danny as a reflection of myself and wondered if I looked that desperate.

Truth was, I felt desperate. I had hoped to run into Jake every time we went somewhere, but he never showed. I refused to ask Issy about him. I already knew her feelings on the subject. With each day that I didn't hear from him, I started to second-guess everything that had happened.

Thankfully, I had kept the drinking to a minimum, unlike Issy who was truly a fish. It was no wonder she had already blown through her allowance this month and needed to do some serious groveling.

I thought of our conversation this morning.

"What will you do if your mom doesn't give it to you?"

She tapped her chin and shrugged. "I'll just go see my dad. He feels guilty for abandoning our family when I was twelve, so I can usually say a few key words and get what I want."

"Why not just go there first?"

"Because, there is nothing more excruciating than

my stepmom. She goes on and on about her and my father's son—Mr. Perfect. Barf. Then I'll get the lecture about my clothes and hair and how college will be over soon, and I need to get focused. Like I said, only if I'm desperate." She was randomly balling up her clothes and stuffing them in her duffle bag.

My type A instincts screamed at me to grab her bag away and fold each item she threw in there, but I refrained, suddenly putting two and two together.

"Wait, isn't your father's son… your brother?"

"Don't ever call him that again." It was the first time I had heard a tone from Issy that wasn't playful. A glimpse of hurt flashed in her eyes, but it quickly disappeared. "Now you, young Padawan, keep yourself out of trouble while I'm gone."

I laughed out loud. "No worries there." Truth was, I had done nothing but get into trouble since I met Issy.

The shuffling of books woke me up from my daydream. Class was over. I looked at the board and saw four problems assigned.

Ugh. I rolled my eyes and wrote them down. I hated my classes. I was already behind in my two hardest ones, and we were having a quiz on Monday.

Last year, my engineering classes were my favorite, but last year I didn't have a life.

"Hey, Avery." I looked up to see one of my classmates waving me over to the group. "We're putting together a study group on Saturday morning around ten if you want to come. We figured we could knock out these problems and then focus on our Statics quiz."

The nice thing about engineering was that most of us took the same classes each semester, so we'd end up helping each other a lot throughout the year.

"Sure, that sounds great. I'll be there."

I left class and walked through the center of campus on my way home. It was beautiful this time of year. The campus had no shortage of trees and they were turning every shade of orange, yellow and brown. The grassy center of the quad was covered in students studying, sunbathing or catching a quick power nap.

A group of fraternity boys were doing a step routine outside the library that was drawing in a large crowd.

Normally, I would have stopped to enjoy the show, but today already seemed like it had lasted a lifetime.

I got home, relishing the silence I hadn't heard since I moved in, and checked my phone one more time to see if Jake had tried to call. Nothing.

How was it that he hadn't thought to call even once? It didn't make sense!

I walked in my room and glanced at myself in the mirror.

I looked horrible. I hadn't run in three days, and my pants felt way tighter than usual. I lifted up my shirt and started to find every bulge that existed around my torso. I swear my butt looked huge today too… and not in a good way.

My eyes zeroed in on the scale. I shouldn't get on. It would only depress me. But I did anyway and saw I had gained a pound.

My throat tightened, constricting my air flow. How is that possible? I just weighed two days ago!

Tears sprang to my eyes. I knew temptation was coming, and panicked sweat slid down my face. I wanted to escape; I wanted to get this weight off of me. I wanted to disappear.

I got on the scale again—sure I had read it wrong the first time. I hadn't.

Desperation, like hot, thick lava poured over me.

I tried calling Cara.

Voicemail.

I started to pace the apartment, telling myself it wasn't worth it, that it wouldn't make me feel any better, but I knew it would help. Help ease the ever-increasing panic and make me feel like I had control of something in my life.

I opened the cabinets and refrigerator. Inside was cereal, little chocolate snack cakes and ice cream.

That would work. None of those things would hurt on the way back up. I closed my eyes, willing myself to be strong, and slammed the doors shut. I ran back in my bedroom and shut the door, fighting with everything I had. I didn't want to do it here. Not here.

Fifteen minutes passed and I started to believe the worst was behind me. I walked back to the living room and attempted to study, but the draw of the kitchen was just too strong.

Tears filled my eyes. I hated that I needed this, hated every part of me that enjoyed each bite I took. But with each one, my body started to relax and turn numb.

After ten minutes, I'd eaten two large bowls of cereal and was on my second snack cake. My stomach was full… so full, and it was screaming at me to give it relief.

My heart raced, blood pumping in my ears. I was at that critical point.

I gulped down a coke. Carbonation rose in my throat, and I leaned over the toilet and let it all come out. My body heaved and heaved as it got rid of all the food I had just stuffed into my stomach.

Relief echoed in my empty stomach. My throat burned and my eyes watered, but I didn't care. It felt so good to have the calories out of me.

I looked around at the mess I had made and immediately started cleaning.

The anxiety was gone and the desperation had finally passed, but with it came the reality that I had yet again failed. My lungs swelled with guilt and shame. Once again, I lost my resolve and gave into the temptation, the easy fix. How could I expect Jake to want me when I was so weak and disgusting?

I glanced at my phone. Cara had called me back; I didn't want to talk anymore.

Instead, I stayed rooted in self loathing.

I walked back into the kitchen and realized I had nothing to lose. The damage was done.

Apart from a small slip up when I got back to Winsor, I hadn't had an episode in two months. I had been so sure I was healing—that I was strong. What a lie.

Tears clung to my cheeks. It was out of control.

I poured the last of the cereal in my bowl and started the process all over again, hoping it would somehow take the pain away. It wasn't until I'd eaten all the snack cakes and had a bowl of ice cream that I finally stopped.

In the end, I had thrown up five times. Five times I had intentionally wrecked my body. Stuffing it to the point of capacity and then forcing myself to vomit.

My throat was completely swollen, and my gums were throbbing. I brushed and flossed my teeth and crawled into bed. I let my tears flow freely, wanting nothing more than to get this miserable day over with.

When I awoke Saturday morning, the events of the night before came rushing back.

Ugh. What was I thinking?

I went to the kitchen and scrubbed all the dishes. Then, into the bathroom and cleaned it from top to bottom.

Feeling a little better, I made sure all the empty containers were put in the trash and took the bag right out to the dumpster. I threw on my clothes and made a quick trip to the mini mart to buy replacement food.

Once home, I opened all the new items and took out what I needed to make them look like they hadn't been touched all weekend. I dumped the trash once more and finally relaxed.

Everything was as it used to be, and no one would ever know.

I looked at the clock… it was 9:30 a.m. My study session started in thirty minutes.

I needed the help, but I couldn't be around people yet. I texted the group and made my apologies, using some lame excuse about not feeling well. They offered to send me their answers so I could check my work. What a great group.

Cara had called three more times last night.

I didn't feel like talking. She knew me too well, and I wouldn't be able to fake it. Exhaustion hit, and I crawled back in bed, wanting to escape to another world. One where I was perfect, and Jake would profess his undying love.

Issy threw open the door. "I'm back!"

I was sitting on the couch finishing up the last thermodynamics problem. My afternoon had been surprisingly productive, and I was almost feeling like my old self again.

"Was your mission successful?"

"Of course it was. I didn't even have to see my

dad. Turns out my mom is dating a hot new guy from work, and she is exceedingly happy. We had the best time ever! I love new guys. I get a whole new wardrobe when they come around!" She danced and twirled her way into her bedroom to drop off her bags and then climbed over the back of the couch to sit next to me.

"I totally have us all set up for tonight. I met these two guys at the post office who are gorgeous, and they are a part of Lambda Sigma, the hottest fraternity on campus. Anyway, you and I have a double date for dinner and drinks tonight at Sammy's. Yay!" She clapped her hands and jumped back off the couch. "By the way, I am totally picking out your clothes tonight. You were way too conservative last time we went out."

Issy was back in her room before I could refuse. Truth was, even if she had let me speak, it wouldn't matter. Issy did not take "no" for an answer.

Part of me was glad. I had been locked away in this apartment for over twenty-four hours, and I was feeling a little cabin feverish. "Do I have time for a run?"

"Yes, but make it a short one. We're meeting them in two hours!"

I seriously started to wonder what I did for fun before Issy came along.

We walked into Sammy's and immediately spotted

our dates. They were both cute, but in that, I-look-like-a-member-of-a-boy-band kind of way.

Issy had staked claim to Pete on the way over, so that meant I had the one named Bobby. He seemed alright, nicely dressed and stood up when we got to the table. Neither of them held a candle to Jake, though, and I knew it within the first five minutes.

We ordered our food, and Bobby started talking about school. He was in his second year of law school and felt the need to explain every mundane detail.

I was amazed at his ability to continue talking without so much as a breath. I wondered how many different interested faces I could make for him before he took a break. I had made it up to number seven, when his hand on my leg brought me screeching back to reality.

Bobby started to lean in. "You're an amazing listener," he said in a sultry voice.

Bile sprung to the back of my throat. I was desperate to leave, but Issy was in full flirt mode with Pete and had scowled at me every time she saw me looking at my watch.

The check finally arrived, but not before Jake walked in the door, stealing every ounce of oxygen from the room.

He wasn't alone.

Standing next to him was a beautiful brunette with long straight hair and a perfect body. She was stunning.

Hard nails scratched the inside of my heart. I

immediately turned my head to try and focus on anything else in the room.

Issy gasped. "Oh, crud, here comes Jake. Boys, be on your best behavior."

In a flash, she was out of her chair and giving Jake a big hug. "When did you get back in town?" she asked innocently.

He looked at the table and, without acknowledging any of us, turned back to her. "What are you doing with these guys? They are way too old for you."

He had grabbed Issy's arm tightly and was pulling her away from the table. His date stood there awkwardly, unsure of where to go.

I stared at her, comparing each of her assets with mine. She won, hands down.

Issy jerked her arm away. "Jake, back off. I'm not a kid." She grabbed her bag and headed out the door. Pete cleared his throat and took off after her.

Meanwhile, I was living out my worst nightmare. We were all frozen in painful silence until my date asked, "You ready?" and we politely excused ourselves.

I peeked over my shoulder on our way out the door and made eye contact with Jake for just a second. He looked furious.

I couldn't wrap my head around the difference between him now and the other night. Issy was right. I got only a small glimpse of the real Jake. The caring, affectionate guy I fell for was gone and this other person was there instead. It felt tragic.

In the parking lot, Issy was back to her old self, hugging and kissing Pete with full abandonment. I could have sworn she was upset, but you'd never know it from her charming smile and excitement. When she saw me, she grabbed me by the arm. "I'm going to let Pete take me home, do you mind?"

"Issy, we live five blocks away from here. Why not just come with me?"

"Because, with you I can't make out in the car. Please. I'll be home in twenty minutes, I promise."

She gave me a quick hug and was gone.

Forty-five minutes later, she still hadn't made it home. I had already gotten ready for bed, cleaned up the apartment, and now was pacing. I checked my phone and texted her for the third time.

Come on, Issy, where are you?

I didn't know how the time clock worked in Issy's world. Did twenty minutes mean an hour? Should I be worried? Was this a normal thing for her? She had never ditched me like that before.

Minutes later, the door unlocked and loud voices filled the hallway.

"Jake, I've had it!"

Jake dragged her into the apartment despite her cries.

"I am almost twenty years old, and I don't need a chaperone."

"You could have fooled me! That guy is twenty-four, Issy, and has a horrible reputation! What were you thinking going to that frat house?" He was matching her anger, pitch for pitch, and the tension between them kept me paralyzed.

"I was having FUN! You remember F-U-N. You used to have it when you were my age, why can't I? Its not my fault you're out of the scene. I like it!"

"You like it? You like dancing on a table in front of ten slobbering guys who are only thinking of one thing? You have that little respect for yourself? No wonder your dad has threatened to transfer you. Hell, I may call him myself!"

That was the last straw for Issy. She slapped him across the face and ran to her room.

Jake turned his rage toward me.

"And you? What kind of friend are you to abandon her like that? You are supposed to take care of her. Watch her back."

I flinched at his tone. "I tried. She wouldn't come home with me."

"How hard did you try? You could have called me, gone with her, or done anything other then leave her alone with a snake!" His body language was vicious, his eyes full of hostility.

The tears were dangerously close to spilling over, but I refused to let him see me cry. "I don't have your number..." I whispered, my eyes transfixed on one of the circles in the carpet.

His tone softened, and he walked over to stand across the coffee table from me. "Give me your phone."

I handed it to him and he added himself to my contact list.

He looked wrecked and so tired that circles marred his stunning eyes.

I hated that I added to his stress. "I'm sorry. I'm new at all of this." My voice was resigned. I had failed Issy and failed him.

He sighed and walked around the table until there was no space between us. He lifted my chin, leaned down and put his forehead on mine.

I held my breath, afraid the moment would vanish if I moved.

My Jake was back, the one who made me feel as if I could leap tall buildings and save humanity.

He pulled me closer and held me, resting his chin on my head. "I feel like I have to be everywhere. That if I let her out of my sight for one second, she'll disappear. You make me feel like for one moment I don't have to be the only strong one. That, for once in my life, someone else could share the burden." He was talking as if to no one, holding me tight in his arms.

He leaned down and kissed me softly, taking in every inch of my mouth. His hands were lightly rubbing my cheeks, then my hair and finally moving down to my back.

I was lost in his arms, letting him drive the moment.

He slowly pulled away and I looked straight at him, keeping eye contact. I wanted to convey all the feelings that my mouth had no ability to say. How I would be there for him, how much I cared about him, how I would do anything to help him.

I wanted his trust. Wanted to be close to him in a way I'd never felt before.

He turned away without a word and walked out the door.

"Lord, I pray You reveal Your glory to her in mighty ways. I pray she sees Your hand in all that nature offers, and she knows that same God has every hair on her head numbered..."

6. ZIP LINE

The next morning Issy was on a tirade, swearing she was going to call the University first thing Monday morning and get our locks changed. I was pretty sure she said the phrases, "How dare he?" and "Who does he think he is?" at least fifty times.

Pete, in the meantime, was excessively texting and calling her. She ignored him, rolling her eyes each time the phone made a noise.

I guess that infatuation was a one-night event. I wished I could be so lucky. I couldn't get Jake out of my mind. There was so much I didn't understand. Who was he with last night, and why was he kissing me when he had just been on a date with someone else?

It took all of my willpower not to ask Issy those questions. But the last thing I wanted was for her to know the depth of my feelings, and she was incredibly perceptive.

Issy fell on the lip love seat and looked at her phone. "Ugh! Stop calling me!"

"Why did you go out with him in the first place?"

"I don't know. I was mad at Jake, and I knew it would bug him."

"Why were you mad at him? I thought you two were bonded by some supernatural force." I was hoping the teasing in my voice would mask my curiosity.

"It's a long story. Let's just say that he and I don't always agree on the 'family' issues, and the older he gets, the more he tries to intervene. It has reached new levels since my Aunt Kathy died."

My heart skidded to a screeching halt. His mom had died. I looked up at Issy. "When?"

"This summer. She had an inoperable brain tumor that slowly took her. Her death was really hard on him and my mom. That's part of why we fight so much. He idolizes my mom because she took care of them. It's like he has this need to pay her back, and that means dote over her and protect me at all costs. And the cost right now is our friendship. Things just haven't been the same since."

My heart was heavy as I tried to imagine his pain. No wonder he was tired. No wonder he was guarded. My compassion for him overwhelmed me.

I looked at Issy with a serious stare. "Maybe you should cut him a break."

"Oh, not you too! Ugh, is there no safe place from him? I told you to stay away from him. You didn't listen." She threw her hands up in surrender. "Do you want to know why Betsy left? She was in love with Jake, and she couldn't take being around him every day when he acted like she didn't exist. He charmed her just like he's doing to you and broke her heart."

"Issy, I don't have to be in love with him to feel bad for him. I just think if you would put yourself in his shoes every once in a while, your relationship might not be so heated."

Issy wasn't hearing it. She got up and left the room.

The tension in the apartment was more than I could stand with my already heightened emotions, so I grabbed my books and headed to the library.

I was thankful to see my study group in their usual corner and joined them. Unfortunately, it soon became obvious that I was days behind. I excused myself, not wanting to hold them back.

A corner table was available in the back of the room, and I set my books out, ready to tackle the impossible.

I worked through five of the twenty practice problems, only having to re-work one of them to get the right answer. I was so engrossed in my studying that I failed to notice my study group was gone, and a guy had joined me at my small table.

He was leaning back in the chair with a book and highlighter. He had on a baseball cap and his face was turned to the side so I could only see his profile. I leaned in, feeling that I knew him from somewhere.

That's when the scent hit me.

I settled back in my chair, not knowing if I should

say anything or not. I had encountered two different sides of Jake, one I adored—the other I slightly feared.

"You go to a whole different world when you're studying, don't you?" His green eyes made contact with mine.

I breathed a sigh of relief. He looked relaxed, even amused.

"How long have you been here?" I asked, my concentration evaporating into thin air.

"At least ten minutes. I was starting to take bets with myself as to whether you were really that zoned or if you were intentionally freezing me out."

I smiled, mostly at the idea that I could ever play it cool when it came to Jake. "What are you reading?"

"It's a riveting book on international finance. What about you?"

I had almost forgotten Jake was still in college. I had yet to see Issy crack a book and was beginning to think I was the only one who had to study.

"Oh, I have you beat. My pleasure reading for the afternoon is statics, the study of physical systems in equilibrium."

Jake lifted his hands up as if to say I had won, his eyes dancing for the first time since he caught me singing in my room.

He eyed my thick textbook. "How much more do you have?"

"Why, have you come to rescue me from my calculator?"

He appeared to be considering it and nodded. "Yeah, let's get out of here. I have someplace I want to take you."

There was no saying "no" to that, even if it meant I pulled an all-nighter to study for my quiz.

"Let's go."

He didn't say much on the drive but kept his hand on my thigh the entire way. By the time we pulled into Pisgah National Forest, my mind was muffled and body enflamed.

He opened my door and I stood in awe. The trees were amazing this time of year, the colors a vibrant red, orange and yellow. The sheer beauty and expanse of the forest made the campus trees look like bushes.

"This is breathtaking," I exclaimed.

"Yeah, I love it. Spent most of the summer up here, just letting nature do its thing."

I wondered if helping him cope with grief was the "thing" that nature did, but I didn't say anything.

We entered the main building, and the guys behind the counter immediately recognized Jake. My mind started registering the harnesses, gloves and helmets on the walls.

I turned my focus onto Jake and caught the last of his conversation.

"I'm going to take her on a few lines, if that's okay?"

The guys waved their hands. "Of course, you know you're welcome to them any time."

My palms started to sweat, panic rising up in my

throat. "Um, Jake, may I talk to you for a minute outside?"

He seemed to sense my panic. After guiding me out the door, he put both of his hands on my shoulders. "You will be fine."

"No, you don't understand. I'm not like you or Issy. I don't take risks, even calculated ones. I can't do this." My heart pounded faster and faster each time I looked toward the building that held my fate.

Jake stared me right in the eyes. I was captivated.

"You will be fine. You trust me, don't you?"

I simply nodded and followed him inside—back in the same trance I felt the first night at the club.

Numbness consumed me as I let the shop guys lock the harnesses all around me, hand me a helmet and give me gloves to wear.

It was a mile hike to the first platform, and the majesty of the area almost made me forget where we were going... almost. I nervously watched my feet as the gravel trail crunched underneath me and wondered how many girls Jake had brought here.

As if sensing my fear, he laced his fingers through mine and squeezed.

My apprehension dissipated until we reached the first platform. I looked over the side and registered how high we were. Knowing I was going to be one hundred feet above the ground and staring at it are two very different things.

"Jake, I can't do this." My voice was barely louder than the wind.

"Yes, you can. I will be right here with you. You can trust me."

I nodded, trying to bury my fear. He strapped my harness to the line and positioned his body right behind me. "Now sit in your harness seat and put your legs straight out in front of you. Grab the top line with your left hand and the bottom line with your right one. Use your right hand to slow yourself down."

I hung on every word.

"Now, Avery, step off."

I closed my eyes and took the leap. My stomach plummeted, but the feeling was spectacular. I had always felt running was like flying when the high took over, but nothing prepared me for this. The trees were surrounding me with their beauty and, for the briefest moment, I felt the freedom I was constantly searching for.

I soared through the air, metal on metal squealing. The wind whipped across my face like the very breath of God.

My feet hit the next platform and immediately strong hands were waiting to pull me in.

I did it!

Jake was seconds behind me.

He got his footing and then looked at me, smiling. "What did you think?"

My inhibitions were gone. I threw my arms around him and boldly kissed him right in front of the world. "It was amazing!"

He pulled me close, looking at me with such intensity that I thought I would catch fire right there. Then he tickled me. "Just wait until you do the next one."

We did all ten of them, each one exceeding the next in height, speed and beauty. The Blue Ridge Mountains could be seen in the distance, and the overall effect was magnificent. As we watched the sun set from the last platform, I was struck with the significance. I had exceeded my own expectations, and the joy and pride I felt changed how I could view the rest of my life.

Jake had given me that moment.

He stood behind me with his arms wrapped around my waist.

"Thank you," I whispered.

He nuzzled my neck, somehow knowing what he had done for me. "You're welcome."

It was as if the trees had bonded Jake and me together. We spent the next two weeks texting incessantly and sneaking off to be together.

Jake and Issy were still not talking, and she wasn't saying much to me either. Issy was a lot of things, but stupid was not one of them. I was sure she figured out that Jake and I were dating.

The euphoria of new love consumed me. I couldn't eat, could hardly sleep, and my stomach was in a perpetual state of nervous excitement.

My schoolwork was also not fairing so well. I had somehow managed to keep a B in Statics, but in Thermodynamics, I was barely hanging on to a C. If I fell below a 3.5 GPA, I would be put on probation.

I knew I should care, but I just didn't. In fact, there wasn't much in my life I did care about right now, except for Jake.

I hadn't run in over a week and got a stern talking to from my advisor about my lack of work-study hours. Even Cara was driving me crazy. It was like they were all bees flying around my head, nagging me to give up the one thing in my life I cherished. I wasn't going to do it!

Jake brought out something in me I couldn't explain. When I was around him, I felt like I took on his qualities. I was more outgoing, funny, and even flirtatious beyond my normal comfort zone. He made me adventurous and fearless, things I had never been in my life.

Cara, as usual, was my incessant buzz kill. "I just don't understand why it has to be 'this you' or the 'old you.' Why can't you be both? You worked hard for that scholarship and this opportunity. All summer long you talked about how much you loved it. I don't understand how it could suddenly mean so little."

"It still matters to me, Cara. It's just not the only thing that matters to me any more. I have Jake now, and he makes me happy."

"Really? You have Jake? When's the last time he's taken you on a real date, or anywhere in public for that matter? Avery, making out in the laundry room at your apartment complex does not make him a boyfriend."

I blushed at the memory that stirred. Me, sitting on the table reading, Jake sneaking up behind me, kissing my neck and pulling me into his arms. He made me feel sexy and beautiful. I felt like he wanted me, and the feeling was invigorating.

"Cara, you just don't understand," I said, sighing.

"I guess not," she responded with equal resignation. After a long, dramatic pause, Cara asked, "So, how is the eating?"

I was taken back by her question, almost forgetting I had shared my deepest secret.

"It's great. I've never felt this good about myself."

"Avery, trading one obsession for another is not healing… it's transference, and it's dangerous."

Anger boiled in my gut. "I didn't ask you to be my psychologist, nor did I confide in you so you could hound me every chance you got. I'm fine, so leave it alone!"

I couldn't remember the last time there was this much tension in our relationship.

"I'm sorry," I finally said after an awkward period of silence. "Let's just talk later, okay?"

We said our goodbyes and hung up the phone, but my heart was heavy. I felt like I was losing my best friend.

It seemed so unfair that I could find such happiness in one area of my life, while all the others seemed to be unraveling. Cara's words bothered me, but I pushed them aside.

Jake cared about me, and I wasn't going to let her question that simple truth!

"Lord, protect her as she navigates through life, bringing forth truths that are so often hidden in the shadows…"

7. UNFORTUNATE TRUTHS

Issy stood in my doorway with her hands on her hips. "I've decided I'm done being angry with you. I miss you too much!"

I was once again attempting to figure out my thermo homework. It was like trying to learn a foreign language with no translator.

"I want you to come out with me tonight. You haven't been out of this house in weeks, and people are starting to wonder what's happened to you." Her whiny voice resembled that of a spoiled child.

My mind reflected on all the fun nights I'd been having "staying in" with Jake. I hadn't heard from him yet today, so it was probably safe to make other plans.

"Okay, I'm in. Where are we going?"

"Do you have to ask? It's Thursday night. Two for one shots at Caesars. Sheesh, have I taught you nothing?"

I laughed at her dramatic tone. "I missed you, too, but if you ditch me again tonight… this will be the last time I ever go."

"Cross my heart!" she promised and spun out of the doorway.

An hour later we were on our way. I felt dressed to kill in a blue, wispy mini dress that hit all the right places.

A few weeks ago I wouldn't have been caught dead in a dress this short. But Jake had changed that. I even weighed tonight and had lost five pounds since he came into my life.

I wore my hair down and matched Issy's strut, step for step. She winked at me when we walked in the bar, garnering all kinds of stares.

Issy, of course, was used to this type of attention. She was practically a celebrity in school, partly due to her father's alumni status, and partly due to her unmatched personality. She was also strikingly gorgeous.

But for me, this was my coming out party. I felt like I could stand on a table and say, "I'm with them, and I belong here."

Issy came back with two drinks in hand. The bouncers at the door stopped carding her a long time ago.

I sipped on the brown liquid that seared my throat and scanned the room. Aaron and Danny were seated at a table off to the side, and I waved at them.

Issy rolled her eyes, but I pulled her that way.

"Danny's nice. You should give him a chance," I scolded.

She sighed. "Okay, but don't say I didn't warn you when that poor boy's heart gets broken."

We walked up to the table and both boys stood up. Issy flirted shamelessly with Danny while I was left to entertain Aaron.

"Avery, you look… delicious," he purred, moving closer to me.

I smiled coyly at him, trying to match Issy's motions. I had no interest in Aaron, but I loved the attention and couldn't seem to get enough of it, which was the total opposite of how I felt the first time I met him.

Issy pulled me onto the dance floor and, song after song, she and I were surrounded. Sometimes Aaron and Danny would cut in, but Issy never liked to stay with one partner for very long.

I began to understand her love for this place. No wonder she had such confidence. Who wouldn't after this?

I scanned the room again, and my heart leapt into my throat. Jake was standing at the bar, looking perfect as always. He had his confident swagger going as he reached out to grab his drink from the female bartender. He leaned in for a European style hello kiss and dropped a bill on the bar.

How did I get so lucky?

He crossed the room, shaking hands and talking with each person he met. People were drawn to him, like kids to an ice cream truck. I was no different.

Pushing through the crowd, I started to make my

way over to him. He turned the corner and found his seat and that is when I saw her.

Light flashed in my eyes, slowing down time.

He had his arm around her and was nuzzling her neck like I'd felt him do to me hundreds of times. She had red curly hair and was wearing a dress so tight it left nothing to the imagination. She was prettier than me and had curves in places I never would.

My drink started to come up, and I made it to the bathroom just in time. Stars danced in front of my eyes, panic in full swing. I tried to get myself together. Tried to stop the tears that threatened.

I looked in the mirror. It was a different picture. The thin, confident woman was gone, and in her place was someone wearing a dress way too short for her imperfect legs.

My hands trembled, the "fight or flight" feeling taking over my entire body.

"You have to calm down!" I told myself sternly. "Breathe in and out, in and out. You can do this."

I managed to pull myself together enough to make it back to the table. Issy was dramatically telling a story about the time she went skydiving and her parachute got jammed. Danny hung on her every word.

Normally, I'd be mesmerized too, but all I could do was tell myself, on repeat, not to turn around and stare at the red haired bombshell kissing my so called boyfriend.

Issy noticed Jake and started eyeballing me.

"You okay?" Her curt voice made me wonder if tonight had been a set up from the beginning.

Did she know he would be here?

"Of course, why wouldn't I be?" I lied with every ounce of conviction I could muster.

"No reason." She paused for a moment but continued to try and read my thoughts. "You want to go say hi to Jake?"

"I thought you still weren't speaking to him?"

"Well, making up with you has been such a success tonight, I figure why stop there?"

She stood and pulled me through the crowd with determination. I had to play it cool. I had to keep myself under control.

Coping had never been my strongest skill. Running and, the *other* thing, were all that worked to take away my anxiety.

But tonight I would have to find a way.

As soon as Issy got to the table, she jumped on Jake's lap and hugged him tight. "I forgive you," she announced, her eyes dancing with amusement.

"Really? And to what do I owe this honor?" He was bantering but relaxed immediately. He hadn't said so, but I knew he missed her.

I tried not to stare, but he looked so sleek and handsome in his pin stripped shirt and jeans. Jealousy burned my insides.

"It's been lonely without my big bad protector. And, honestly, it's not nearly as fun when you don't have someone to tick off," Issy said and then turned to the redhead. "Hi, I'm Issy, nice to meet you."

"I'm Rebecca, Jake's friend. You must be his spunky little cousin I've been hearing so much about." She had a thick southern accent and was rubbing Jake's thigh.

My stomach clenched as icy hot fingers trailed my flesh.

"This is my roommate, Avery," Issy said as she stood up.

I simply gave a small wave and a fake smile.

My voice had failed me, and I feared my knees would follow if I did much more. Jake refused to look at me, but other than that, he seemed completely unaffected by this little meeting.

"Well, we have more dancing to do and definitely more shots to drink, so you cats have fun. Jake, don't you dare start lecturing me until at least 2:00 a.m. That is a perfectly acceptable time for a Thursday night."

He smiled and saluted his cousin, sending a wink her way.

For all of Issy's beauty and confidence, I'd never once envied her. Until that moment.

We walked away, but my ears were still burning. "I think I'm ready for a little of that two for one action now."

She made a beeline to the bar and brought me back two shots that promised to heal my aching heart.

They only made it worse.

We joined Danny and Aaron again, but as much

as I tried to feel better, I couldn't. Even Aaron's crude comments and "accidental" grazes did nothing to improve my mood.

I looked over at the table where Jake was sitting, but they were gone, and so was my resolve. Resting my head on Issy's shoulder like a drunk sorority sister, I begged her to leave.

She patted my face, offering a motherly touch I'd never really known and promised to take me home. Turns out, Issy was a pretty good friend after all.

My depression felt even more constricting when I woke up Friday morning. Class was definitely not happening. I'd just get the notes later. My head was throbbing from the dehydration I knew I was facing after last night's episode.

I checked my bathroom again to make sure all the evidence was gone and re-hid the food and wrappers in my closet.

Issy was in the kitchen making her hangover juice and looked up at me when I walked in. "Wow, you look better than I expected."

"What do you mean?"

"I heard you yakking all night. I almost came in to check on you. I really didn't think you were telling the truth when you said you didn't feel well, but wow, was I wrong. Girl, you are a light weight!"

Time froze…she had heard me. My need to protect myself took over every instinct, and I was able to lie without any of my usual constraints.

"I know. I've never been so sick. What was in those shots?" I paused for dramatic effect and sat down. "There's no way. Had to be something I ate yesterday."

"Well, whatever it was…I don't want it. So take your juice and go on your crazy run, and don't come back until you can promise I won't be doing the same thing tomorrow night!"

Sadness gripped me. *Don't worry, someone like you will never have to do what I did last night.*

She had it all.

After several glasses of water and Issy's famous hangover juice, I felt good enough to go on a long run.

Danny and Aaron were just pulling up when I was about to leave. They honked at me, and I stopped by the car, leaning into their opened window.

"You feeling better?" Danny asked, looking concerned.

My face burned as I lied again. "Yes, I guess I just ate something that didn't settle in my stomach." Wanting to change the subject, I suggestively asked, "Did you have fun last night?"

"Why? Did she say something?"

I thought of Issy's warning and immediately felt guilty. Maybe I shouldn't have pushed Danny on her.

"Sorry, but if it makes you feel any better, Issy never talks about guys."

He looked disappointed. Aaron leaned over him

to talk to me. "How far you running today?"

"As far as it takes to clear my head," I answered honestly before I could stop myself. "I'll catch you guys later."

I took the route around the campus lake and just did an easy pace. It hit me on the trail how disappointed I was with myself. I had walked into this year confident and strong. I had gone months without throwing up and was at the top of my class.

Now, I was barely hanging on in two classes and one of them felt like a lost cause. My confidence was shot, and I had deluded myself into believing that an incredibly hot, kind and extraordinary man could possibly want me.

I passed by the playground that marked the halfway point and stopped. I used to love to swing as a kid. It would make me feel so alive and untouchable. I found an open one in the middle and just started moving back and forth. It was slow and methodical at first, but with each pump, I felt my adrenalin start to increase.

"I thought I might find you here," a voice said behind me.

I just kept swinging, not wanting to acknowledge the source.

He was quiet for a long time, watching me, and then finally spoke up, "So, you're not going to talk to me? Get my side of the story?"

I slowed down enough to look at him, knowing full well I was wearing all my emotions on my face, despite my efforts to hide them. "Not if it's a story. I think I've had enough fairy tales for a while."

We engaged in a staring contest, my mind racing with images of busty Rebecca's hand on his thigh.

He grabbed the chain of my swing. "Seriously, come talk to me. I don't like feeling this way."

It should be illegal the effect Jake had on me, because despite my inner alarm screaming at me to walk away, I followed him to the picnic table.

"It's not what you're thinking. She doesn't mean anything. I go out with these girls to keep up the appearance, that's all. I'm known as a player, and I like that. It keeps my life simple."

I didn't say anything, just kept kicking at the patch of grass I almost had dislodged from the ground.

"I was surprised you didn't say anything when you saw us."

"Why's that?" The rasp in my voice told me tears would be coming soon.

"Well, most girls would have said something. Some try to play it cool, others lose their temper. But you... total silence. Not even a phone call or text. I wasn't expecting that."

I was struck by the fact that this situation was a common occurrence for him.

"What were you expecting? I'm not the kind of girl who throws a temper tantrum in the middle of a bar." I looked at him exasperated, reminding myself to hold my ground and demand more respect.

"I know that," he admitted and ran his hands

through his hair. "That's the problem. You have made my life complicated because, for the first time, there is someone I want to call when I wake up and talk to before I go to sleep."

My heart skipped a beat, and I knew that my resolve was weakening. "How can I believe you? What am I supposed to do with that?"

He inched over to me and moved a piece of hair that had stuck to my tear stained cheek.

"You can trust me, Avery. I'm not going to let you down." He paused for a second, still caressing my temple. "Let me take you on a real date. Things are better with Issy now, and people have already noticed my lack of nightlife these past few weeks."

Tingles danced down my skin at the seductive look in his eyes, my mind replaying the many make out sessions we'd had together.

Very tentatively, he reached out and cupped my face. "I'm sorry." His voice was soft and sincere as he moved in to kiss me.

Resolve gone, I kissed him back with all the longing, need, and hurt I felt until he gently pulled away.

"I didn't like you seeing you out with those guys either," Jake admitted, keeping his forehead on mine.

I looked at him, confused, until I remembered Danny and Aaron. "They are just friends. One is completely in love with your cousin and the other, well, he has LOTS of love interests."

Jake kept his piercing eyes on mine. "I still didn't

like it."

He pulled me on his lap, and we made out shamelessly in the park.

Finally, I pushed him away and looked around, feeling a little embarrassed.

"Tonight," he said gruffly before getting up.

I just nodded.

When I declined a ride home, he drove off.

I was still in a daze as I showered and dressed for the day. I had missed my first class but could make it to my second one if I hurried.

My phone rang as I walked out the door, and I spent the next five minutes detailing the evening's events to Cara, who already didn't have a high opinion of Jake.

"So, did he say you guys were exclusive then?" she asked with an air of irritation in her voice.

"No."

"Did he at least say he wasn't dating those girls anymore?"

"No."

"Avery!"

"What? I don't care, okay? He likes me. He practically said I was the one he thought about when he woke up and went to sleep. Besides, I'm a private person too. I totally get him not wanting to expose his personal life to the college paparazzi."

I was so exasperated with her interrogation that I was speed walking to class.

"So, how did you cope when you saw him at the

bar? Any relapses?" She hesitated as she asked me that, and my guilt and shame over my continual failure all manifested in anger.

"Why do you always have to go back to that? No, I told you, I'm doing fine with it. Sometimes I wish I had never confided in you. It's like we can't talk about anything else now."

"Avery, we talked about it all summer. You told me to ask you. Why are you being so defensive?"

"Because it feels like all you do is judge me now. It's like having a third parent."

I knew I was being unreasonable. She was only trying to help, but it didn't matter. It was my life, my secret, and I didn't need her intrusion.

"That's not what I'm trying to do. I don't know how to be here for you anymore," she explained with a catch in her voice. I had hurt her.

"Just laugh with me and be happy for me. Can you do that?"

"I'll try." She was quiet and then attempted to change her tone. "Call me later and tell me how the date goes, okay?"

"Okay. Talk to you then."

I let out a sigh and sat down in my class chair. My conversations with Cara were just getting more and more trying. I felt horribly guilty for lying to her, but I didn't want to talk about it. I had it under control, and she would just freak out.

My class did nothing to improve my mood as the professor worked problems on the board with such speed I had no hope in following.

I left class feeling miserable and anxious as I tried to mentally and emotionally prepare for the evening.

The afternoon flew by, and before I knew it, it was only two hours before *the date*.

I was at my wits end on what to wear. Nothing looked good, and I was bloated. Issy had ordered takeout for lunch, and I ate way too much. I felt like a stuffed pig. How was I supposed to go on a date with Jake tonight feeling like this? I heard one door shut and then another outside my room.

I poked my head out. "Issy?"

No answer.

Oh, thank goodness!

I ran to my bathroom, shut the door, and forced myself to get rid of my lunch. I knew it didn't help—that I never really lost weight by throwing up, but it made me feel better. It calmed me down and allowed me to see rationally instead of emotionally.

Tonight was my first real date with Jake, and I had to look perfect.

He was charming and deep, more handsome than any man I'd ever known, and for some reason he wanted to be with me.

I thought of the two other women I had seen him with and looked at my body in the mirror.

They were flawless, and I was not.

The mirror magnified every imperfection, and tears consumed me as I covered myself up.

"Lord, I know Satan is like a roaring lion, waiting for someone to devour. I pray you protect her from those who will harm her…"

8. PUSHING LIMITS

The night was serene and slightly cool, with just a light breeze. I was living out the perfect romance movie when Jake came to pick me up. He looked totally dapper in tan pants and a fitted V-necked sweater.

I settled on an Audrey Hepburn look, classy yet sexy, sporting a fitted black dress with a thin belt around the waist. The dress fit my body well. I ran my hands over any area that felt soft and tried not to fidget.

His reaction melted my heart and made my confidence soar. He grabbed me by the waist, pulled me close and kissed me on my neck. "You look perfect."

We had dinner reservations at an Italian restaurant in Asheville that came complete with beautiful music and candlelight. The food was delicious, although I did more picking than eating.

Jake and I made small talk all through dinner, mostly sharing funny Issy stories. The mood was relaxed and lighthearted.

I looked at him from across the table. I had only known him a few weeks, but in that time he had taken residency in my thoughts and heart in such a way I didn't know how I could live without him. I wanted him to feel the same way, where he would talk to me and confide in me. I longed for the closeness.

"I realized when I was getting ready tonight that I don't really know anything about you. Not even what you want to do when you graduate," I said, hoping to seize the opportunity.

The past few weeks together had been less about talking and more about making out and sneaking around.

Jake smiled flirtatiously, as if reading my thoughts, and settled back into his seat. "I'm hoping to get into stock trading, maybe even dabble a little in international stocks."

My brow furrowed. I hadn't expected that answer. "Why the look?"

"I'm just surprised that a guy who labels himself as the ultimate caretaker wants to get into such a cut-throat business."

He placed his hand on the table, his words rushed. "But that's exactly why stocks appeal to me. The business is all about making money. The more selfish you are, the better. It's a nice change."

"I guess I didn't realize that you didn't like doing it." I couldn't figure out why that disappointed me.

"Taking care of people?"

I nodded.

"It's not that I don't like it. I mean, with my mom and Issy, I wouldn't want anyone else doing it. But sometimes I just feel, well, trapped."

His words hung in the air, leaving us in awkward silence until the waitress came and filled our glasses.

"Is this your idea of light dinner conversation?" He had humor in his voice, but I changed the subject anyway. I wanted our night to be perfect.

"Issy said you are in a fraternity. Do you like it?"

"Was in a fraternity, not anymore."

"Why not?"

"I grew up. I mean, I just kind of got my priorities straight this summer and realized I had to focus and finish school. My mom never even graduated from high school. She got pregnant with me and did what she had to in order to survive."

He didn't mention his dad, so I assumed he was out of the picture. "Your grandparents didn't help?"

"They were pretty old when my mom was born. She was a surprise, so by that time, they really weren't able to help that much. Mom wasn't really the type to ask anyway; she was pretty self-reliant, felt she could do it on her own. I guess I know who I get that from, right?"

He was trying to lighten the mood, bring us back to that playfulness we had earlier, but my heart felt too heavy. I had to say something.

"Issy told me she passed away this summer. I'm really sorry. She sounds like a wonderful woman." I was cautious as I spoke, wanting to convey my compassion, but not wanting him to feel like I was overstepping some imaginary boundary.

"Thanks. Yeah… not the best three months of my life." He moved around the remnants of food on his plate, and I reached over to squeeze his hand.

Haunted eyes met mine. "Why do I feel like I'm bearing my soul every time we talk?"

My pulse quickened. "I want you to. I like listening to you."

He leaned up on the table, closing the distance between us. "I think we need to do more kissing and less talking."

I followed his lead, putting less than an inch between our faces. "Maybe it's time you were with someone who could do both."

Something flashed in his eyes before he kissed me, and I wondered if he felt it too. Love. He pulled away and my eyes searched his. Nothing. Just the return of Jake's relaxed, nonchalant demeanor.

"You have gorgeous eyes." he said casually, still staring at me. "They are so light they look like blue ice crystals. I've never seen anything like it."

I blushed and turned away. "They're too big for my face."

He lifted my chin back, his eyes like lasers into mine. "They're beautiful."

My breath hitched. Everything around me became a blurred mess except Jake.

"We should get out of here before my thoughts get us in trouble," he whispered. "Besides, I want to show you where I live."

He grabbed the check, and I stood up and followed him out, excited, but nervous to be alone with him in his apartment.

Jake lived in a studio apartment only two blocks from the restaurant. The décor was pretty modern, and I knew without asking that Issy had been involved in the decorating. The only piece of furniture that looked like Jake was a long, soft leather sofa that nuzzled around me when I sat on it.

I glanced up and saw a staircase leading to a small bedroom loft.

My stomach tumbled. I had no idea what to do in this situation. I had never been in a guy's apartment alone before, and had never gone further than kissing.

I felt completely out of place, putting my hands in my lap to try and settle the shaking.

Jake grabbed us a few drinks out of the kitchen and turned on the TV. A basketball game filled the screen. Jake hit mute, but the blood pumping in my ears was deafening.

He slid behind me on the couch, tucking me between his thighs and against his chest.

"You're so tense," he said, rubbing my shoulders.

"Sorry, I'm just not used to being so alone with you. In my apartment, there was always the thought of Issy walking in to hold us accountable."

He started moving my hair and kissing the back of my neck. "We don't have to do anything you're not comfortable with."

He continued to move up my jaw line to my ear.

Every nerve ending in my body was on fire, and I was acutely aware that his free hand rested on my exposed thigh.

My breath came out in labored puffs. "That will become a very short list if you keep kissing me like that."

"You promise?" His words were so soft they could have been the whisper of butterflies, and his touch so tender that I wondered how anyone could have such gentle lips.

He started to unzip the back of my dress and I froze, completely terrified.

The zipper suddenly went back up and Jake chuckled, making me feel like a frigid school girl.

"I'm sorry."

"Don't apologize. I love your innocence." He stroked my arm. "You don't see that much anymore."

I turned around and kissed him with all the desire welling up in me. He let me drive the moment, continuing to be a total gentleman.

When I wanted to stop, he just held me close while we talked for hours. I knew right then that he was all I wanted, in every sense my match. I also knew without question that I was completely in love.

Jake became the perfect boyfriend after our dinner date. Even Issy noticed his devotion and stopped giving me the warning speeches each morning.

He'd call or come by every night, and we'd talk for hours about anything or nothing. It didn't matter. Mostly we'd talk about school or his internship. But sometimes, on rare occasions, he'd open up about his past. With every new insight, I fell harder and harder.

"I found my father, you know," he said, stroking my arm one night while we were lying in my bed. "My mom didn't think I knew who he was, but the town she lived in wasn't that big, and it's amazing what's on the Internet."

"Did you speak to him?" I asked cautiously. Jake always clammed up when I pushed too hard.

"No. He was living in Atlanta, working for a media-marketing firm. I had decided I would confront him; force him to deal with what he did to my mom. I told Issy we were going on a road trip, and we drove all night. I parked outside his office building and watched people go in for two hours, wondering with each passing figure if it was him."

"What happened?"

"Nothing. I left and haven't been back." He was staring at the ceiling, his eyes lost in a world I couldn't see.

I had learned with Jake that there were only two options when he talked about his past, stay quiet or say something witty. If I said anything serious, he would immediately shut down and change the subject. I chose wit.

"Issy really let you sit there for two hours? I didn't

know she sat still that long."

Jake smiled and kissed my nose. "It was six in the morning when we got there. She was still asleep. She woke up two hours later and insisted on breakfast. If not, I might have stayed all day. I just want to know how he could walk away and never once think to check on her. But something wouldn't let me out of that car." He was lost again in the past, watching the scenes in real time on my ceiling.

I stroked his face, trying to offer comfort.

He turned to his side and pulled me close, kissing me softly at first, but then with growing intensity.

Jake had been sleeping over a lot lately, and each night we seemed to go farther and farther physically. He made me lose my senses and question every boundary I had set on intimacy.

He was especially aggressive tonight, moving his hands all over me.

My mind was at war with itself. I wanted to succumb to the sensations, but I had always pictured myself waiting until I was married. I wanted my first time to mean something.

I loved him. I knew that, even though I hadn't told him yet. He was my everything.

Jake started to unbutton my shirt. "Jake, I don't know…"

"Shhh, just for a little while. I want to feel close to you." He kissed my neck and mouth with pure hunger, and I felt hypnotized.

I started to question why I was even waiting.

Most girls my age had gone this far with a guy many times.

Jake stopped kissing me, and we locked gazes, each saying all we needed to with one look. He gently touched my face and whispered, "You're so beautiful, Avery."

His eyes penetrated mine, and I was so enthralled by his sincerity that I allowed him full access to my body and soul. I knew in that moment I wanted him to be my first and my last. I responded to every one of his touches, and Jake immediately sensed my wavering.

He hesitated for just a second. "Are you sure?"

My body was on fire, and I had no ability to resist.

"Yes," I answered, breathless. "I'm ready."

He leaned back in, his mouth consuming mine, and no more words were spoken.

Jake was still asleep as I studied him. He looked serene and beautiful. I softly ran my fingers through his hair, feeling that our souls were now connected.

Last night wasn't exactly what I'd expected. Jake was careful and soft, and when I looked at him, everything else seemed to disappear.

But the euphoric, out of body experience I had been promised in books and movies wasn't there, and sometimes it even felt painful.

I pushed those thoughts aside and focused instead on how much I loved the man in my bed. He was warm and caring and made me feel like I was special.

As if he knew I was thinking of him, he opened his sleepy eyes and looked at me.

"Hi," he said with a slight grin.

"Hi," I whispered back, my stomach in knots.

"Are you okay?" he moved a piece of hair off my cheek.

"I'm fine."

His eyebrows peaked.

"More than fine," I corrected, laughing.

He drew me into a bear hug and kissed me hard before getting up. He walked around the room picking up his clothes, and I turned my head, embarrassed at his exposure.

Insecurity gnawed at me. "Do you want breakfast?"

"No, baby, I wish I could, but I have to get home. Big test tomorrow." He got dressed like a man running from the law.

I tried to settle the growing uneasiness in the pit of my stomach.

"I'll call you later." He gave me one final kiss and was out the door.

I stumbled into the bathroom, still in shock over what had just happened.

"Lord, I know there will be times in her life when she feels lost and broken. I pray in her weakness that You become her strength…"

9. HEARTACHE

My imagination was running wild, even though my heart kept telling it to stop. Jake had been by every night this week, but I couldn't suppress the feeling that something was different.

He seemed agitated and distant, leaving at midnight every night, as if he would turn into a pumpkin if he stayed.

I felt too insecure to ask him about it and instead pretended everything was okay.

Issy was nowhere to be seen. She had finally agreed to a date with Danny, and I guess she had fun because she'd been sleeping over there ever since.

The hole her absence left was staggering, and I realized how much her cheerful banter did to lighten the mood.

After five days of short answers and distant touches, I couldn't take any more.

"Jake, are you upset at me?"

"No, baby, I'm just stressed. I bombed my finance test on Monday."

I knew the feeling. Thermodynamics had gone from bad to worse. I got a D on my midterm, and even my study group stopped calling me because I so often showed up without the work done.

Even though his words were terse and his back was rigid, I snuggled up next to him on the couch, kissing his neck. "We could study together. I have a class that's on the brink myself."

He stood up briskly and started pacing the room.

Nerves pricked at my arms. I couldn't lie to myself any longer. He hadn't so much as touched me beyond the required boyfriend hello and goodbye kisses since our night together. I was starting to question if he enjoyed it, or if he was even attracted to me anymore.

"Please tell me what's wrong." My voice was laced with desperation, and Jake flinched at the sound.

"Nothing...I'm just feeling smothered, that's all."

"By me?"

"Yes. I mean, no. Just by everything."

Fear replaced the nerves.

He continued to pace, pulling at his hair. "I just feel like you are putting pressure on me."

Where was this coming from? A week ago we were locked in each other's arms, him telling me how close he wanted us to be.

"Jake, I have never pressured you. I've never asked for anything." My voice hitched, and I knew I was seconds from losing it.

"You think I can't tell? That I don't see

everything you are thinking when you look at me? You wear your feelings on your sleeve, Avery, and I can't measure up." His hostility startled me, his voice getting louder with each sentence. "You think I'm this perfect guy without flaws and I'm not."

The room began to spin.

"I just think I need to take a break for a while, get re-focused."

Surely my ears weren't working, because the idea of taking a break from him was like asking a bird to fly without air.

I looked down at my chipping toe nail polish. He was breaking up with me.

Jake walked over and knelt down, taking my hand in his. "This isn't a breakup, okay? I care a lot about you. I just need to spend time in my own place, doing some guy things for a while."

I didn't fight. Didn't beg him to come back when he walked out the door. I just sat there, already knowing what he must have finally seen.

There was nothing here to love.

I spent the next two weeks in isolation, only leaving the apartment to go to class and work.

With Issy gone, episodes became part of my daily ritual, the one thing I looked forward to every day.

It was the only thing that brought me peace, and I refused to feel guilty about it when my life was in such turmoil.

The bubble I was living in worked well until the harsh reality of school popped it wide open.

I sat quietly in the waiting room chair, staring at the note I got from my advisor. Our appointment was at four o'clock, and I was dreading it, knowing full well what we were going to discuss.

Thanksgiving was next week, which left only two weeks before finals, and my grades were abysmal.

"Dr. Davis will see you now, Ms. Nichols," the receptionist said in a sweet voice. She looked like she was in her mid sixties and had probably been working in this same office since the university started.

She had a kind smile, almost apologetic, as if she knew what I was about to face.

I walked into the office that used to bring me comfort. Dr. Davis had been my advisor since freshmen year, and we had always gotten along. It felt different in his office today, smaller, as if the walls were slowly closing in on me.

"Have a seat, Avery, I'm just going to pull your file." His voice had the same calm, melodic tone it always had, but I sensed a bite in it.

He sat down across from me and got right to the point. "You're having kind of a rough semester, aren't you?"

I nodded, too embarrassed to look up at him.

"I also see that you only have one hundred hours of work study done, which is well short of where you should be right now. Anything you want to talk about?" He sat back and took off his glasses, waiting for me to respond.

I simply shook my head as I unsuccessfully willed the tears to stay back.

Dr. Davis sighed and then continued on, "I've seen your grades. I think it's safe to say that you will be on probation next semester. You might want to consider your future plans."

I continued to look down at my hands, as I alternated wrapping a string around each one of my fingers.

"Avery, I need you to take this seriously." He was getting agitated with me.

"I am," I whispered. "I just don't know what to do. I got behind early and was never able to catch up."

He pinched the bridge of his nose while I grabbed a tissue.

"We have a one-time grade replacement program here at the university. Mostly due to students like you who show great promise but have one rough semester. I highly recommend you retake Thermodynamics and use it. It's your only shot to get your average back up to where it needs to be."

I nodded. "I can do that."

"You will have to pay for it, though. Your scholarship doesn't cover repeat courses."

"I understand," I said, having no idea where I was going to get the $2500 I needed for the class.

"Also, I'm not giving you a pass on your work study hours. I warned you a month ago that you had to get serious. My grad student said you've been flaky at best and often incompetent. I was sure he had the wrong student, but he assures me it was you."

His words punched me in the gut. Never in my life had I been such a disappointment to someone.

I was the stellar student, daughter and friend. I prided myself in always being the best in the class and constantly exceeding expectations. Yet, as I sat there, I realized how far I was from that person.

I hadn't spoken to Cara in weeks, and even before, I didn't think to ask her anything about her life, just clambered on about mine.

Issy no longer asked me to go out with her, knowing I would sit and sulk the whole time.

Dr. Davis cleared his throat. "Are you staying on campus for Thanksgiving?"

"I hadn't decided yet."

"Well, I recommend you do. You have fifty hours left in your work study requirement, and I expect you to honor those. Thanksgiving break will be a great chance to get in some hours, and my grad student needs the extra help with it being the holidays. He was less than thrilled when I said you would be the one helping him, but I assured him you would be the perfect assistant."

He blurred in front of me. "I will. I promise. I don't know what to say except... I'm sorry." My voice cracked a little as I choked out the words.

"I know you're better than this, Avery. We'll talk again after finals and figure out the way forward from there."

I nodded and stood to leave, giving his receptionist a little wave on the way out. I didn't know what to do. I didn't want to go home and face the loneliness that waited for me there.

I needed Jake. I needed him to tell me it was going to be okay. I needed to feel his arms around me one more time, just so I could feel worthy again.

Before I even registered my actions, I was on my way to his apartment. I had never just shown up there unannounced before, but I knew he cared about me and would understand when I told him what I was facing. Wasn't he the one who said it wasn't a breakup?

I walked to his door and lightly knocked, my stomach turning inside out with nervousness.

He answered the door and my breath caught. I had almost forgotten how beautiful he was. Bare from the waist up, he looked like he had just woken up for the day.

He squinted at the light and then tensed when he recognized me. "Avery, what are you doing here?"

"I just needed to see you. Do you have a minute to talk?" I was careful as I glanced at him, silently urging him to let me in, but not wanting to give away my feelings as easily as he said I did.

I heard a noise in the background and immediately placed that thick southern accent.

He wasn't alone.

The pain that ripped through my chest rivaled

that of a flogging. Backing up, I would have taken off in a full sprint if I could only get my legs to work properly.

Jake grabbed me by each arm and turned me around. "I never meant to hurt you."

My mind was in a daze. The pain making it impossible for me grasp what I had just seen. "I just don't understand what happened. Was it all a lie, everything you said to me? Was I just some conquest for you? I cared about you. I loved you."

I sounded jilted and desperate, but I didn't care. My world was crashing all around me.

"That's exactly why this doesn't work, Avery. I'm not that guy. I never have been, and you look at me like your world is somehow complete because I'm in it. I'm done being what everyone wants me to be. That part of my life is over!"

His words were like bricks, each chipping away pieces of my heart.

I looked at him through my tears. "I never asked you to be anything but who you are. All I wanted was to be there for you, to help you."

He pushed me away, letting go of the death grip he'd had on my arms. "I don't need your help! I'm not this wounded soul you've made me out to be. I'm just a guy in college who likes to have fun and isn't interested in being tied down right now."

Lightning snapped through my veins. "You said I could trust you! That I was special. I thought you cared about me. My God, Jake, you pursued me!"

I continued to stare at him, searching his eyes for any remaining feeling that might be there, but there was nothing.

"You were special, Avery," he said, exasperated.

He ran his hands through his hair as if remembering. "You were this shy and innocent girl who charmed me with her wit. You were strong on the outside, but so soft and caring on the inside that I found you irresistible."

I gripped his shirt. "Jake, I'm still that person."

He removed my hands and stepped back.

"Something's different, Avery, maybe it's you, maybe it's me…"

I willed my ears to stop working, knowing his next words before he said them.

"…but I just don't see that girl anymore."

That was it, the final blow. The crushing brick that you don't recover from.

I looked up at him, this man who held my heart, who I unashamedly gave everything to, and saw him for the first time. I wanted to vomit, to tear every inch of skin off my body. Anything that would replace the devastating pain that had taken over my heart.

I didn't remember walking to my car or driving home. I existed in a state of shock, going through motions without registering them in my brain. I didn't remember walking across campus, but somehow here I was, standing in the quad.

Nothing made sense; nothing was in focus. I sat

down, hoping to somehow end the crushing pain. I didn't know who I was anymore. Everything I once valued and held true, I had discarded without any regard for the consequences.

I could sense people around me, some even staring in my direction as I sat frozen to the bench I was sitting on, but I didn't care.

Numbness stretched over my shaking body, leaving me cold and empty. If only it would reach my mind, consumed still with thoughts of him. Thoughts frozen in permanent rewind, reminding me over and over again of how much I had failed.

There was music playing around me, and I tried to get my ears to focus, to hear anything that might help me stay above the gripping, smothering nothingness that was everywhere around me.

How did I get to this point? How did I let the chains get so tight that they were crippling every part of my body, dragging me further and further into this pit?

I heard screaming in my head, begging for me to let out its fury, but I just sat there, unable to move, trapped in a silent prison of my own making. The truth glared at me, mocking me for denying it for so long.

I had become nothing… and he knew it.

The air was getting thicker, and I felt the heaviness start to choke me.

Just breathe…in and out…just breathe.

The tears were fire racing down my cheeks,

provoking me with each drop. I sat, gripping the bench until my knuckles were white.

Come on, Avery…just breathe.

The bench shifted slightly, and a warm hand covered mine. Looking up through my tears, I saw warmth and compassion in the eyes of a stranger.

Sounds returned with a flash. I was in the middle of an outdoor concert, and the band was just finishing. A man in jeans and a button up shirt walked to the podium and started to read from a book.

His voice drifted slowly in the air and penetrated the very depths of my heart.

"Even the darkness will not be dark to you; the night will shine like the day, for darkness is as light to you. For you created my inmost being; you knit me together in my mother's womb. I praise you because I am fearfully and wonderfully made."

The words rolled around in my head and suddenly, deep down, I felt a spark. I had forgotten the feeling, as it had been so long since I'd felt anything other than despair, but it was there… hope, just a glimmer, but hope all the same.

"Lord, You know our needs and our hurts. Guide her as she grows, learning which path You have for her..."

10. GLIMMER OF HOPE

Minutes felt like hours, and hours felt like years, but somehow I managed to survive for two days after my crushing breakup with Jake without another major breakdown.

The pit was still surrounding me, but each day I survived, it felt like I was one step closer to that promised light.

Opening the door to the engineering lab, I thought about the concert and the stranger who had been so kind to me. He never said a word, just waited until I calmed down and then patted my hand to say goodbye. His mannerisms somehow conveyed that he was sorry I was hurting.

The concert had gone on for another hour after he got up, and it held a combination of music and speaking. The music was great, but a lot of the words didn't make sense to me.

My time there was a good reprieve, though, because Jake had tried to call three times. He wanted to make sure I got home safely, he had said on my voicemail.

I immediately deleted it, feeling total hatred.

My anger had subsided a little the last couple of days, but now the sadness was taking over.

The sadness of what I had lost—my dignity, my future and my body. All of which were choices I had made with no regrets at the time. I was feeling regret now. In fact, I was feeling it so strongly that I could taste its bitterness.

The timer buzzed, and I immediately took the samples out of the freezer and ran the required tests.

When I finished, I signed out in the log and headed home, dreading every step. How had it only been four months since my first day when everything looked so promising?

I pulled out my phone as I walked, knowing I had to make this phone call. I hadn't told my parents I wasn't coming home for Thanksgiving, and while we weren't close, I knew my mom would use this opportunity to pry.

The phone rang, and I took a deep breath to control my nerves.

"Hello?" My mom answered in her usual sweet tone.

"Hi, Mom. How are you?" My voice was steady despite my anxiety.

"I'm good, Avery. How are you? Are you heading our way tomorrow?"

"Actually, that's what I was calling about. I'm not going to make it home this year. I have a lot of studying to do, and I volunteered to help out with some lab testing over the break." Lie number one.

"Oh, okay, dear. So where are you going for Thanksgiving?"

"Um, the campus has a big dinner they put on. I'll be fine." Lie number two.

"Well, just remember that Thanksgiving isn't a license to let yourself go. You don't want that college fifteen to sneak up on you. Have you still been running?"

I rolled my eyes, wondering how my mom could take any conversation back to my eating habits.

My anxiety was getting worse, so I closed my eyes and took two deep breaths. "Yes, I've been running faithfully every day, and my diet is perfect." Lie number three.

"Good. I'm glad to hear it."

We continued our conversation a while longer, with her doing most of the talking. She told me all about the latest fad diet she and my sister were doing and promised to send me all the information she had on it.

I feigned interest but felt more and more stressed as I talked to her. Finally, after I had remained on the phone an appropriate amount of time, I told her I had to go.

"We'll miss you."

I doubt it. "You too, Mom. I'll talk to you later."

We said our goodbyes, and I hung up the phone, feeling more beat down than I had in two days.

I looked around, trying to find anything that would bring me peace.

The sun was starting to set and the sky was amazing, full of reds and oranges as if a sun goddess was streaking across the clouds in a wonderful dance.

I found my bench (the one from that fateful night) and just stared up at the sky, hoping to find that same spark I had felt there just two days ago.

The bench moved slightly, and I peeked up to see a familiar face looking at me.

"We really should stop meeting like this," he offered, his eyebrow shooting up.

My cheeks flushed, heat searing the back of my neck. The last time he saw me I was on the verge of a complete emotional breakdown.

"You must think I'm crazy." I drew out the words and forced myself to face him.

He was actually really cute, a thing I had no ability to process the first time I saw him. He had sandy blond hair that was cut pretty short and dark blue eyes.

"Nah, we've all had our moments. I mean, I've actually seen people start banging their head against the wall during finals week." He was trying to make me feel better, which was sweet of him.

"Thanks."

Normally, I would feel uncomfortable talking to a stranger in the quad, but the smile that moved across his lips was so genuine and honest, I immediately relaxed.

"I'm Parker. My first name, not my last. It confuses people sometimes. It was my mom's maiden name and now is a source of constant explanation for me."

He was leaning up with his elbows on his knees and looking around the campus as he spoke. When he finished, his eyes rested on me. "And you are?"

"Avery. It was not my mother's maiden name," I teased.

"Good to know."

He had a charm about him that was refreshing. It wasn't the intense attraction I had with Jake, where I wanted to crawl inside of him and get lost there, but I felt at ease with Parker.

"Can I walk you somewhere? It's starting to get dark, and I'd hate to think something might happen to you." He stood and hiked up his backpack.

"You don't need to. I'm just going to University Apartments; they aren't that far."

"I don't mind… if you don't?"

"Um, okay." I got up, and we started to head towards my apartment. He was taller than me, but not by a huge amount. He was certainly shorter than Jake, but stockier. His t-shirt pulled against his chest, exposing an athlete's body.

Comparing Parker to Jake made me sad. I hated that Jake was now my standard for all guys. Hated how he made me believe I was important to him when it turned out I was just like everyone else.

"Are you always this quiet when you walk with

someone?" Parker asked.

I hadn't realized that my mind had wandered for so long.

"I'm sorry. I just have a lot on my mind right now." Attempting small talk, I asked, "Do you live on campus too?"

"No, I have a place in Asheville that I rent with another guy. He's pretty cool, so the arrangement works well. Do you have roommates?"

"Yes, I do. One of them I've never met. She's in Portugal on exchange. The other is amazing. Her name is Issy, and she is fun and exciting, but not around much lately. I kind of miss her."

The words came out before I could stop them. What was I thinking telling a perfect stranger how I was feeling?

"Yeah, I can see that. I'm not much for being alone either; I'm kind of a people person, you know."

"Really? I couldn't tell." My voice hitched, letting him know I was teasing, and his shoulder hit mine in a friendly bump.

It took me a second to realize I was smiling and had been for a while. "Have you been at Winsor long?"

"I'm a junior. Working on pre-med. I really thought this semester would be easier for some reason, but I think that was wishful thinking. The ladies in the library are starting to ask me how my parents are doing… using their first names."

He saw my confusion and explained. "I get bored

easily so I tend to find people to talk to. Sheila works nights in the medical section. She is a single mom with two kids. I find her inspiring, though. She's the only person in her family to graduate high school, and now she's working on her English degree. She wants to be a teacher. Isn't that cool?"

He was unlike anyone I had ever met. Just cheerful and honest, like we had been best friends for decades. I didn't know who Sheila was. I had never once stopped to notice any of the people who worked at the library, despite the hundreds of hours I had spent there.

I studied him, my eyes questioning if it was possible for someone to be this nice.

"So, which one is yours?" he asked, his head tilting toward the buildings.

I hadn't noticed we were here.

"Building 1, my stairs are right there."

"Great! Well, Avery, it was so nice to finally meet you. And now that I know you are safe, I'm going to drag myself back to my car with much less enjoyment than I had walking you home."

His face lit up with animation when he spoke, and his genuine smile nudged a little at my hardened heart.

"Thanks again… and I'm really glad I met you, too."

"You sound surprised."

I laughed and then admitted, "Okay, maybe a little, but pleasantly."

"I can live with that! You have a great weekend,

Avery. Oh, and keep smiling like that. Your eyes light up when you do." He winked at me and turned to leave.

He walked away and I realized that his car was in commuter parking, the other way across campus. His chivalry had added over a mile to his walk.

I felt good as I walked up the stairs, almost happy. Maybe this weekend wouldn't be so bad after all.

As always, I spoke too soon, because staring back at me when I entered my apartment were Jake's stunning green eyes.

He was sitting on the couch with Issy, watching a movie.

"Hey, guys," I somehow managed to say through my disbelief. The crushing pain from the other day returned, and I felt myself stumble back down into the pit. My heart broke all over again as I watched his cool confidence, empty of any feeling he used to have for me.

"Avery, hi!" Issy yelled, jumping off the couch to give me a big hug. "I feel like I haven't seen you in ages! We've decided to do a marathon of *The Office* this weekend since the nightlife before Thanksgiving is nonexistent."

She sat back down by Jake, who hadn't moved since I walked in the door.

The sliver of happiness I felt with Parker vanished, and my bitterness came rushing back.

"Sounds like fun," I muttered and went to the kitchen. I refused to hide in my room just because

Jake decided to show up at MY apartment. "If I made popcorn, would there be any takers?"

Issy put her hand up enthusiastically.

"Jake?" I asked coolly.

"Yeah, I'll take some." He didn't move his eyes from the TV.

I threw the popcorn in the microwave. *What a coward.* How did I not see it before? Every time there was an uncomfortable situation, Jake would check out.

I put my books in my room and then passed out the popcorn before sitting down. The tension between me and Jake was as thick as the dense fog in my photograph.

"Where's Danny tonight?" He and Issy had been inseparable for weeks.

"I wouldn't go there if I were you." There was a hint of amusement in Jake's voice that, a week ago, would have sent flutters to my stomach. Tonight it just made me angry and sour.

"Danny's over," Issy said nonchalantly, and then started hysterically laughing at something happening on the screen.

"Why? I thought you liked him."

"He said the 'L' word." She said the letter "L" with such disgust that I thought she might lose her popcorn.

"The 'L' word? Am I missing something?"

"Really, Avery? I've obviously left you alone way too long. L-O-V-E. Yuk, I can hardly say it."

It took me a second, but then it struck me. I did the same thing to Jake. Love must be a bad word in their family, because both of them ran from it like sprinters in the Olympics.

I wanted to scream at her for hurting him. Scream at Jake, too, for just sitting there as if he hadn't crushed my world. But I didn't say a word and focused on the screen.

I lasted an hour but then excused myself, saying there was only so much "Michael" I could take. The truth was, there was only so much Jake I could take without completely breaking down, and I had had my fill.

The only positive thing…I didn't throw up. That marked three days. I decided to take joy in the small victories and internally patted myself on the back when I turned out my light.

Around two in the morning, I heard a knock on my door. "Avery, are you awake?" Issy whispered.

"I am now. Come in," I sat up in bed and turned on my lamp. "Is something wrong?"

"No, I just wanted to talk to you, and knew I had to wait until Jake was asleep." I peeked out my door and saw him passed out in his usual position on the couch.

"What about?"

"I just wanted to see if you were okay. You were acting a little strange tonight. I tried to talk to Jake about it, but he got defensive like he always does when he behaves badly with a friend of mine. I just don't want you to leave like Betsy did. It's partly why I tried so hard to keep you two apart."

I sat silent for a while. That speech was the most serious dialogue Issy had ever given, and I didn't quite know how to respond to it.

Part of me wanted to tell her everything, to confide in her about my struggles with food and about the horrific way Jake ripped my heart out. But that would require vulnerability, and I was still healing from the last time I had given it to someone. So, instead I deflected to something true, but much less honest.

"Issy, you don't have to worry about me leaving, well, unless my grades don't come up." I sighed and then lied through my teeth. "I'm not upset about Jake. I was never that serious about him anyway. It's my grades that have me on edge. I'll be on probation with my scholarship next semester, and if I don't get them back up, I'll lose it for good."

"I'm sorry. I had no idea."

"I have no one to blame but myself. I knew it was going to be a hard semester, and I chose not to make it a priority. I'm just going to have to really buckle down next semester. Which, of course, means much less partying."

I tried to give my voice a teasing edge to let her know I didn't blame her, and then I changed the subject. "So, what really happened with Danny?"

"It just got too intense. I like to have fun. I'm kind of a free bird like that." Her face stayed completely void of any emotion.

"Is he upset?"

"I don't know. I stopped taking his calls."

"Issy, that's horrible! You didn't even tell him why you were breaking up with him?"

She cocked her head to the side as if talking to a five year old. "You have to be dating in order to break up, Avery."

"You've been sleeping over there for weeks. That's dating."

Issy just shrugged. "Maybe to you. I don't do relationships. Anyway, when are you leaving for Thanksgiving?"

"I'm not." Irritation burned in my stomach. She was no better than Jake.

"Ohhh, you should come with me!"

"No way."

"Come on, Avery, you've never met my mom, and there is no way I can deal with my dad without you there. You have to come!"

The thought of eating Thanksgiving dinner with Jake made me ill. "You have Jake. You don't need me."

"Are you kidding? That's exactly why I need you. I hate Jake when he is around my mom, and he can't stand my dad and refuses to go over there with me. I need a buffer. Please. Pretty please."

There was no way I'd let her talk me into this, but

I was edgy and too tired to argue. I'd put my foot down tomorrow.

"I'll *think* about Thanksgiving Day only. I'm working the rest of the week."

"You're the best, Avery! I'm so glad you moved in!" She jumped off my bed and said good night.

Avery Nichols, I mused. The world's biggest pushover.

"Lord, set her feet on level ground and let her walk in Your truth. Show her Your love is ever before her and lead her to a place where Your glory dwells…"

11. VORTEX

Jake was gone before I woke up on Saturday. Issy was still avoiding Danny, so we spent the afternoon shopping in Asheville and doing other "girl" things like getting our nails painted. It'd been a while since I had good, carefree fun, and it felt refreshing.

Issy spent most of the time giving me the background on her family drama, so I wouldn't be surprised on Thursday. I still wasn't sure how to tell her I wasn't going, but I'd deal with that later.

Her mom and dad met in college and got married young. Issy came along after they had graduated, and her mom opted to stay home with her while her dad got into the business world. To hear Issy's point of view, you'd think her dad was a monster.

"He got into the habit of buying my affections around my fifth birthday, and I've taken full advantage of that since. He topped it all, though, on my twelfth birthday," Issy said as the massage chairs kneaded out the tension in our backs. "He had promised to take me to a concert that night, but was running late, as usual. My mom decided to drive me to his office to save him the commute time—or so she said—and that is when we got to see him and his assistant going at it. Talk about a quick way to have the birds and bees conversation with your kid."

"Oh my gosh! Did your mom suspect?"

"Of course she did, but I don't think she expected us to see what we saw. Even she seemed shocked. Needless to say, I didn't get to go to the concert. Instead, I spent the next year going to custody hearings and counselors. Fun year." The sarcasm in her voice was potent, but her face concealed any emotion.

"How do you do that?" I asked, amazed at her ability to detach.

"Do what?"

"Be completely apathetic, like you're telling me a story of someone else's life? Jake would do something similar, too, except his was more of a zoning, while your face just stays vacant. I can't master that. I'm a total open book."

Issy chuckled. "Yes, you are, and worse, you are a terrible liar. But that's beside the point. I'm vacant because that is how I feel… empty. There is no emotion there because I feel nothing for my father. Jake zones because he's stuck in the past, trying to figure out what he could have changed."

I cursed Issy in my head. I didn't want to hear that. I didn't want to feel sorry for Jake or see anything redeeming in him. It was too painful.

"See! There you go again!" Issy said, pointing. "Your face totally shifted. You thought something and it immediately reacted. Don't tell me Jake didn't hurt you. I know you're lying."

"Fine, he hurt me. What does it matter?"

"It matters because I don't want you to change."

"I'm afraid it's too late for that, Issy. Life changes you. It just does."

She leaned back in her chair, knowing full well I was right. We finished the rest of our pedicure in silence, neither one of us wanting to talk about the men in our lives who hurt us.

We had about two more hours before dinner, so we decided to hit some of the art galleries in town. Looking at art was by far my favorite thing to do in Asheville. I had always been blown away by the creativity of others. I didn't have an eye for such things and was inspired when someone could take a simple object and make it look spectacular.

Issy bored pretty easily and didn't understand why I spent so much time on each picture.

"I guess I just don't see what you are staring at," she said, mimicking my intensity. "I mean, it's a picture. You look at it and move on. What are you trying to find? Is Waldo in there or something?"

I couldn't help but laugh. Issy looked at life though the eyes of a child, seeing only the obvious and stating it as well.

"I like to imagine what they were thinking when they took the picture. Why they chose that angle and how the lighting sets the mood. There is so much more to the pictures than what you see at a glance."

"Okay then. What does this picture say? To me, it says 'I'm a spiral staircase with people on me.'"

"Actually, it's the image he created that's so awesome. He used shadows and textures to create what looks like a spinning vortex. The addition of people makes the staircase appear so large that it could swallow them up whole. Kind of how life seems sometimes."

She looked at me and then at the picture again with new insight. "That's amazing."

"Yes, it is," a masculine voice agreed behind us.

Issy and I both turned around and, to my surprise, Parker was peering over our shoulders at the same picture.

"I thought that was you," he said. "This is one of my favorite galleries."

He looked exactly like he had the other day—jeans, t-shirt and a black backpack, although his t-shirt was an army green today instead of red.

A comforting warmth washed over me as I met his smile.

"You two know each other?" Issy asked looking back and forth between us.

"Yes, in fact, you must be the fun and exciting roommate Avery told me about. I'm Parker." He reached out his hand to shake hers.

She took it and flashed a just-wait-til-I-get-a-hold-of-you smile. "We are on our way to grab some dinner, wanna come?"

A strange feeling of possession hit me as Issy's eyes roamed over Parker's solid chest.

He looked at me for a confirmation, making me feel a little guilty for not being the one to ask.

I quickly agreed. "Um, yeah, you should come. We were just going to the sandwich hut down the street."

"Hey, I should call Jake and see if he wants to join us."

I flashed her a panicked stare.

"I'm sure he has other plans," I stammered, unable to process why Issy would be so cruel after our earlier conversation.

"Too late, I've already texted him, and he is on his way there." Her eyes were gleaming, and I wanted to crawl in a hole.

"Okay then." I gritted my teeth, doing my best to keep a smile plastered on my face. "Let's go."

Issy was in true form as we walked to the restaurant. She latched her arm through Parker's and started giving him the third degree. "So, how did you meet our Avery?"

"We actually met in the quad. She was sitting there, looking very lovely as she watched the sunset, and I just had to say hi."

I hadn't realized I was holding my breath until I finally released it. He didn't mention that fateful night, or my total meltdown. I was once again impressed with his character and how he had gone out of his way twice now to spare my feelings.

"You're a student at Winsor then? What major?"

"Pre-med."

"Wow, pre-med, what made you decide on that field?" I hit Issy discretely and gave her the look that said, *What are you doing?*

She ignored me and continued to wait for his reply.

"I love people, and I thought, what better way to make a difference than to help them when they need it most? People are vulnerable when they're sick. I want to give them peace, and if I'm lucky, healing too."

"You will love my cousin, Jake, then. He always says he's the ultimate caretaker."

My throat constricted at her words, causing a coughing spasm so severe we had to quit walking. All I could think of was how much I wanted to be in the photograph getting swallowed up by the vortex.

Parker immediately came to my aid, patting my back and handing me a bottle of water he had in his backpack.

"Thank you," I said between coughs until I finally got myself under control. "I don't know what happened."

Parker walked into the restaurant to get us a table, and Issy whispered in my ear, "He's cute! Why didn't you tell me about him?"

"Because there is nothing to tell," I fired back. "I'm going to kill you, by the way!"

Parker returned and, despite my irritation, I met him with a smile.

"They have a table ready now if you want to go in."

"Great. Lead the way."

I was seconds from a full-fledged panic attack. I had no idea how I was going to react with Jake in the room, and how much more awkward it was going to feel with Parker sitting right there.

He pulled my chair out for me and then sat down adjacent to it, all under the watchful eyes of the always-perceptive Issy.

To the unaware bystander, it looked like Parker and I were on a date.

"So, Issy, you heard all about me. What about you? What are you studying?" Parker asked.

"I'm in the undecided category." She ripped open a packet of sweet-n-low and dumped it in her tea. "I figure there's no reason to commit at this stage. I'm going to take all the classes I like now, and then my senior year, I'll just figure out what major I can use to graduate and declare that one. My theory is that I'll really like that major because I picked those classes by choice and not off some degree plan."

Issy's logic was remarkable. She was so convincing, I almost thought it was a good idea.

The muscles around Parker's mouth tightened and I could tell he was trying not to laugh. I didn't see judgment in his eyes, though, just humor.

"You'll have to tell me what you ended up

declaring or it will bug me for the next ten years."

She eyes him suspiciously. "You don't think I'm crazy? Huh. I pegged you as the over achieving type."

His head fell back with laughter. "You are absolutely right, but I think originality is a gift, and you certainly have plenty of it."

Parker's tone was totally complimentary and authentic, as if he was validating her right to be her own person.

"Thank you," she said with a hint of pride.

I wasn't sure how he did it, but Parker had a way of making you feel really good about yourself, like your individuality made you special and unique.

"What about you, Avery? We never got to that on our walk the other day."

"I'm in engineering. I'm not sure what specialty, yet. I don't have to decide that until next year, but I'm starting to think I may go into civil. I'm kind of fascinated with different types of structures."

"Ah, that explains your love for the staircase in that picture."

"Yeah, maybe so." I was surprised he had remembered such a small detail.

Issy battered him with questions again. By the time she was finished, I'd learned that Parker was from Boone, North Carolina, which was about two hours from Asheville. His parents had been married for twenty-seven years, and he had an older brother who did missionary stuff overseas.

I never thought hearing about someone's

hometown would be so interesting, but Parker had us falling out of our seats laughing at the stories he would tell. I was having so much fun, I almost forgot Issy had texted Jake until we heard him move the chair out and sit down.

"What's so funny?" he asked, giving Issy an annoyed look.

She wiped the tears out of her eyes. "Parker was telling us stories from his hometown, and they are hilarious. The one of Mr. French and the cat…" Fits of laugher took hold again, and Jake looked considerably put out that he wasn't included.

"I'm sorry, Jake. I guess you had to be here," she said with a hint of "oops" in her voice.

"Well, I'm here now. So, what's for dinner?" He grabbed a menu and began looking at the specials.

I couldn't believe he didn't introduce himself to Parker. In fact, I had never seen Jake so off his game before. He looked uncomfortable and antsy. I took that as a direct slam against me and realized that Issy probably didn't mention my being here.

The chains started to crawl up my legs, pulling and tugging again. I looked down at my trembling hands and wondered how I ever thought Jake cared about me.

"You okay?" Parker whispered in my ear, sounding genuinely concerned.

I met his eyes and nodded, trying to give a convincing smile. I would have to do a better job at the whole hide-your-feelings thing.

Jake stared at the exchange between me and Parker, and his jaw went rigid. Not wanting to look at him, I focused on Issy, who appeared very pleased with herself.

She took that opportunity to make introductions. "Jake, this is Parker, Avery's friend from school. Parker, Jake."

The guys nodded at each other, the way men tend to do when uncomfortable, said muffled hellos, and then went back to their menus.

The air grew thick around me, and I felt that horrible sensation start in my gut. My heart followed and was soon knocking against my chest in an erratic drumbeat. I cursed myself, begging internally to calm down.

Parker's hand reached over and found mine, just like it had in the quad. The effect was immediate. My heart rate slowed, my breathing became normalized, and I could feel the color returning to my face.

He let go as soon as I had calmed and smiled up at the group. "I know what I'm having, how about you?"

We ordered our food, and Jake excused himself to take a phone call. I was visibly more relaxed as soon as he left the table.

"I'm assuming there's a backstory there," Parker said gently, once again leaning into me.

"It's complicated… and not at all an interesting story." I was trying to downplay the tension and my strange response to it.

Parker's face said he knew better, but he dropped the subject.

Turning his attention back to Issy, he asked her what she liked to do for fun. I don't think he had any idea what an open-ended question that was, because all Issy did was "fun." It defined her life.

They were actively engaged in stories of road trips and adventures they wanted to take when Jake returned to the table.

He had his old swagger back, like he had pulled a telephone booth transformation. He grabbed his chair by the back of it and slid it over in my direction before he sat down. Our knees touched, and I felt his hand settle on the inside of my thigh.

My back went board straight when he began rubbing his finger up and down, so lightly and provocatively that my body immediately responded.

I looked up at him, confused, irritated, and totally lost. The heat in his eyes had me blushing and wondering if Parker or Issy had caught our exchange.

Luckily, they were still engaged in animated story telling, so they didn't think it was odd when I excused myself to the bathroom.

I grabbed both sides of the sink and glared at myself in the mirror. I had to calm down; I had to find some control. How was he able to affect me like that… with just one touch? It was ridiculous!

I splashed some cold water on my neck and gave myself another pep talk before making my way back to the table.

Our food had come, and I dreaded the idea of eating in such a stressful environment. There was no question I had a love/hate relationship with food.

Life would be so much easier if I just never had to eat again, but here it was, surrounding me as always, mocking me with the realization I would never be free of its hold.

I moved my chair away from Jake and sat down, which by default meant I was almost touching Parker's leg. He smelled really nice, like an airy freshness that comes after a morning rain, but masculine enough to make your senses alert.

His tender smile eased my tension, and he filled me in on their conversation.

"I was asking Issy how you two met."

"Oh, no, what did she say?" I was terrified to relive that first day through her eyes.

"Why would you ask that? I was perfectly complimentary." Issy pouted like a scolded toddler.

"She was very complimentary," Parker assured me. "Said you were shy and timid, but she could see you had lots of heart. She also said she had never seen anyone run as much as you did."

I glanced at Jake, thinking of how many miles were driven by the excitement and anticipation of seeing him. I rolled my eyes. He was texting on his phone under the table as if we were having the most boring conversation in the world. *Jerk.*

I averted my eyes right as Issy pointed out that Parker was a runner too. "He's in some kind of military fraternity, and they run all the time."

Parker's eyes sparkled with humor. "They're not exactly a fraternity, but we do run." He turned to me. "Maybe we could go together sometime?"

My stomach fluttered. "Sure."

Jake chose that moment to come back into the conversation. "I'm ready to go. You guys finished?"

"Avery hasn't had a chance to finish eating yet, besides I'm having fun," Issy whined.

"No, I'm done. I'll just get the rest to go."

"Where's your car, Issy? I'll take you back to it." Jake was trying to hurry us, as if he had somewhere to be… or someone to be with.

"Actually Jake, you and I need to plan our Thanksgiving meal. Mom promised to let me pick all the dishes this year, and I need your input."

Issy threaded her arm through his and pulled him out the door. "You two go ahead and keep talking, we'll meet you back here in a little while."

And like a puff of smoke, they were gone.

I didn't know whether to feel nervous or excited about being left alone with Parker. Honestly, it just felt nerve wracking, like I was on a first date or something.

Parker chuckled and turned back to me. "Issy is amazing."

"She's something, all right. You just never know what to expect next." I was shaking my head, but my voice held nothing but affection for my quirky roommate.

"There's a coffee shop on the river if you want to go. They have the whole area lit up this time of year for Christmas, and it's a really beautiful walk."

"I'd love that," I said, eager to get outside where the fresh air could wipe away all my confusion.

I texted Issy the new plan and let Parker guide me out the door.

The walk was every bit as he described. Trees were lined with white lights, each placed in perfect, equal distance from the other. The walls along the river were decked out with red light wreaths twinkling against the night sky.

It's beauty touched something in my heart. It was a feeling of hope. I looked at Parker, wondering if he was the common denominator.

The air was crisp, a perfect fall night that made you wear a jacket and scarf, but didn't chill you to the bone.

Parker started giving me the background of the city and why they did the Christmas lights each year.

As we walked, the heaviness of what wasn't being said started to get to me.

"You like to look beyond the obvious, don't you?" My question came out more like an accusation.

Parker tilted his head. "What do you mean?"

"You never seem to take anything at face value. You have some story that goes along with it, whether you're talking about Sheila in the library or a walkway by the river. Even me. I was a wreck when you saw me, on the edge of a complete meltdown, but you act like that horrible moment never happened."

I couldn't figure out why I was upset. He'd been nothing but completely nice to me since the first moment we met. Maybe that was the problem. I was broken, and he was acting as if I were whole.

I looked down at my feet, stopping our walk. I was so sick of crying. So sick of who I had become.

He took my hands in his. "Avery, you weren't wrecked when I saw you, and your story doesn't define you."

I shook my head. "I still can't understand why you would even want to talk to me after seeing that."

"What I saw that day was a girl who wasn't afraid to examine her life and figure out how to move forward. I sat there watching you and couldn't take my eyes off you. The anguish was real, and I just wanted you to know someone cared."

"That's so pathetic," I scoffed, angry at myself for being so transparent.

"No, it's not; it's remarkable. Do you have any idea how many people never get to that point? How many go through life never stopping to realize that they've fallen? Avery, those people can never get up. You can." He was intently looking at me, pleading with me to believe him.

"I wish you could see yourself through my eyes," he finally said when I turned away from him. "That night I saw you watching the sunset, it was like a ray of sunlight had descended. You looked so beautiful sitting there waiting, anticipating an answer from the sky. There was a hopefulness that drew me to you—a glimpse that something great was happening within you."

He moved in closer to me. It was as if my body didn't know that I was wounded. It responded to him like we'd been cut from the same cloth and were ready to be stitched together.

Confusion tugged at me. I was completely struck by the difference of how I felt with Parker versus Jake.

He pulled my hands up to his face and lightly kissed my fingers. It was soft and lingering, and warmed me to the core.

"Don't sell yourself short, okay?" He searched my eyes.

"I'll try not to."

He turned to continue walking, but kept his hand securely in mine, lacing our fingers together.

Jake and Issy were already at the coffee shop waiting when we got there.

I quickly took my hand out of Parker's before we walked over to their table. If it bothered him, I couldn't tell.

He just said cheerful goodbyes to everyone and then turned to leave, giving me one last smile on his way out the door.

I sat down at the table and Issy got up to get a refill.

"What are you doing?" Jake scooted himself over so we could whisper.

"What do you mean?"

"I mean having Issy text me just to parade another guy in front of me."

I was horrified at his implication. "Jake, I had no idea Issy would call, and I certainly wouldn't have let her if she had asked. You and I both know Issy does whatever she wants to."

"And the guy?"

"Seriously? Are we living in two different realms of reality? You are sleeping with someone else. I don't owe you any explanation." I knew my tone was cold and accusatory, but I didn't care.

"For the record, I am not sleeping with her. You judge things too quickly, Avery. I never said I didn't care about you, just that I needed some space. I didn't see that as a license for you to go hook up with a new guy." He sounded furious at me, which only added to the chaos in my head.

"I'm not hooking up. We just met, and it's nothing more than friendship at this point, anyway."

"Avery, that guy does not want to be your *friend*."

I'd studied Jake's eyes a million times, could recite every emotion I'd seen in them. But the bitterness I saw tonight was new and chilling.

He had grabbed my arm sometime during the exchange, and I suddenly felt very uncomfortable this close to him.

I pulled my arm away. "Why do you even care?"

He didn't answer, and I was weary from our staring contest. I got up to leave, not saying another word.

He stormed away from the table and out the door, leaving me to do nothing but wonder how it was possible to send so many mixed signals.

"Lord, I pray she knows Your unfailing love and how to find refuge in the shadow of your wings. I pray she knows you delight in her and that in Your light, she will see the true light…"

12. PARKER

The air hung thick in the apartment on Sunday as I tried to forget the weekend. I'd had another episode and was still reeling from my disappointment. Failure should be etched on my forehead.

Danny was calling constantly, and Issy was getting more and more agitated by it.

"Why don't you just answer it and talk to him?" I asked after she dramatically turned off her phone and threw it in her room. "Maybe if you just explain things it won't be so hard."

Issy sent me an frustrated look. "I did. The idiot cornered me in the laundry room this morning."

She examined my face, apparently reading my concern for Danny. "Don't look at me like that. I warned you this would happen."

"I guess I don't get it either. You were with him for weeks, and you even told me you don't do more than one or two dates. Obviously you felt something for him."

Issy stood up and crossed her arms. "I guess I'm

just going to have to spell this out for you. I never felt anything for Danny. I don't feel anything for guys, okay? Nothing. He was convenient. You were all brooding and sad, and I couldn't stand to be in the apartment anymore. Aaron is funny, and Danny is sweet. That's it. The fact that Danny fell for me is an unfortunate side effect, but I was very clear with both of you from the beginning that I don't do relationships." She drew out the last four words with a hard undercurrent in her tone.

I knew that Issy had to practically take out a restraining order to get men to stop calling her, but I had no idea she could be so cruel.

Reality struck me like a dart to a bulls-eye. I was Jake's Danny. That was what Issy had been trying warn me about from the beginning. They were exactly the same.

"You're right, Issy. You did tell me. I'm sorry I pushed him on you." Knowing how easily Issy could toss Danny out just further confirmed how little Jake ever felt for me.

It was a game of chess, and Issy and Jake were the victors.

Satisfied I wouldn't bug her anymore, she held up two different movies for me to choose from. I picked the comedy. My own drama was enough in my life right now.

"Hey, I left driving directions on your desk for Thursday. I'm leaving in the morning, and the phone will get you lost," she said as she loaded the DVD.

I was dreading this conversation, but I had to tell her I wasn't going. "Issy, about that. I really don't think it's the best idea if I go. It will only be awkward with Jake, and that's the last thing you need while you are there. I'm really good just sticking around here."

Issy completely turned her body to look at me. "No way. You said you were coming, and I do not have the strength of mind right now to be in my dad's house without some backup."

Issy was hard to turn down when she was being playful, but I decided turning down serious Issy was simply impossible.

"Okay," I resigned. "I'll come."

The campus was eerily empty Monday morning, with all classes cancelled for the holidays.

Determined to make the most of the week, I found my favorite table in the library and got each of my books and papers set up exactly how I liked them.

I knew I couldn't recover from my grade in thermo, but I figured the more I learned this semester, the better I'd be for next term.

For some reason, though, I couldn't concentrate. Maybe my brain needed a break. I had just spent the last four hours studying in the lab.

I walked around the library, not sure what I was looking for until I found myself on third floor with all the medical references. I convinced myself that I was seeking out Sheila, eager to meet the woman Parker so admired, but deep down I knew I was hoping to run into him.

I looked around the room filled with shelves of reference material and there he was, leaning over the counter talking with someone.

A warm wave ran though my body, and my mood immediately brightened.

He looked exactly the same: jeans, a black t-shirt and his typical smile that made the whole world seem right.

My reaction to him was so different. I didn't feel nervous or lose all control of my mind and body. Instead, I felt a comfort in his consistency and strangely self-assured.

He caught a glimpse of me and waved me over. He seemed genuinely glad to see me as he gave me a sideways hug when I walked up.

"What a wonderful surprise! Avery, this is Sheila," he said proudly, as if to validate everything he had told me about her.

I smiled and shook her hand. She was a petite woman in her mid-thirties, with dark skin and a kind smile. Her face was full of character, indicating she had been through a lot in her life.

"It's nice to meet you," I said. "Parker, here, is your biggest fan."

She waved her hand as if to bat away the compliment. "He's not so bad either, although I get nothing done when he's here. This one's a talker, let me tell you."

Parker pretended to be hurt, and we all laughed, knowing she was right. We said our goodbyes, and Parker walked me over to his table.

"I didn't mean to interrupt," I said, suddenly feeling unsure about seeking him out.

"Are you kidding? You're the best thing I've seen all day. Anatomy is about to suck the life out of me."

I looked at his table and saw papers everywhere. It was a stark difference from my perfectly organized study setup. "How can you even study in this mess?"

"I have a method to my madness, I promise. You just can't see it with the naked eye."

"Really?" I dropped my elbows to the table and set my chin on my hands. "So, where can I pick up the super spidey glasses that make sense of all this craziness?"

"Are you calling my notes crazy? I am violently offended. Just for that, you are forced to stay here with me as I muddle through this mess."

It was cute how he asked me to stay in such an clever way. His easy mannerism and humor made me feel special and wanted.

"Well, sir, my books are downstairs, so I will have to get a pass in order to retrieve them."

"I guess that is a valid reason, but since you are a flight risk, I insist on escorting you to the area. Agreed?"

I laughed and stood, acting resigned to my punishment.

His eyes sparkled, telling me he was enjoying our

bantering.

I wondered to myself how I never noticed how special his eyes were before. They were a dark midnight blue and didn't hold any of the darkness that Jake's did.

We walked downstairs, continuing to kid around as I grabbed my things.

"I must warn you, though, thermo has been known to put me in a very bad mood." There was definitely truth to that comment.

He leaned into to me as we were walking and whispered in my ear. "Then I'll just have to be extra charming today."

Bolts of electricity ran from my ear, down my neck and through my legs. I'd never seen him be anything but charming, but I was surprised by how much it affected me. Maybe I wasn't doomed to love Jake forever.

We made our way back to his study table. He cleared a space for me by moving all of his notes into a pile. I had to look away from the chaos, focusing instead on getting my system set up again.

Parker watched me with fascination.

"What?" I asked.

"Nothing. It's just you are so careful about where you set everything. It's interesting."

"It's obsessive, but it's the only way I can study. Must be my control freak self coming out to play. You've met her before. She's the one who always seems to lose her mind when she feels powerless in a situation." My voice was full of sarcasm, but Parker still picked up on the truth of it.

I always said too much with him.

"Like at dinner the other night?" The mood suddenly shifted from fun to serious.

"Yeah, like at dinner the other night," I said quietly, using my pen to draw a perfectly square box on my notebook.

"So, you and Jake, did you date?"

He was being careful with his questions, trying to gage the situation without looking too nosey. I figured we were going to have this conversation eventually, so I may as well get it over with.

"Date may be too strong of a word. We went out for a while, off and on. Things just didn't work out." I was being cryptic and not fully honest, but I didn't really feel like telling him the extent of my feelings for Jake.

"How long were you two 'off and on' for?"

"Not long, really, just this semester. It's really not a big deal. We just haven't found our way back to being 'just friends' again."

His face appeared skeptical, but he dropped it all the same, opting instead to make a joke about something he had to memorize for class.

I watched him as he studied and wondered how he learned anything. He was constantly fidgeting or messing with his papers. About every fifteen minutes, he would come up with something to ask me or would start telling me something interesting about what he was learning.

I looked at him, feigning exasperation. "I'm not going to get anything done like this!"

"Sorry. I'm a loud studier. I'm done. Not another word." He made the motion like he was locking his mouth and throwing away the key.

I shook my head affectionately and then returned to my books, starting again in chapter one. Back to the basics.

I was on my fifth problem in the chapter when Parker leaned over and drew a little smiley face on my paper with the word "hi" underneath it. I looked up. His eyes mirrored a lost little puppy.

"I've never seen anyone with such concentration. That was the longest half hour of my life."

I couldn't help but laugh. I had a whole new appreciation for what Shelia was talking about.

"Let's get some air," he said.

Parker and I always seemed to do our best talking outside. The quad was normally packed with students, but today the entire place belonged to only us.

"So, any big plans for Thanksgiving?" he asked as we found a nice spot on the grass and sat down.

"Well, I've been suckered into going to Issy's house to be a buffer between her and her dad, so I'm not especially looking forward to the holiday."

I didn't mention the fact that Jake would be there as well, not wanting to revisit our earlier conversation.

"It's nice of you to go, though. I get the sense that Issy is lonely."

I looked at him like he was crazy. "Issy? The girl literally has a phone call or text every second, and I'm not exaggerating. She's anything but lonely."

"Huh. Maybe you're right. I just got that vibe the other day. Of course, popularity doesn't necessarily equate to friendships. It just means you know lots of people."

I pondered that thought for a minute and then dismissed it, remembering how easily she had dumped Danny the minute she had no more use for him. There was no way that Issy was lonely.

Thinking of Danny reminded me of how easily Jake had discarded me, and I decided I wanted to change the subject. "What about you? Are you going home?"

"Oh yeah, or the wrath of my mom would overtake me. Actually, I really do love Thanksgiving… almost as much as Christmas, but not quite." He looked up at the sky like he was reliving fun family memories. "We usually have lots of family over and watch football. We also have our annual football game in the afternoon, which can get pretty intense."

"How so?"

"My mom has two brothers, so between all of us, there are eight testosterone-filled guys on the field, and the game can get competitive. My first broken bone came from one of those games. I was twelve."

"You're kidding! What did you break?"

"My finger." I started laughing at him. "Okay, so

it wasn't a major injury, but the break hurt all the same." He bumped me with his shoulder and laid back on the grass, covering his eyes to shield them from the sun.

"This is one of my favorite things to do. Just lie here in the quad and soak up the heat."

I followed suit and laid down next to him. I had seen students do this a lot but never took the time myself to come out here. I always had somewhere I needed to be or something on my mind that I needed to do. Truth was, it was really hard for me to just be still.

The sun felt warm on my face, and I could feel the grass through the back of my shirt. It smelled like summer, even though it was cold. The scent of the fresh grass took me back to being a kid, when life was so full of promise and excitement, and part of me wanted to stay there forever.

"I can see why you like it. Do you do this a lot?" I was curious about his thought process. He was so different from anyone I knew.

"I don't know. It comes and goes in waves. I enjoy letting the world stop around me. Laying here often brings me clarity and focus."

"Is there something you need clarity on now?"

He rolled over to his side and rested on his elbow. I did the same and faced him so he would know I was listening.

"Well, there's this girl I met who I can't seem to get out of my head." His voice was playful, but I got the sense he was being serious.

My pulse quickened. I wanted to be that girl. "Why can't you get her out of your head?"

He inched himself closer to me and looked deep into my eyes. His look wasn't intense or sensual, just appreciative. "She's spectacular, and even more amazing, she doesn't know it."

He leaned in slowly and time ceased to exist. I felt his breath first. It was minty and warm. Then his lips touched mine. Soft and careful. It mirrored his treatment of me, reverence, respect, and only lasted a few seconds.

The chill in the air was gone, replaced only by a cocoon of tenderness.

My eyes opened. He was staring, his face full of care and concern.

Goose bumps sprung up on my arms even though I felt nothing but warmth.

"You're not so bad yourself." I whispered.

We rolled to our backs, and Parker's hand moved over to mine.

He was right; there was something very calming about sitting still and even more so about his presence. The comfort level I had with him seemed impossible, and yet here I was, feeling a serenity that surpassed my wildest expectations.

"Lord, I pray Your strength be upon her and that You will rescue her when she needs it from the mouth of the lion. I pray she is able to stand firm and put her hope in Your unfailing love."

13. THANKSGIVING

Today was Thursday. I sat up in bed, dread covering me like a blanket, and realized that I would have to be especially on guard today.

The last few days were like a nice dream. I would run in the morning, work in the lab, and then meet Parker at the library to study.

We would talk about our families and what we wanted for the future. I learned that the Air Force was paying for his schooling, and that they were also sending him to medical school after graduation.

Since Winsor didn't have an active unit at the school, he would drive to Charlotte once a month for training.

Parker was so careful with me, whether it was holding my hand or stealing a kiss. He always did so with such consideration. He made me feel precious and valued, like his world revolved around making sure I knew how special I was to him.

The realization hit me that, for the first time in months, I didn't think about throwing up.

What I found amazing was not that I was able to resist it, but that I felt a calm that negated the desire to do it at all.

I felt healthy.

Of course, it had only been four days, but considering I had been alone in the apartment all that time, it was a pretty big feat.

I looked at the clock and groaned. I promised Issy I would be at her house before noon. I didn't want to go. I wanted to throw the covers back over my head and sleep the day away.

There was nothing to look forward to. Parker had left last night for his parent's house. Issy was probably going to be very high maintenance, and Jake... well who ever knew with Jake.

Would he be my kind, loving, sweet Jake? Or the angry, rude and emotionally unavailable Jake? Part of me didn't know which one I would prefer. It was a no win situation for me.

I sighed as my alarm continued to ding at me. *Let's get this over with.*

The drive was relatively quiet and really pretty. Issy lived an hour from school, down predominately back roads. Trees lined the shoulder as far as the eye could see and almost created a hypnotic setting for the driver.

I pulled off the main highway onto smaller roads and finally into a gated community called Season Oaks. The houses were spectacular, at least twice the size of my house in Georgia. I followed the curvy road, in awe of every house I looked at, each having its own character and design.

Issy's house was by far the most grand in the neighborhood. It sat on a half-acre, off the street and was tall enough to be three stories, although, on closer examination, I saw it was only two.

There was a circle drive in front, with four white columns flanking wide steps that led to the front porch, which was scattered with luxurious outdoor furniture.

I was awestruck as I walked to the door, realizing how dramatically Issy had downplayed her family's wealth.

Issy flung open the door before I could knock and rushed out to give me a hug. "There you are! I was going crazy!" Her voice was as dramatic as ever.

"Issy, I'm thirty minutes early." I patted her back, trying to hold in a laugh.

"Really? Goodness, this morning is taking f-o-r-e-v-e-r."

She grabbed my bags and led me through the door.

I could hardly move as I took in the beauty.

The ceiling was at least twenty feet high, with a huge chandelier in the entrance. The flooring was a pristine Carrera marble that reflected the light perfectly. The entry fed straight into a huge living room with hand-scrapped dark wood flooring and a stone fireplace that ran all the way up to the ceiling.

The room was impeccably decorated with dark

wood furniture and mushroom colored couches. Everything about the place screamed luxury and comfort, an impossible combination.

Issy began to get annoyed with my gawking and started to pull at my arm. "You're upstairs, Avery. This way."

"I'm sorry. You just have a beautiful home."

She rolled her eyes as if I had said the most ridiculous thing ever and practically pushed me up the stairs.

My room was the second on the left, next to Issy's. It was perfect. The walls were two-toned, with soft white on top and dark taupe on the bottom.

A large bed sat square in the middle, but the best touch of richness was a beautiful taupe ottoman that held bath towels and a perfectly placed mint. I felt a little like royalty.

"Avery… really. You need to snap out of it. It's a room."

"Issy, you may see stuff like this all the time, but not everyone grew up in a house this beautiful. I'm just taking it all in." I carefully set down my bags so I didn't add any clutter to the immaculate room.

"If you are this crazy over my mom's house, just wait until you see my dad's." I looked at her in disbelief. "It makes this house look tiny."

She grabbed my arm and pulled me into her room, which looked like an 80's video. There was a large, red platform bed, with white sheets and a black coverlet.

Two of the walls were stark white with large windows and the other looked as if Issy had flung every color of paint she could find at the wall.

She sat on her bed, held a fuzzy lip pillow and started filling me in on her "horrific" week.

After a few minutes, I realized the gist of it was that she had been stuck in her mom's house all week with Jake, and they were making her crazy. New guy was out of the picture for her mom, which meant lots of alcohol and Valium.

"I swear, Avery, I've watched enough internet TV to be considered a hermit." Issy had the typical whine in her voice that comes when she doesn't get her own way, and then it changed abruptly. "So that is why I have tonight all worked out." Her mischievous voice was out now, which was always the one that got me in the most trouble.

"Issy, the whole reason I came was to go with you to your dad's house tonight. What on earth do you have planned now?"

"An after party," she stated simply.

"Who has an after party on Thanksgiving?"

"Ben. His parents spend every fall in Europe, and it's become a solid tradition around here." She was going on as if it was the most practical thing in the world.

"Wait a second, ex-boyfriend Ben?"

She nodded and pretended she was fascinated by something in her magazine.

"Issy, no! That has 'regret' written all over it."

She set down her magazine in a huff. "I seriously could care less about Ben. I've gone to that party every year but last year, and people will talk if I miss it again. They expect me to be there."

"Who does?"

"Have I not taught you anything? The same expectations I have at school, I have here. I'm the social dictator. If there is a major party, and I'm not there, what does that say about me?"

"I don't know… that it's Thanksgiving!" I paused for a second, waiting for Issy to come to her senses.

Then I realized that Issy and I operated in such different universes that there was no possible way to get through to her. I only had one choice… to go.

"Okay, fine, we'll go, but how are you going to get through Jake? He'll never go for it."

"He'll never know. We'll be at my dad's, remember? Ben lives right down the street, and if I act as annoying and rude as I always do over there, by nine o'clock he'll be begging for me to go back to my mom's house…"

"…which, of course, we won't do until much later," I reasoned.

"You are so smart! So, I already packed a bag for us and put it in the car. You will wear what I picked out." She gave me a stare so severe I didn't respond.

Instead, I let her believe I would change, knowing that I probably wouldn't.

An odd feeling of excitement shot through me. For some reason, every time I was with Issy, I felt like

I was doing some form of espionage.

"Isadora, honey, where are you?" Issy's mom called from the bottom of the stairs.

"Isadora?" I questioned.

"It's better than Kaitlyn, and she refuses to call me Issy," she explained as she headed to the door. "I'm up here with Avery. We're on our way down now."

Issy motioned for me to come and led us down the stairs. I quickly realized I had no idea what her mother's name was. "What does she go by?" I asked quietly.

"Call her Diana. She stopped using my dad's name a while ago, and her first name makes her feel younger anyway."

We walked in the kitchen, which was as grand as the rest of the house. Issy had on a smile so fake I was sure it was done just to annoy her mother.

Diana didn't seem to notice and instead was pulling the turkey out of the oven. Jake was getting the carving knives out of the drawer when he looked up and saw me standing there. My heart leapt into my throat upon seeing him, and I secretly cursed my body for reacting.

"Avery, you're here." Jake dropped the knife and fork and came to give me a big hug and a soft kiss on the cheek. I stood frozen, wondering who this person was.

"Diana, this is our Avery, Issy's new roommate." He announced me proudly while keeping one arm

153

around my shoulders as if there was some relationship still going on between us.

I looked up at him in total confusion, wrestled my way out of his grip and walked towards Issy's mom. "It's very nice to meet you. Thank you so much for having me. Your home is absolutely beautiful." She smiled at me warmly and seemed to beam with pride when I mentioned the house.

Issy's mom was the picture of beauty and grace. She had Issy's dark hair and green eyes and carried herself like an aristocrat. Every inch of her was perfectly manicured, and not even one hair was out of place, despite obviously being in the hot kitchen for hours. While Issy was close to the visual replica of her mom, the stark contrast of their mannerisms and style was almost unnerving.

"Well, we are so glad you are here. Jake has told me all about you. We're so lucky that Issy got such a great roommate this year." She turned back to the turkey, and I looked at Issy with a mixture of shock and disbelief. She just rolled her eyes and left the room. I felt like I was in some episode of the *Twilight Zone* and was really wishing I had learned to say "no" to Issy. The only positive was that Jake was being cordial, which I decided was much better than the silent treatment I usually got.

"Can I help with anything?" I offered, feeling like I needed to say something.

"Can you fill the glasses? There's water in the fridge and red wine on the bar in the dining room."

I grabbed the pitcher of water and walked into the dining room. In the center was a long mahogany table that easily had to seat twelve guests. It was beautifully decorated with a fall centerpiece, which included pinecones, candles and small pumpkins. On the far side sat our four place settings, consisting of fine china atop gold chargers, real silver, and crystal water and wine glasses. I poured the drinks, careful to place everything back in its perfect location, and returned to the kitchen.

Diana and Jake had all the dishes ready to go, and I helped them bring the feast to the table. There was more than enough food for an army, let alone four dinner guests, but I didn't say anything except to compliment on how lovely everything smelled. Again, Issy's mom beamed with pride and smiled.

"Isadora, we're eating, dear," Diana called out to the living room.

Issy came bouncing in and took the far seat, leaving me next to Jake, who was at the head of the table, and facing her mom. Jake reached over, covered my hand with his and shot me a breathtaking smile.

I quickly looked down at my plate and put my trembling hands in my lap. My stomach was in full turmoil at this point. What was he doing?

Issy's mom said grace and then started serving the plates.

"Avery, Jake says that you are an engineering student. That is wonderful, dear. I have been trying to get Isadora to declare a major for a while now."

Diana's voice was as sweet as honey, but I knew her words were meant to sting. I suddenly felt very protective of Issy, as I hated when people were passive aggressive like that.

"Well, I think Issy's theory on choosing a major is brilliant. If I wasn't on scholarship, I'd totally do it her way." I thought of Parker's words and continued, "Originality is a gift, after all, and Issy never ceases to amaze me." I tried to match the sweetness in Diana's voice but wasn't quite as good at it.

Issy hit my leg under the table and tried to hold in her laughter. Diana quickly moved on to other subjects, mainly Jake's internship at the stock company. Seeing his eyes light up as he talked about it, reminded me of the hours we would spend in my bed just sharing our day together. I willed the tears to stay back and took a deep breath.

Issy was no help. She ate in total silence. In fact, I had only seen Issy this quiet when she was sleeping, and even then she made more noise.

"So, Avery, are you also going to do an internship your junior year as well?" Diana voice continued to sound angelic.

"Um, no ma'am. I work at the engineering school now as part of the program I'm in. It's been a great experience for me." I was totally lying, but I didn't feel like saying that I hated every second I was in there.

"I didn't know you had a job," Jake said, looking at me with a mix of surprise and admiration.

I wanted to say, *Of course you didn't. You didn't take the time to know anything about me before you decided you needed space.* Instead, I shot him a sweet smile. "Well, now you know."

I could almost feel my life being sucked away as we finished our meal. Jake was watching my every move, while Diana continued to interrogate me on my plans for the future. Every minute felt excruciating, and I was starting to think that Issy actually hated me, otherwise she wouldn't have forced me to sit through this.

I was hungry but could hardly eat under all the scrutiny. Diana ate like royalty, finely cutting each piece and delicately placing it in her mouth, while Jake took every opportunity to secretly touch some part of me during the meal.

Issy hung her head over her plate and just started shoveling food in as fast as possible. The tension between her and Diana was so intense that it seemed to suffocate any other thought in the room.

Finally, the meal was over, and we excused ourselves. I realized after I cleared my plate that I had drunk the entire glass of wine I'd poured, and I had new appreciation for Issy's love for alcohol.

We dropped our plates in the sink, and Issy made a beeline for the door. "Shouldn't we help with the dishes?" I whispered.

"You can, I'm not. I've done my time for the day." She jetted out right as Jake and Diana made their way into the kitchen. I smiled and complimented her again on how good everything was, not sure how to make the great escape myself.

"Diana, you worked so hard. Let Avery and me clean up for you while you rest," Jake offered as he took the plates out of her hand.

"Oh, I couldn't, Avery's our guest."

"Are you kidding, she insists." Jake looked over to me expectantly, and I quickly agreed, having no idea what was going on. Diana took the out and headed to her bedroom, looking as fragile as a child. I turned to the sink and started running water for the dishes, hoping to keep busy enough to avoid small talk with Jake. Suddenly, I felt his arms wrap around me from behind and his lips touch my neck.

"I'm so glad you're here. I couldn't wait to get you alone," he whispered as he began to kiss my ear and my jawline. I quickly turned around and attempted to move him off of me.

"What are you doing?" I hissed. "You are acting like we are a couple, when we are hardly speaking!" I was so taken off guard by his affection that I didn't know how to process it. Part of me was still so angry with him, but part of me still loved him and felt connected to him.

"Only because you aren't speaking to me. You know how I feel about you." He was flashing me his sexiest smile and closing the gap between us again where I was locked between the sink and his body. His smell brought back memories so vivid that I felt almost woozy.

"Jake, you wanted the break. You said I wasn't the girl for you. I don't understand what you are doing." I was feeling nauseous and claustrophobic under his weight.

"I'm doing what feels right." He was still kissing my neck and whispering in my ear. "You belong to me. My sweet, innocent Avery."

I wondered how much wine Jake drank before I got here today. His body pressed against mine, closer and closer. "I knew as soon as I saw you with that other guy that I wasn't letting you go. You bring up feelings in me I can't explain. And now, seeing you here, in this house, it just confirms that you are everything I need." He took my face in his warm hands and looked deep in my eyes.

My legs felt weak, and my senses were so scrambled from his kisses that I almost gave in.

"Jake, you have to stop. I can't do this with you again," I begged, trying to break the eye contact.

"Yes, you can. I know you want to. Just give me some time to remind you. Remind you of how amazing we are together." He whispered in my ear again, and I was steadily falling under his spell.

He reached down and kissed my lips, full of passion and intensity, just like it had always been between us. My body reacted and I hated it for doing so. Jake could set me on fire with just a touch, and I didn't have the power to resist it. Despite my inner voice screaming at me, I kissed him back with everything I had, and all the emotion I had locked away for weeks came rushing back as I poured myself into him.

A ding from my phone brought us out of our trance, and I realized what I was doing. I detangled myself from his grip and walked to the door, my breath labored from our kissing.

"I'll come back later to finish the dishes. I'm sorry." I practically ran upstairs to my bedroom and tried to collect my thoughts. I looked down at the phone and saw a text picture from Parker. It was him and his brother doing a strong man pose in their flag football gear. The caption below said, "Wish me luck, while I wish you were here." I smiled and felt tears invade my eyes. I didn't answer back, just lay on my bed, holding my phone.

I sat there for a while, wallowing in confusion and frustration until I realized how ridiculous it was. I was not going to let Jake determine my happiness anymore! I'd given him everything, and he let it go. Words. He was always so good at saying the right words but never doing the right things. I was done.

I got out of bed and headed to the bathroom to get ready. I had come here for one reason, to help Issy deal with her dad. I was not going to let my drama affect my friendships or my life anymore.

With my pep talk finished and my mind almost convinced that Jake no longer affected me, I went through the motions of getting ready for dinner. I opted for black dress pants, with a sleeveless cream and gray ruffled blouse that would work for the party if I needed it. I pulled on my gray cardigan sweater to make the look dinner worthy and touched up my makeup. My hair was a disaster, so I twisted it up with a clip to keep the wildness under control. One last look in the mirror, and I knew I was ready.

I was slightly petrified of this dinner, especially considering that lunch had been a nightmare, and this wasn't even the house that Issy was worried about. I knocked on Issy's door to see if she was ready and almost fell over when she opened it.

Issy had gone out of her way to take her punk look to the top of the charts. Every inch of her hair was a neon pink fuchsia color that had been flat ironed straight to reach her mid back. She had a black dog collar around her neck and a stud nose ring in that I had never seen her wear before. Her outfit was even more shocking.

She had on gray and white striped knee-high stockings that stuck out a good six inches above her high heeled combat boots. Her flare skirt was gray pin-striped with an attached chain dangling from it, and the skirt length barely hit her mid thigh. The most conservative thing on her body was the long-sleeved black sweater with a red and orange flame that ran across the side of her torso.

Before I could even utter a word, Issy looked me up and down and scoffed, "You look like my mother. Don't even think you are wearing that to the party." She had her hand on her hip like she was lecturing me.

"First of all, I thought we were changing before the party, and second… you can't possibly wear that to your dad's house," I exclaimed, still reeling from the look.

Issy pulled me into her bedroom and shut the door. "I decided we're not going to change. If I'm going to get lectured and judged, I want to make it worth it." She walked over to her bag on the bed and pulled out a sage green shirt that looked like it only had material on one side of it.

"Your pants are cute, but you are wearing this top. You can keep your cardigan on until we leave my dad's, but it's coming off as soon as we get to Ben's."

I held up the green top. It was a beautiful silky green halter with fine beading woven throughout. It was cut with three crisscross straps along the back and fell just an inch below the waistline of my pants.

"Issy, this had to cost a fortune. You sure you want me wearing it to a college party?" I was being practical, as usual, and Issy's response was one of exasperation.

"Just put it on so we can go. Oh, and the hair comes down."

"Issy, it's a mess."

"Better than looking like a frigid CEO!" she retorted as she pulled the clip out of my hair.

I could feel my frustration starting to get the better of me, but I pushed it down and took a deep breath. Issy's spunk was what I loved most about her… except when it came to dressing me.

"Much better. I don't know why you complain about your hair so much. Most women would kill for half of it." She was done with my look and went about putting her things in her purse. She grabbed her car keys and spun around. "Let's go!"

"I don't think so. I'm driving," I said taking her keys from her. Previous experience had taught me never to rely on Issy for a ride, especially when going to a party that included unlimited alcohol.

"Works for me." She smiled sweetly and bounced out the door. I grabbed my sweater and purse to follow her, hoping we'd get out of the house before her mom saw what she looked like. We weren't so lucky.

Jake and Diana were sitting in the living room, Diana with a novel and Jake with his laptop open. He looked up first as we hit the bottom of the stairs, and his face immediately became rigid. Diana was the next to look up, and her face held a mix of shock and horror at the same time.

Issy didn't seem to register any reaction and walked over to kiss her mom on the cheek.

I watched from the bottom the stairs as Diana simply shook her head and returned to her book, not saying a word. I quietly followed Issy and almost made it out the door, when I felt Jake grab my arm.

"I want to talk to you," he whispered, scowling, as he pulled me onto the porch and closed the door.

My frustration hit a boiling point. Between Jake's earlier advances, Issy's absolute control over my clothes and now the lecture I knew was coming, I just lost it.

"What do you want?" I yelled at him. "I have no control over her, and why you have this expectation that I do is beyond me. This sick relationship you two have… just leave me out of it!"

Jake's face looked stunned and then a little amused, making me even angrier than I already was.

"What is so funny?" I blurted, still folding my arms and staring at him in utter defiance.

"Nothing. I just think it's cute that you thought my reaction was for Issy."

I stared at him, totally dumbfounded.

"It's for you. You look way too hot to be going anywhere without me tonight, even if it is just to dinner." He winked at me and then closed the space between us again, wrapping his arms around my waist and pulling me to him. "We never finished our earlier conversation."

Issy honked the horn from the passenger seat and yelled, "Let's go! Jake, leave her alone; we're going to be late."

I detangled myself from his grasp and walked off the porch, trying my best not to look back over my shoulder at him. My hands shook, and my thoughts were going a mile a minute. I gripped the steering wheel with both hands, making the leather stretch as I twisted it. Taking a calming breath, I turned to Issy. "Okay, tell me where to go."

"Wow, you are getting good at this," she said

nodding, shooting Jake a final goodbye wave. "If your face wasn't a complete give away, I'd almost think you were over him."

"I am over him," I lied, hating Issy for being so incredibly perceptive.

"You're doing better than most girls. I actually think he wants you back. I've never really seen him pursue a girl more than once before. This is new territory for me." Her tone implied that she was impressed, but it didn't make me feel any better. I had just spent the last four months on a downward spiral, with Jake being the center of all of it. Now that I was finally seeing some light in the dark tunnel, he was back, like my kryptonite, making me fall for him all over again.

"Issy, be straight with me. Do you really think Jake will ever be more than the sporadic boyfriend he was before?" It was the first time I'd ever asked Issy for advice on Jake, but I had to know. He was invading my thoughts again, and my stomach was still in knots from his scent when he held me on the porch.

"I think Jake is complicated." She was matter of fact and honest, yet it left the door open. My inner voice was yelling at me, but a smile crept on my face regardless as I thought, *You never know.*

"Lord, I pray You keep her eyes firmly open so that she can see when others are there to deceive or hurt her."

14. AFTER PARTY

I was laughing hysterically as Issy belted out another Madonna song at the top of her lungs. It wasn't that Issy had a bad voice. It was just that it was a loud voice, and not fully in key.

Her lightheartedness had improved my mood drastically. I didn't even try and kill her when she grabbed my phone and texted Parker back for me. They engaged for barely a minute before he wised up. I was actually impressed that he knew me well enough to call it. He ended their conversation with a "good luck with your dad, and give Avery back her phone!"

"Amazing," Issy said as she set the phone down. "He totally nailed me. I thought for sure you two were well into the dirty talk phase."

"Oh my gosh, Issy, what did you text him?"

"Just that he looked sexy in his shorts and that I looked forward to rubbing out all of his hurt muscles." Her voice was pure innocence as she turned up the stereo.

I couldn't help but laugh, mostly because Parker

already knew it wasn't me. The thought did make me blush, though. Parker was sweet and kind, and I really liked him. But the only person that popped into my head when I heard "sexy" was Jake. My smile remained until Issy got to the chorus of *Like a Virgin*, which quickly brought me back to reality. I hit the power button as fast as I could.

"Hey, I was singing that!" Issy yelled as she reached for the stereo.

"No, we have to focus." The forty-five minute drive to Issy's dad's house was almost over, and I needed some preparation this time. I walked into a lion's den with Issy and her mother, and I refused to do it again. "What should I expect here? You made it seem like all was peaches and cream with your mom, and you two hardly said a word to each other."

"What to expect?" Issy sighed, posing in the thinker position. "Okay, well, my dad will act like we are best friends. I will play along. My stepmom will say all the wrong things, and I will either ignore her or say something rude. Her son will likely be reading a book or playing a video game, so he is a pretty low threat. In all, it will feel like a perfectly dysfunctional meal."

"Okay, then clarify for me, please, why you wanted me here? I thought you and your dad didn't get along." I was totally confused at this point. It seemed more that her mom was the estranged one.

"Avery, just have my back. My stepmother tends to bring out the worst in me. You seem to bring out the best in me. I was just hoping they would balance each other out."

Her comment surprised me, but I finally understood. Sometimes you just need a friend to be there, even if they don't do anything at all. Maybe Parker was right about Issy.

I followed her instructions down a long driveway until out of the trees loomed the largest house I'd ever seen. No, house wasn't the right word… it was a mansion.

Issy punched some numbers on the keypad and the gates opened, giving us access to the front drive. The house was split level and three stories. It was a butter-yellow color with cream trim and had multiple balconies on each level. The entire yard was filled with tall trees and plush landscaping, making it seem even more expansive than it was.

"Oh, here we go again. Avery, you really need to stop gawking."

I shot her a dirty look and parked the car, carefully watching her body language as she got out of the car. I'd known Issy for months and had never seen her so tense. She grabbed her purse and whispered under her breath, "Here we go."

As if given new resolve, she shot me a big smile and pointed to the front door. I followed slowly, turning around with every step to take in the beauty.

The door opened before we even got to it, and a young man in khaki slacks and a cotton button-up dress shirt and tie stood there smiling. He was handsome in a rugged kind of way, and his broad face and tussled hair didn't seem to match his preppy attire.

"Issy, the prodigal daughter returns." His voice was full of humor but also had a tension to it. He watched Issy carefully as if trying to read how she would respond to him. I quickly deduced that those two didn't get along.

Issy walked past him without a word and waved her hand to dismiss him. I watched his face tense as he shut the door behind us and walked away.

"Your butler?" I asked as he disappeared around the corner.

"No, silly, we're not that rich. He's my dad's assistant. My stepmom is obviously smart enough not to let a woman have the job again."

"You weren't very nice to him," I reminded her.

"That's because he's a jerk and not really worth my time or energy," she explained, but I noted a slight catch in her voice and the way her body stiffened when she first saw him.

"Issy!" Her father said as he approached her with his arms spread wide. He was a mass of a man, well over six feet and relatively built for someone his age. Issy was a good foot shorter than him and seemed to get swallowed up in his huge hug.

"Hi, Daddy," I heard her say in a muffled voice.

"You look beautiful, as always, and I love the pink much better than the blue from this summer." He was touching her hair as he said that, and I almost lost my composure. I guess Issy's look didn't have quite the effect she wanted.

His attention was suddenly diverted to me, and his massive presence was such that I pulled my sweater tighter around me, hoping to find some comfort.

"You must be Avery."

"Yes, sir, thanks for having me."

"Of course! Any friend of Issy's is always welcome here. Shall we go see Anna?" He wrapped his arm affectionately around Issy and led us though the enormous foyer.

I glanced up at the set of stairs that each curved up to the second story like mirror images of themselves. My eyes squinted as I thought I caught a glimpse of someone peaking through the rails, but he disappeared so quickly, I was sure it was an illusion. I turned back to follow Issy's father, not wanting to lose them in the vastness of the house.

The décor of his home was drastically different from Diana's. Everything here was rich and ornate, with lots of gold and wood tones. There wasn't a piece of furniture that didn't look like it was taken from a mid-century European castle. I felt uncomfortable in the space, like I was a tourist who shouldn't touch anything.

We finally made it to the living room, which was no different from the rest of the house. The floors were gold marble, and the walls and ceilings were lined with intricately carved walnut paneling and gold leaf. The furniture was a royal purple with gold trim and looked horribly uncomfortable.

Anna was moving around a vase of flowers as we walked in and practically squealed with delight when she saw Issy. Her mannerisms were eccentric and borderline obnoxious as she grabbed Issy in a bear hug.

"We are so glad you are here! It's been way too long!" Her voice sounded odd as if it had been trained to hide the southern accent that was all too apparent. She had bleached blond hair, and her dress was so incredibly short and tight that I could see her string underwear beneath it.

I was sure I stood there with my mouth wide open as I took in the sight of it all, because I didn't even notice the assistant walk up behind me until I heard him say, "Don't worry, it's a lot to take in all at once." I turned to look, and he winked at me before fixing the vase that Anna had just left dangling too close to the edge of the table.

Issy finally detangled herself from the clutches of her overzealous stepmom and came to stand beside me. I took one look at her and almost couldn't control the giggles.

Her face was red with fury and the likeness to her hair was quite a sight. Tears threatened my eyes as I tried my best to maintain my composure.

When Issy saw me, she started laughing so hard that I had no more resolve, and the room came to a halt as everyone watched us succumb to gut-wrenching fits of laughter. I looked up, and Anna seemed annoyed, making it even harder to stop.

The only one who didn't seem taken aback by our outburst was the assistant, who watched with a sparkle in his eye. I was making a horrible first impression, but it didn't matter at the moment.

We finally got ourselves under control and wiped the tears out of our eyes. The room was silent for only a moment and then Issy's dad clapped his hands and said, "Let's eat!" as if nothing had just transpired.

Issy grabbed my hand and bounced into the dining room, starting to look a little like her old self. We sat opposite of Anna and her son, who seemed to appear out of nowhere, and Issy's father sat at the head of the table. I was surprised when his assistant excused himself and didn't join the family for dinner.

I leaned to Issy and whispered, "What's he do again?"

"Oh, just about everything. Grant's my dad's right-hand man," she whispered back.

"Why didn't he join us for dinner?"

"Would you, if given the option?" she replied with such sarcasm that the giggles almost returned.

"Yeah, I see your point," I whispered back and turned my attention to Anna who was tapping her wine glass with a fork.

"I want to make a toast to Issy," she said, standing. "To a beautiful girl with so much spunk and unrecognized potential." She raised her glass and drank a sip, acting as proud as if she had delivered the

Gettysburg address. Issy's father beamed with pride, and I couldn't imagine how a man so obviously smart in business didn't just catch the way his wife subtly insulted his daughter.

I saw Issy get up from her seat, and I immediately sensed trouble.

"To Anna," she began, holding her own glass. "A woman with impeccably bad taste and even worse table manners."

I closed my eyes, sure I had heard incorrectly, but the audible gasp from her stepmom and the stern, "Kaitlyn Isadora!" that followed proved me wrong.

"What?" Issy shouted, her jaw rigid. "Insults are only allowed if they are underhanded?"

"I want you to apologize right now," Issy's dad demanded with full authoritative measure.

"Tell you what, Daddy, I'll apologize to her for being honest, when she apologizes to me for sleeping with my mother's husband," Issy retorted, and the room got so quiet we could have heard a pin drop. I looked down at my plate, wanting to disappear. I was wrong, the silent tension with her mom was a hundred times better than this moment.

Anna stormed away from the table, and Issy's dad put his head in his hand and started rubbing his temples. Issy sat down, and I could feel her shaking, but her face was stone cold, devoid of any emotion whatsoever.

"Kaitlyn, I don't know what I'm going to do with you." Her father's voice was resigned and lost.

"Don't call me that," Issy said flatly, not even acknowledging his comment. "Are we going to eat soon? I'm starving."

Her dad looked up at her, and Issy flashed him an innocent smile. He excused himself from the table, not saying another word.

It was just us three left: Issy, myself and her quiet little half brother who couldn't have been more than six or seven years old. He was perfectly adorable, with straight brown hair combed over to the side, and he was wearing thin, round glasses. His resemblance to Harry Potter was striking.

"Are you okay?" I whispered to Issy, not sure what the next step in the protocol might be.

"I'm fine, just hungry. Let's eat."

"Without your dad?" I asked, feeling really uncomfortable eating their Thanksgiving meal without them.

"Oh, they'll be back shortly. Anna's going to have a temper tantrum, he'll console her, and then they'll return. Better to shut her up now than hear it all through dinner," Issy said flippantly as she filled her plate. I watched her brother do the same, careful to not make a sound. I wondered how she could say all of that in front of him with no remorse. I felt sorry for the little guy and was disappointed in how Issy was acting.

"Hi," I said, addressing him with a smile. "I'm Avery. Did I see you peeking through the stairs earlier?"

He looked down sheepishly and nodded his head.

"I bet you are a master at hiding, especially in this big house. Are there any secret hiding places I should know about?" I asked the last part in a whisper, as if we were having a secret conversation.

He took the bait and nodded enthusiastically, "There's one door from my father's study that leads right to the kitchen. I sneak in when Rosa's not looking and get her homemade chocolate chip cookies."

"That sounds fabulous! Is Rosa a secret spy?" I asked, playing along.

"No." He chuckled. "She's my nanny, but she's strict on the sweets."

He was an adorable kid and super sweet. I looked over at Issy, who was eating her food in silence, intentionally ignoring the whole conversation. I rolled my eyes and returned to her little brother.

"I told you my name, what's yours?" I asked.

"It's Andrew, after my father, but everyone just calls me Junior."

"Junior, it's very nice to meet you," I said, and was just about to reach my hand out to shake his, when Issy's father and Anna returned to the table.

Anna had obviously been crying and was still carrying her tissue. Issy's dad looked more irritated than ever but quietly served up his plate. The silence went on for what felt like hours, and then suddenly the focus was on me, the one neutral ground in the room.

Soon came the onslaught of questions about my school and classes, where I was from and how I liked Winsor. I was really starting to hate talking about myself and felt like I had been through two exhausting interviews today.

I attempted to change the subject by asking Issy's dad if he enjoyed Winsor when he went there. He seemed genuinely happy to talk about his experience, until Issy piped in about how much her mom also loved the school, even though she sacrificed her education to raise her daughter on her own.

The room was silent again until Rosa brought in the dessert and refilled the wine. I was careful this time not to drink too much but did notice that Issy was working on her third glass.

"So, are you two heading back to school tomorrow?" Issy's dad asked.

"Yes, sir, I've got to get back. I'm not sure about Issy."

"Nope, it's Black Friday, my favorite shopping day of the year." Issy suddenly came to life as if she got the escape route she had been waiting for all evening. "In fact, Daddy, I promised Mom I'd ready before the sun comes up, so I better make sure I get home in time to get a good night's rest." She already had her napkin on the table and was standing up.

"But you just got here. I thought we could take a walk by the lake. I was really hoping to talk to you." He seemed genuinely disappointed she was leaving.

"Next time, Daddy, I promise." She walked over, kissed him on the cheek and left.

I excused myself, thanking them again for a lovely dinner and followed her out of the room. Never in my life had I experienced anything like this day. I had sat down for two Thanksgiving dinners and was leaving hungrier than before either of them. How anyone could eat under that kind of strain was beyond me.

Grant was standing near the foyer as we headed to the front door. He was watching Issy closely, and I saw her immediately tense as he smoothly asked, "Running away already?"

Her eyes became like daggers as she hissed, "Go to hell!"

Seconds later, she was practically running out the door to my car. I watched as she stood with her hands on the roof for just a second and then turned around, her face completely blank. "Let's go! I'm dying to get this party started!"

I got in the car but refused to turn on the ignition. "Issy, you were deplorable in there… to everyone. I've never been so uncomfortable in my life." I didn't mean to lecture, but I was really upset.

She sighed and put her head in her hands. "I know. I'm sorry."

I didn't know what to say, didn't know how to even begin to be there for her. I drove out the gate and waited for Issy to point me in the right direction.

Ben lived only five houses down, but it was a mile

down the road. His gate was open, and we could hear music through the car windows before we even got to the house. The music snapped her out of her daze, and Issy looked up with a huge grin.

"Please don't be mad at me," she begged, wanting me to smile too. "I promise, first thing tomorrow, I'll call my dad and apologize, okay? Besides, you get to meet all my old friends tonight, and I really want you to have a good time."

I couldn't resist smiling as I watched her animated apology. I had to admit, it felt good to get out of the stuffiness of Issy's world and see something that felt more like Winsor.

We got out of the car, and Issy made me take off my sweater, even though it was easily forty degrees outside. A few steps later and we were entering the second biggest house I'd ever seen in my life. Issy was right, I was starting to become numb to the extravagance and just noticed the mass of people that covered the place.

There were makeshift bars set up in three locations, complete with a vast array of liquor, blenders and pumpkin shots. Before we had made it five feet, someone had put a bottle of beer in each of our hands and a pumpkin shot in the other.

Issy slammed them both back in a matter of seconds and raised her arms up over her head with a proud scream. She was immediately surrounded by people and looked happier than ever.

I took a sip of the shot, more out of curiosity, and

recoiled. It tasted good, like pumpkin and cinnamon, but that couldn't mask the strength of the rum underneath. I set it down, knowing one of those would ruin any chance of us making it back to Diana's house tonight.

I looked around, having lost Issy in the crowd, and saw her on the dance floor with a guy I was sure had to be Ben. He was extremely good looking, almost movie star handsome, with dark hair that was styled to perfection. He had defined cheekbones and a strong jaw that appeared chiseled. His eyebrows were straight and dark, bringing all attention to his sultry eyes that screamed sexuality.

Seeing the two of them together was breathtaking, because their beauty perfectly complimented one another.

As I watched Issy dance with him, I lost any thought that she felt nothing for him, and it was glaringly obvious that he too was still mesmerized by her. They were so lost in each other that I had to look away, feeling as if I was intruding on their intimate moment.

I was suddenly aware of how isolated I was, even though the room was full of people. There was not one familiar face, and everyone at the party looked as if they stepped right out of a fashion magazine.

By midnight, I had finally had enough. Issy had introduced me to all of her old friends including Ben, who I immediately did not like. He was arrogant and snobbish, meeting every stereotype I'd heard about spoiled rich kids.

Issy seemed to be having the time of her life, floating between partners on the dance floor, but always ended up back in Ben's arms. The drunker she got, the more inappropriately he touched her, and I was starting to worry a little about leaving her alone. I excused myself from another pointless conversation and went to get her off the dance floor.

"Issy, it's time to go," I said, pulling her off of Ben. She was barely coherent and was having trouble standing on her own.

"Oh, don't be a party pooper," she slurred as she draped herself on me.

"Yeah, Avery, she's just fine," Ben agreed with a devilish look in his eyes as he pulled her back to him. I glared at him and put her arm around my neck.

"Do I need to call Jake, or can you help me get her to the car?" My voice was stern, letting him know I wasn't bluffing. The mention of Jake's name sobered him up pretty quickly, and he let go of her waist, leaving me to bear her entire weight.

"Fine, take her home. She was getting on my nerves anyway."

I watched him walk away and felt sickened. Issy was way too good for that jerk.

Luckily, another of her friends saw me struggling and helped me walk Issy out to the car. We laid her in the backseat, and she was out before I even shut the door. I said my thanks and goodbyes, so ready to leave I was practically running to the driver's side.

I started the car and pulled out of Ben's driveway, heading back towards Issy's father's house. When I got to his gate, I pulled over and tried to pull up the GPS on my phone. No cellular data. I cursed under my breath, realizing that I had no idea how to get back to her mom's house.

Feeling panicked because it was really dark and spooky, I considered for a moment calling Jake, but immediately changed my mind as I thought back to the many times he had scolded me for not taking better care of his cousin. A party at Ben's house would be unforgivable.

I took a breath and texted Parker.

Me: Are you awake? If so, can you call me?

It only took a minute for my phone to ring, making me feel more relieved and relaxed than I had all day.

"Hey! Thanks so much for calling me. I know it's really late," I said apologetically as I answered.

"Sure. Is everything okay?" He sounded tired.

"I was wondering if you could do me a favor. We were at this party, and Issy had way too much to drink. We're still forty-five minutes from her mom's house, and I have no idea how to get there. We're out in the middle of nowhere, and my cell isn't picking up any data. Could you look it up online for me and just get me to a main highway somewhere?" I could feel myself rambling as I tried to justify needing him in the middle of the night.

"Of course. You sound upset." His concern

registered through the phone. "You haven't been drinking, have you?"

"No, I'm fine. Just a little spooked," I answered and then gave him her dad's address as the start point and then her mom's.

Parker looked it up and carefully guided me to the highway where Issy's written directions could take over. As soon as I turned on the well-lit road, I could feel the tension start to ease. Dark woods and two girls alone at night was not a good combination.

"Parker, thank you so much. I should be good from here," I said, not wanting to keep him any longer than I already had.

"Why don't you stay on the line with me until you get there. I won't be able to sleep until I know you are safe, anyway," he admitted, and my heart melted.

"That would be nice. How did the game end up?"

"It was a disaster. We lost twenty-one to seven, which meant we had dish duty for the entire day. I think my hands are going to be permanently wrinkled. What about you? How did Thanksgiving go with Issy's family?"

"Honestly, it was a total nightmare!" I exclaimed, laughing, finally able to step out of the situation and see the humor in it all. I went on to tell him every detail of the day, leaving out the parts about Jake, of course.

He seemed as stunned as I was at the extreme dysfunction of Issy's home life. As always, talking with Parker made every situation seem manageable.

We laughed together on the phone, making jokes about Anna and the taste level of their house. We took turns trying to guess the prices of some of the items I described, with Parker even looking up a few of them online. Talking with him was exactly what I needed, and the drive went by so fast, I was almost disappointed when I pulled in Diana's driveway.

"Well, I'm here. Safe and sound, thanks to you," I said appreciatively.

"Good. Now I can go to sleep and dream of large purple couches." We laughed some more and then he got serious. "All joking aside, I'm really glad you called me. I will always be here for you, any time. You know that, right?"

"I'm starting to. Thanks again."

We said our goodbyes, and I went around to the back door to try and wake Issy up. She wouldn't budge, just batted my hand away when I tried to shake her. I knew I couldn't leave her in the car but was at a loss as to how I could get her into her house.

"I've got it from here," I heard Jake say over my shoulder, and I almost screamed from being so startled.

"Sorry," he said, laughing. "I didn't mean to scare you."

My heart finally started to settle as I watched him carry her to her room. I locked up the house and walked to my bedroom, setting my purse and sweater on the bed. I could feel the tension return and ran my fingers through my hair, closing my eyes as I tried to

183

get myself to relax.

I opened my eyes again when I heard a light tap on the door. I looked over and Jake was leaning against the frame watching me. He was rugged and more handsome than I had ever seen him. He was wearing a gray tank and black boxers, which only accentuated his strong, chiseled body.

His normally manicured hair was messed up and kept falling in front of his eyes. I tried not to stare, but he looked emotionally exposed and that was always when I was at my most vulnerable with him.

"Rough night?" he asked softly.

"You could say that." I turned away and began taking my shoes off. I didn't want to talk to him, feeling the way I did.

"I wanted to apologize for earlier. I had a little too much to drink and came on way too strong. It wasn't fair to you." He was being so careful with his words, which was not like him at all. In fact, he hadn't said a word about Issy being wasted out of her mind on my watch either, which really wasn't like him.

I shot him a look that must have said all I was thinking, because he walked toward me carefully and sat on the bed. "Can we just talk? Like we used to?" he asked, taking my hand in his.

I didn't know what to say, so I just sat on the bed next to him. He moved up to where his back was resting on the headboard and pulled me between his legs. My back was resting on his broad chest, and his arms were wrapped tightly around me. I closed my eyes, taking in his perfect scent, sure I was in a dream.

"This was my first holiday without her," he explained quietly, still holding me tight. "I thought I'd be fine, but really, neither of us were. Diana was a mess today, trying to make everything perfect so I wouldn't miss her so much, and I pretended with everything I had just to make her feel better. As hard as we tried, though, it wasn't enough. Her absence was everywhere." His voice trailed off and he buried his head in my hair.

I didn't know what to say. My anger towards him had completely melted, and I wanted more than anything to take away his pain. I shifted my body so that I could reach him and ran my fingers through his hair while he continued to rest on my shoulder.

He was still for a long time and then whispered in my ear, "Can I just stay with you tonight? We won't do anything. I just need to feel you next to me." He looked up at me and I nodded, lost in his eyes, remembering all the reasons why I fell in love with him to begin with.

He smiled at me, almost as if he could read my mind, and got under the covers. He was on his back and I rested my head on his chest as he held me. It felt so familiar, so right, that I fought sleep as long as I could for fear it would all disappear in the morning.

The sun coming in my window woke me from my sleep as I felt around for Jake. He was gone, and just as I feared, my heart suddenly felt very empty and cold again. I went next door to Issy's room to check on her, but she was gone too. I knew she was planning to go shopping but never imagined she would actually make it. I shook my head; Issy never ceased to amaze me.

I showered and cleaned up the room, trying to make it look as perfect as it had when I got there yesterday. I glanced at the bed one more time before I turned out the light and shook my head. So much of my relationship with Jake was a mirage, so real when I was in the midst of it, and then gone in an instant.

I walked into the kitchen and left Diana a note, thanking her for her hospitality. The comfort and warmth I felt when I walked in yesterday was gone; it just felt dark and empty now.

I felt depressed as I drove home, the weight of the week suddenly weighing on my shoulders. My phone beeped, and I grabbed it as quickly as I could, hopeful that it was Jake. It was just the grad student, reminding me to take the sample today, as if I could possibly forget. I rolled my eyes and threw my phone down. I hated today.

I got home and unpacked, but my mood was still foul. Parker was getting back today too, and we had talked about meeting up at the library again and possibly going to a movie. For some reason, it didn't have the same appeal. I sighed, frustrated with myself for being such an idiot, and left to go take samples for the fiftieth time. The whole walk to the lab, I could feel my conscience gnawing at me, but I pushed it down.

I daydreamed of Jake, remembering our kiss in the kitchen, his broken manner in my room last night. It was consuming me. He was consuming me, just like before. I tried to make sense of him, why he was so mysterious. How he could turn it on and off so quickly and effectively. He seemed to need me, to want me, but yet he was gone… again.

The hours in the lab dragged on forever, but finally my time was up, and I trudged back to the apartment feeling just as defeated as I had earlier. I approached the building and immediately noticed that Danny was sitting on the top step near our landing. My heart constricted for a minute. He looked just as miserable as I felt.

I sat down next to him and patted his leg. "You doing okay?"

He let out a heavy sigh and looked out over the lake. "Not really," he admitted. "Did she say anything to you?" He turned to me, his eyes almost hopeful. I didn't know what to say. How could I tell him it was all just in his head, and Issy felt nothing for him but irritation?

"She just mentioned that you two weren't seeing each other anymore," I lied.

He shook his head and then ran both of his hands up through his hair, leaving it standing straight up. "It makes no sense. Things were amazing. I mean, more than amazing, and one morning she was gone, and that was it."

I didn't know what to say, so I just ran my hand along his back, attempting to comfort him.

He sent me a weak smile and continued, "It's my own fault. I mean, she told me the first night that she didn't do serious. I didn't care at the time. I mean, being around her is intoxicating and, in the midst of it, you don't even think about the hangover. Then she just kept saying yes when I'd ask her to do things and when things, between us got physical, I just assumed we were on the same page." He grabbed his hair in frustration. "One stupid word!"

Watching Danny was like watching myself through a different lens. I had thought the same thing, so sure Jake was my forever.

"Danny, I know this won't make you feel better, but I don't think that one word changed anything. It may have sped it up a little, but in the end, Issy is Issy."

"So it's really over? She won't change her mind?" he asked sadly, as if realizing it for the first time.

"Well, I wouldn't dare to ever guess what's going on in Issy's mind, but chances are more likely that she won't."

He let out another sigh and then stood up. I followed suit, and he squeezed my arm before ascending the stairs to his floor. The defeated way he walked matched my own as I unlocked my apartment and slid into bed. I felt too depressed to cry. Just wanted to sleep.

It was six o'clock on a Friday night, and I was still lying in my bed. It was pitiful, and I was at my wit's end with it. I got up, determined to be a stronger person, a better person. I made my bed and threw on some decent clothes. I would go into Asheville and walk the gallery strip, knowing that I would feel better tomorrow.

My mind lingered on the closet. I still had food in there. It would be so easy. Issy was gone until tomorrow, and no one would ever know. I looked at the calendar. It had been six days, the longest I had gone since breaking up with Jake. I took a breath and pushed the thought out of my head. No! I was not going to do it!

I grabbed my coat, determined to escape the temptation and almost ran right into Parker, who was about to knock on the front door.

"Hey!" he said, obviously surprised to see me in such a rush. "I was worried about you. I thought you were going to meet me?"

I backtracked into the apartment, feeling more uncomfortable around him than I ever had before. I turned and set down my coat, trying to stop my hands from fidgeting with my shirt.

"Yeah, sorry about that. I just wasn't up for studying today," I lied, still not making eye contact with him.

I heard him shut the door and walk towards me. "Your place is great. No wonder everyone fights for these apartments. It's twice the size of mine." He put his hands on my arms and I jumped, heading right into the kitchen.

"Do you want a drink?" I asked, trying to sound natural. He gave me a confused look and then went over to sit on the lip love seat, running his hands back and forth over the upholstery.

"Let me guess… Issy?" he asked with grin. He was trying so hard to lighten the mood, and each time he did, I felt more horrible. It was like there was a chasm between us that I couldn't cross, and suddenly the guilt of Jake started to overwhelm me. I stood in the kitchen, not saying anything, and he got up again to walk over to me.

"Avery, what's going on?" he asked, careful this time not to touch me.

"Nothing, I'm just tired," I lied. "It was a rough couple of days, and I'm really not up for doing anything tonight." His proximity to me made me sad. The comfort and closeness I'd always felt with him wasn't there. Tears threatened my eyes, and I walked away again to my bedroom. I heard Parker sigh and then footsteps behind me. I didn't know why he wouldn't just leave.

"You're starting to worry me. Did something happen last night after we got off the phone?" He took my arms in his hands again, firmer this time, so he could turn me around to face him. "You can talk to me."

I looked down at my feet, unable to look him in

the eyes. He was so good, and I knew I had to tell him, even if the consequences meant I'd lose him. I moved out of his arms again and sat on the bed, still fidgeting.

"Parker, I don't know what we are to each other, and because of that, I don't know what's okay and what's not okay." I took a pause, knowing I wasn't making any sense. "I wasn't totally honest with you when I told you I spent Thanksgiving with Issy."

"How so?" he asked, pulling up my desk chair so he could look me in the eye.

"I didn't just spend Thanksgiving with Issy. I also spent it with Jake." The words came out just louder than a whisper, and I looked down at my feet, not wanting to see his reaction. He stood up and walked across the room. His stride was rigid, and I watched as his hand began to rub the back of his neck.

"So you two are back together," he said flatly.

I stood up quickly. "No, we're not. It's not like that at all." I paused again, knowing I had to tell him, but not wanting to. "But, we kissed. And I've felt so guilty about it, I didn't know how to be around you." I didn't know why, but it was like the minute I told him, the chasm closed. I felt his comfort again, even with his back to me, and wanted more than anything to touch him and somehow convey to him what I was feeling.

"Anything else?" he asked, turning to look at me. He was visibly hurt, which stabbed at my heart more than I expected it to. I wanted to say no, to end the conversation, but I knew I had to tell him the rest.

"We slept in the same bed."

He ran his hands over his eyes and behind his neck, as though he was trying to relieve the tension he was feeling.

"But nothing happened," I added. I wanted to make it better—to take it away somehow. "I'm sorry, Parker. I didn't plan on it. I didn't even really want to. It was like a freight train that, once it got started, I couldn't seem to slow it down." I knew I was trying to justify my actions, to make them less offensive, but nothing I could say would do that.

"Then why did you?" His question was direct, honest, and I didn't know how to answer it.

"I don't know," I said, frustrated. "I still care about him. I don't want to, but I do. But we're not back together, nor are we ever getting back together. It was just a slip." I looked him right in the eyes, wanting to get back to that place where he would hold my hand and make the entire world seem possible. "I'm really sorry."

It was as if my words healed the wound, because he walked right over to me and hugged me so tightly I wanted to cry. I had missed him and didn't even realize how much until that moment. He released me and cupped my face with his hands.

"I don't know what we are either," he admitted, intently looking at me. "But I know one thing, I have no desire to kiss anyone else, and I definitely don't want you kissing anyone else. Why don't we start there?"

I looked at him and smiled, feeling the tears bombard my eyes. "That sounds great."

He leaned in and his warm lips softly covered mine, sending electricity all the way to my toes. There was no desperation when I kissed Parker, only sweet comfort. We stayed locked together until he pulled away and wrapped his arm around my shoulder, guiding us back into the living room.

"So, are you going to take me to a movie, or what? Because you bailed on me today, and Sheila wasn't there, so I had no choice but to study in silence the whole time. It was pure torture!" He was back to his old self and I laughed, so happy that things felt normal.

"Quiet in a library? Oh, the horror!" I teased as we walked out the door. Maybe I didn't hate today so much after all.

"Lord, we all fall and make mistakes. I pray she turns to You during those moments and knows that You are her wonderful counselor and prince of peace..."

15. MOMENT OF WEAKNESS

It was finals week at Winsor, which pretty much meant the world came to a screeching halt. The library was packed, and I even saw Issy reading on the couch this morning.

"Oh my gosh! Is that a book in your hand?" I teased as I made myself a bowl of cereal. "I did not think you owned a textbook."

"Shut up," she said, throwing her highlighter at me. She tossed her body across the couch as if she was fainting and sighed. "I HATE FINALS!"

"Don't we all," I agreed, laughing. My mood had been nothing short of chipper since I got back from Thanksgiving. I had a wonderful guy who adored me, and everything just seemed to be going perfectly.

"Your mood is almost annoying, you know," she said as she sat back up. "I think Parker's a bad influence on you." I knew she was teasing, because Parker had charmed her too, just like he did with everyone. "Speaking of which, are you two rendezvousing again tonight?" She had a devilish tone, and I threw her highlighter back at her.

"It's not like that, and you know it," I said.

Parker had been hanging out with us every night, but he never stayed over. In fact, he wouldn't even let us go in my bedroom alone. I asked him why and his response was, "You're a beautiful woman, and I'm a guy. There's only so much temptation I can handle. I want to take things slow with you. Enjoy the little things." He nuzzled my neck affectionately after he said that, making me feel like the most valued person in the world.

The only dark spot in the last two weeks was the bond I still felt with Jake. It seemed that no matter how hard I tried to push thoughts of him out, they would come back the minute I spent any time with him.

He didn't come over as much with Parker being here so often, but the late nights with Issy never changed. They would get in at two in the morning, and Jake would crash on the couch. He would still be there in the mornings when I got up to run, and I would watch him sleep, taken by his ability to look confident and vulnerable all at the same time. As much as I tried to deny it, he still had an effect on me.

It took a week before Jake talked to me again after our night at Diana's house. It was another late night with Issy, and earlier that evening he had ignored me when he came to pick her up, a situation I was getting used to by now. I sighed as I remembered the conversation.

"Avery, are you awake?" Jake asked as he sat on my bed. It was three in the morning, but I had woken up when I heard him and Issy come in the apartment.

"Yeah, I'm awake. Are you okay?" I was uncomfortable with him in my room, mostly because I knew there would always be a part of me that missed him being there.

"I wanted to explain the other night and this week," he whispered. The light from the living room allowed me to make out his face, and the shadows of it only added to his perfection. I could smell a hint of alcohol on his breath and wondered if he would even remember the conversation in the morning.

"You don't have to explain," I assured him. "It's not a big deal." Truthfully, I didn't want to hear it. I knew he had just used me the way Issy used Danny, and despite that knowledge, having him actually say it would be heartbreaking.

"You're always there for me, even when I don't deserve it." He was looking intently at me, searching my eyes for something and then turned away disappointed.

"I was lying on your couch last night, just staring at your closed door. You were so close, yet I couldn't get to you. It made me angry, and I thought, 'What the hell? There's a million more like her.' So I went out tonight and met them all, and not one held a candle to you." He turned to look at me, and my heart started racing.

So many nights I had dreamt of this moment,

when he would realize I was the one and come back; but that was Jake. He always seemed to know right when I was getting over him, as if he could pinpoint the precise moment and do something to draw me back in.

"I don't know what to say, Jake. We've been down this road…and it never ends well for me," I said softly.

He seemed surprised by my honesty and got up to walk over to my desk. There was a picture of Parker and me that I had just framed and set out. He stared at it for a long time and then turned it over on the desk. He squared his shoulders and sat back on the bed, closer to me this time, his hand tentatively reaching up to gently stroke my cheek.

"I know I'm not the man I need to be for you yet, but I can be. I can be everything to you that he is, only better, because it's us, and you can't fake that kind of passion and chemistry."

I didn't want it to, but my heart tugged. He sounded so sincere, so genuine that I caught myself, for just a moment, looking at him the way I used to. Seeing all that was good in him and all that we could be.

It was as if he sensed the change, because he pulled me in. I realized what I was doing right before our lips touched and pushed him away.

I looked down at my hands and shook my head, unable to say anything. He hung his head and settled for a kiss on my forehead. "You'll see," was all he said before he left and closed the door.

"AVERY!" Issy yelled as I snapped back to reality. "Sheesh, where did you go?"

"Sorry, just was thinking about something. What were you saying?"

"I was asking about Christmas. When are you leaving?" She sounded exasperated like she always did when I failed to give her my undivided attention.

"I don't know. We have a month off, but there's no way I'm going home for that long. What about you?"

"Are you kidding? Did you forget everything you witnessed? I'm not going back until Christmas Eve. And that's just to get my presents," she said, putting her book back on her lap as if she was actually going to read it.

"Whatever happened with that, by the way?"

"With what?" She looked up at me like I'd lost my mind.

"I mean with your dad! Things were totally intense when we left there. I actually thought the vein in his neck was going to pop." I started giggling again at the visual.

"Oh, it was fine. I called on Saturday and told him I was sorry. I told him I was extra sensitive because Mom had been so hard on me earlier about declaring a major. He felt sorry for me and asked if I had fun shopping. I lied and told him no, and that I couldn't even enjoy it because I felt so bad." Issy smirked the whole time she spoke and reached in her purse to pull out a card. "Two days later, I got a $300 gift card to my favorite store. My dad is so predictable," she said rolling her eyes.

I was stunned. Here I was trying to find the courage to tell my parents about having to repeat and pay for Thermo, and Issy got paid for being a total brat.

"Don't judge," she demanded, looking at me, and I had to smile. Issy could see right through me.

"Fine, but I should at least get a set of earrings out of it, since I had to sit through that nightmare with you." I was totally kidding, but Issy perked up and reached back into her purse.

"I'll do you one better. It's all yours," she offered, handing it to me with a smile on her face.

"Issy, I was kidding. I don't want your money. That's not why I went."

"I know that. Take it anyway. I don't want it. In fact, looking at it just makes me mad." She was pushing the card on me, and I felt horrible, like I had just lessened the value of our friendship in some way.

"I'm not taking it. I went because I'm your friend, and despite the horror of the day, I'd go again. Okay?"

She nodded and put the card down. Issy's rebound time was typically no more than a few seconds, so she was back to her playful self before I could even take another bite of my cereal. Something about her face gnawed at me, though. I wanted to ask her probing questions, but I was all too aware of the time and that my Thermo test was in less than two hours.

I put my dish in the sink and headed to my room to change, preparing my mind for the inevitable failure that I was about to embark on.

Over the last two weeks, I had made great progress in recovering my status as a "reliable student" and was even praised by Dr. Davis' grad student on the work I'd done in the lab. But as much as I tried, Thermo was just too far gone.

Despite knowing that, I still spent six hours last night cramming as much information in my head as possible. I wouldn't even let Parker near me, knowing full well he would do nothing but distract me. He feigned being hurt, but deep down I knew he couldn't stand it when I was physically next to him but mentally somewhere else.

I walked to class deflated, taking as much time as I could to get there. The worst ten minutes for me were right before the test was passed out. My stomach would start to flip, and I would second-guess all my studying and convince myself I would fail. I would spend the next five minutes doing breathing exercises to relax myself. Thinking about it, it really was ridiculous how much pressure I put on myself to be perfect. No wonder I never measured up.

The air was chilly this morning, and my nose was already red and numb from its bite, but I still sat on a bench in front of the engineering school to wait it out. I didn't want to get into class until exactly ten and still had twenty minutes to kill. I looked around, watching each student as they passed by. Most looked as stressed as I was feeling, but some were laughing and chatting in groups, comparing answers or arguing about how to solve a problem.

I started to wonder if each of their lives were as complicated as mine, if they struggled like I did to fit in or feel self-assured. I looked especially at the girls and wondered if any of them had made themselves throw up like I did last night just to settle the panic of a failing grade. I shook my head, not wanting to revisit the fact that I had thrown away weeks of progress because of one moment of weakness. I looked down at my watch again. My time was up. Let's get this over with.

"So, how did it go?" Parker asked as he sat on the grass next to me. I had just finished my test, and it was as miserable as I had expected it to be. I was lying in our favorite spot in the quad, trying to stop myself from rethinking every problem. I opened my eyes to look at him tenderly. He was so handsome, and just seeing his face relaxed me. I reached up to pull him close to me and kissed him.

"That well, huh?" he asked, smiling, taking the opportunity to smother my neck with kisses and tickle me.

"No, it was awful!" I said through my laughter, trying unsuccessfully to push his hands off me.

"STOP!"

He finally did and then propped up on his elbow, so we were face to face. He was staring at me with total adoration as he moved a piece of hair off my face. Sometimes I wondered if he would still look at me that way if he knew all the secrets I kept hidden in my thoughts.

"Come home with me," he stated as if he just decided to ask.

"What?" I asked, sitting up.

"You said you weren't going home until right before Christmas anyway, and I don't want to be away from you that long. Besides, I want you to meet my family."

I suddenly felt stressed. "I don't know, Parker, they're going to think it's weird, me coming to their house around Christmas when we haven't even been dating that long."

"Are you kidding me? My mom has not stopped hounding me about it since I told her about you at Thanksgiving. In fact, I don't even know if I'll get my Christmas presents if I come home empty-handed. Just spend a few days with us before you go home, please?" He was looking at me with puppy dog eyes, and I knew I was going to cave.

It wasn't that I didn't want to meet his family. I really did. I just didn't know if I was ready for it. Everything with Parker was all in, almost to an overwhelming measure. He never did anything halfway, and there was still a part of me that I wasn't ready to give him.

I smiled at him and gave him a light kiss. "I'll think about it."

He lay back on the grass next me and we just stayed in silence for while. His hand was covering mine like he always did, and I wondered if life got much better than this. Parker made all things seem possible, even when I knew they weren't.

I sighed, not wanting to end the moment, but also unable to fight my own practicality. "Don't you have a test in an hour?"

"Oh, the bitter words of reality," he said as he sat up. I felt a shadow cover my eyes, and I opened them in time to see Parker's beautiful blue eyes as he leaned in to kiss me. It was passionate and full of wanting, and took me off-guard for a minute because he had never kissed me with such intensity before. I looked at him questioningly, but he didn't say anything—just grabbed his stuff and shot me a wink before he headed off to class.

I lay on the grass a few minutes longer, enjoying the heat of the sunlight against the cold breeze of the day. It suddenly hit me that finals were over, and I was free from the pressures of school for the next month. The realization sent a wave of ease through my whole body, and out of the blue, I felt so energetic, I wanted to get up and run home.

Christmas was coming in a few weeks, and I hadn't done any shopping. Asheville was the perfect place to go, and I couldn't wait to get there where I knew that each little store downtown would smell like cinnamon and be filled with the wonderful sounds of the holiday. I still hadn't decided what to get Parker. My budget was pretty slim, especially with the tuition payment looming over my head, and I wanted it to be meaningful, to somehow convey thanks for all he had done for me this year.

I walked through several stores, looking at knives and watches, each more than double what I knew I could spend. I was starting to feel frustrated and opted to take a break so I could walk through my favorite gallery. They had updated all the photos on the walls, and I was blown away by some of the new pieces.

My eye caught one piece in the corner that attacked my heart with a flood of memories. It was a black and white close up photo of a zip line. The background was fuzzy, but in crisp focus were the line and a gloved hand solidly grasping it. The picture was angled on a diagonal and felt like you could jump right into the photo.

As if in a daze, I asked the lady at the counter if they had any smaller prints for sale and within minutes had purchased an eight by ten copy. I found a beautiful black frame at the next store I went to, and the effect was breathtaking. I convinced myself I was giving it to Jake as healing for his mom and nothing more. After all, this would be his first Christmas without her.

I ended up agreeing to go with Parker to meet his family before heading home for the holidays. He was picking me up at one, and I knew I should get up and pack. I stayed in bed longer, wanting to ease the anxiety that was starting to fill my chest. Meeting parents was a big deal. What if they didn't like me? What if I didn't like them? I brushed the thought aside. Parker's parents had to be wonderful. He turned out way too good.

I threw off my covers, knowing full well I had to at least get a short run in today or I would be a total mess. I got dressed and stepped out of my room, quietly shutting the door so I wouldn't wake Issy or Jake, who had only just gotten home a few hours ago. To my surprise, the couch was empty, and Jake was moving around in the kitchen.

As always, my body had a physical reaction to seeing him, and I hated it. He wasn't wearing a shirt and his jeans were slightly open at the top. His hair was going in every direction, and I smiled, knowing I preferred it to the perfect styling he usually had. He looked up, catching me staring at him and grinned.

"I thought you'd be getting up soon," he said in a cheery voice.

I walked tentatively toward the kitchen to make my energy drink for the run and was taken aback when Jake slid it to me at the bar. I looked up at him questioningly.

"You drink those before you run, right?" he asked

as he started to wipe down the counter. "I've been watching you in the mornings, and it seems to be your ritual."

I wasn't sure what to say and stood there staring at him in disbelief.

"How many miles are you running today?" he asked while he continued to work.

"I don't know, I haven't decided yet," I whispered, unable to find any volume in my voice.

He leaned over the counter to look at me, resting casually on his elbows. "Why do you always look so surprised when I do nice things for you?"

"I don't know," I answered, finally getting my vocal cords to work. "I guess we never really got to this part." I knew Jake was aware of how uncomfortable he made me. He seemed to relish it, like my uneasiness around him gave him confidence. He came around the bar and stood so close to me that I could feel the heat radiating off his chest.

"I meant what I said the other night," he said quietly, the sparks between us so extreme that I literally felt frozen in his presence.

"I'm leaving today," I finally said as I took a step backwards, looking for any excuse to put some distance between us. "And I probably won't see you until after Christmas." I walked back in my room, grabbed the perfectly wrapped present, and handed it to him. "So here. Merry Christmas." I was trying to be as nonchalant as I could, but my heart was slamming against my ribcage to the point where it almost hurt.

He seemed startled by the gesture and began opening it, taking care not to tear any of the paper. He turned the frame over to see the photo and quietly ran his hand over the glass, stopping on the gloved hand in the picture. His eyes said it all when he looked up. They conveyed his pain with such ferocity that I wanted to take him in my arms and tell him everything would be okay. But I didn't. I just stood there in silence, waiting.

He closed the space between us and hugged me with such sincerity that I had to fight the tears invading my eyes.

"Thank you," he whispered in my ear, burying his face into my hair as he held me. I hugged him back, but with much more reserve, remembering how quickly Jake could muddy my senses with his touch.

He slowly released me but didn't step back, instead he stared into my eyes, searching as always for some unknown thing. "Spend the day with me. We'll go do the lines again just like before."

"Jake, I can't."

"Just as friends, I promise. Your parents won't care if you go home today or tomorrow. Give me this." His urgency surprised me.

I hesitated and moved away, grabbing my headsets for the run. "It's not my house I'm going to," I explained softly.

Understanding registered on Jake's face, and I saw his jaw tighten. I moved towards the door, all the sudden feeling suffocated by the room. "Have a wonderful Christmas, Jake. I mean that."

"Avery," he called as I was about to open the door and was next to me in an instant. I could feel his breath on my forehead, and I closed my eyes, unable to manage the way his scent overwhelmed me. I felt his hand move over to my wrist and capture it, rubbing two of his fingers across the inner skin as if to check my pulse. I knew my heart was still racing, giving away the effect he had on me. "You forgot your phone," he said quietly and put it in my hand. "Have a wonderful Christmas, too."

I looked up at him, and he was smug, obviously pleased at my reaction. I couldn't seem to get out of the door fast enough and could hardly catch my breath once I did. It was unfair how I was feeling. Unfair to me and to Parker. I took off at a sprint, ready to escape the crushing truth that part of my heart still belonged to a man who was fully capable of destroying me.

"Lord, I pray she knows You as her rock and her salvation. I pray she trusts You at all times and pours her heart out to You…"

16. GAS STATION SCAVENGER HUNT

My apartment felt different when I returned, darker somehow, like the footprint of Jake was everywhere. The pit felt closer than it had in weeks, and I knew it was my fault. I had given in when I bought him that picture, and allowed myself to feel for him all over again.

I looked at the picture of Parker on my desk, and tears stung at my eyes. He deserved so much better than me, and I knew it. I set the picture down and got undressed to shower. My reflection in the mirror stopped me as I started to examine everything that was wrong with my body. I pinched at each bulge, disgusted by it.

No matter how hard I tried, how much I ran, it was never enough. The tears were freely flowing now as I stepped in the shower, letting the steaming hot water run over me, praying it would sear off everything I hated about myself.

Two hours later, I was dressed and ready to go,

eagerly anticipating Parker's arrival. I was still feeling panicked from earlier and had barely managed to keep myself from the kitchen. He had insisted we ride together, even though it meant he had to bring me back here in a few days to get my car. "I don't mind," he had said. "It's totally worth the drive to get you to myself for a little while."

I practically jumped at the knock on the door and ran to open it, relief flooding my body when I saw him. He barely got in the door before I tackled him in a hug so fierce that he had to brace himself.

"What's this for?" he asked, chuckling, as I held on for dear life. I breathed in his scent, so different from Jake's, and just relished the feeling of comfort and warmth I felt in his arms. I didn't want to let go, wanting instead to get lost in the peace he brought to me. I knew if I continued to hug him, he would start to ask questions, and I didn't want to talk about the events of the morning, so I reluctantly released him.

"Nothing. I'm just happy to see you. That's all."

He kept his arms locked around me as he leaned down to kiss me. "Me too. Now let's get this show on the road before my mom starts blowing up my phone."

He picked up my bag, and I shut the door, glancing back one last time at the apartment that had hours before felt like a prison, grabbing at me, trying to pull me back down into its pit. It looked different now, safe once again.

We pulled out of the parking lot, and with each

mile of distance between me and Winsor, I started to feel at ease, even excited about seeing Parker in his hometown.

He smiled at me and then got a childish grin on his face. "I have a ritual on road trips that started way back when I was a kid. You think you can handle it?"

"Um, sure?" I answered with hesitation apparent in my voice. "It doesn't involve doing anything that will get us arrested does it?"

"No, nothing like that. It's just that I get antsy, well you know that from our many study sessions, and so my mom created road games for us to play the whole time we traveled. Now, I'm hooked."

"What, like I spy?" I teased, thinking how cute he looked when he was being playful.

"Insulting. I'm a professional, Avery." He was feigning seriousness, and my curiosity rose.

"Since it is only a two-hour drive, I kept it simple," he went on. "So we are sticking only with gas station scavenger hunt."

"What?" I asked laughing, sure he was kidding. The mischievous look on his face told me he wasn't. "Okay, how do you play?"

"It's easy. There are ten gas stations between my parents and us. I put a list of twenty random items in this bag. At each stop, we have to pick one item. The first person to find it and purchase it gets to ask the other a personal question. One they would never ask in normal conversation. AND, the other person has to answer it 100% truthfully. Oh, you can't ask anyone for help, either."

I looked at him in disbelief. "That took a lot of preplanning. How did you have time during finals to come up with this?"

"Avery, I planned this out when I came home for Thanksgiving."

"But we weren't even together. I mean like really together," I recalled, surprised at his answer.

His tone suddenly got more serious. "Avery, I knew I wanted you with me the first time I saw you. From that point on, you've never left my mind." He reached over and squeezed my hand, smiling. He was so good to me, always seeing only the best. How I wanted to believe him, but I knew better. I had a secret, a cruel, overwhelming secret that I would never tell him, could never tell him. He would never see me the same if he knew the extent of my emotional weakness and my reliance on food to settle it. But I didn't want to think of that now, just wanted to enjoy this time with him before I inevitably ruined it.

"Okay, I'm in," I agreed, smiling. "But I must warn you… I'm very fast."

"We'll see about that," he challenged as he winked at me. "Our first stop is right now."

I reached in the bag to pull out my card and scowled. It was canned soup. What gas station carried that?

Parker pulled in front of the station, and I was out of the car before he even got into park. I was rushing down the isles hysterically laughing as I watched him practically knock down a man in a business suit on his way to the fountain drinks. I found the "household items," but there was no soup. I went down another aisle, frantically searching, and spotted a soup to-go on the bottom shelf. I grabbed it and ran up to the counter, but it was too late. Parker was already leaning on the counter, casually sipping on his 40-ounce drink.

"I win," he announced with a smile.

I scowled at him and set down the soup. He put his arm around me and walked us back to the car. Now I was kind of dreading this game. Parker was way too insightful, and I knew his questions would be also.

We got back on the highway and he turned to me. "My first question is a hard one, because I don't know if I'll win again," he explained as if to justify it. "What happened that day you came to the quad? It doesn't matter to me; it can be anything, but I just want to know." His eyes were sincere, and I knew he was asking so he could be closer to me, not to judge or pry.

I took a deep breath and then told him everything, well, almost everything. I told him I met with my advisor and learned what a colossal disappointment I was, how I went to see Jake for comfort and he was there with another girl. "When I confronted him, he basically told me that I wasn't the girl he first fell for, that I had lost what made me special." My voice trailed off at that point, not wanting to remember the words. "I just kind of went numb after that. I felt like I was consumed in darkness, because I had lost so much of who I was, and I didn't know how to get it back. I honestly don't even remember getting to the quad. I just kind of was there. That's it." It was amazing how quickly the pain resurfaced as I spoke the words.

Parker was quiet for a long time and then shook his head. "I hate that guy!" He said it so fiercely that I looked up at him startled. I had never seen him angry before. He turned to look at me, deeply searching my eyes. "You know he was wrong, don't you? You are inherently special, and no decision or action you take can change that."

I looked back at my hands and tried to stop the tears that were filling my eyes.

"Avery, look at me," he insisted, and I did. "He. Was. Wrong." Parker said the words slowly and deliberately, trying to make sure I absorbed them.

I smiled and nodded, wanting so much to believe him. I wiped my eyes and took a deep breath. "No more serious questions, or I'm not playing anymore," I threatened.

He smiled at me and squeezed my hand, "You got it."

I was much quicker the next two stops, extra motivated not to be on the receiving end of the questions. I asked Parker what he was like in high school and how he decided on going into the military.

He told me that he was the average jock who loved sports. He knew his parents would be strapped sending him to college, so he really worked hard in school and applied for every type of scholarship out there.

"I never really thought about the military, but when I saw they did medical scholarships, I went ahead and applied. My fitness abilities and test scores got me in, and the rest is history."

The next stop was rigged, because my card said, "sour skittles" and they only had original and tropical. I tried to declare a miss-deal, but Parker refused, happily eating his Milky Way.

"Now it's my turn," he said grinning. "What were you like in high school?"

I visibly relaxed, much more comfortable answering this question than I was the earlier one. "Nothing special, really. I joined the cross country team my sophomore year, and between that and school, I stayed pretty busy."

"Any serious boyfriends?"

I looked at him with a grin. "That's two questions."

"Humor me."

"No, no boyfriends. Guys really weren't that interested in me, and honestly, I was too focused on just getting out of there to mess with any of it."

He looked at me like I was lying. "Not possible."

I hit his leg playfully, blushing at the way he was looking at me. Parker always made me feel beautiful.

He never looked at other girls and was constantly complimenting me. My bad habit of comparing my body to that of every woman I met seemed to disappear when I was with him.

"You have to answer that question, too." I said, hoping his answer was the same as mine. The idea of him caring for another girl bothered me a lot more than I wanted to let on.

"I had one girl I dated my senior year."

"Was it serious?"

"Well, as serious as it could be in high school, I guess. We grew up together in a small town and hung in the same circles. It was easy."

"How did it end?"

He shot me a knowing look, fully aware I was making sure it had ended. "No big event or anything. We both went off to college and mutually knew it wasn't going to work. I still see her around town sometimes, and it's just fine."

It was hard for me to imagine that, because I only had one real boyfriend before Parker, and everything about that relationship was heat and drama. I shot him a little smile and said, "Good." As much as I knew it was hypocritical, I wanted Parker all to myself.

We were an hour and a half into the drive, and I was having a wonderful time. I watched Parker as he drove, singing under his breath to a tune that was on the radio. He reminded me of Issy, but without all the baggage. So comfortable with who he was that the world just seemed to fit around him. We only had two more stops before we got to his house, and I was determined to win. My next card said, "hot dog w/ ketchup," and I easily beat him to the counter while he was searching for cotton balls.

"Okay, my turn again," I said, laughing as he devoured the hot dog. I'd never seen anyone eat as much as he did on this trip.

"How is your relationship with your parents?" History had taught me to always know this answer, although knowing did not help me much with Issy.

"Honestly, it's pretty great. I know most people our age don't like their parents that much, but I really do. We've just always been close. My dad works for the forestry department, and my mom teaches at the elementary school, and while we didn't have a lot growing up, we never wanted for anything. My parents were very active in my life, went to all my games, took us camping all the time and tried to raise us with a strong set of values. Family means everything to me."

"That's wonderful. I really can't wait to meet them."

"Well, they are going to love you. I know that with full certainty," he said beaming, lifting his hand to tickle the back of my neck and rub his thumb over my cheek.

The last stop was a colossal disaster. Parker's card said, "map of North Carolina," and mine said, "toilet paper from the bathroom." He had the map paid for before I even made it to the back of the store.

We piled back in the car, my arms crossed as I pouted. Parker smiled at me, then got lost in thought. I could tell he was trying to decide whether to ask me the question or not. My stomach suddenly fluttered, knowing full well I wasn't going to like it.

He took a deep breath and gripped the steering wheel. "Are you over him?"

I closed my eyes, thinking that was the worse question he could ask, especially in light of the events this morning. "I don't know how to answer that," I said in a whisper.

"Truthfully. I don't want there to ever be secrets between us."

"Even if the answer is no?"

He was quiet for a long time and then said, "Yes, even then."

I looked at his profile while he drove and felt heat run through my body. He was so amazing. I leaned over to stroke his hair and kissed his cheek, lingering on the soft part of his skin under his earlobe. "I'm getting there," I whispered.

He slowed down the car and pulled off the country road we were on. Immediately after he put it in park, I was in his arms and he was passionately kissing me with the same intensity I felt in the quad. It was like the more I knew him, the more he affected me physically, and as we consumed each other in the car, all I could think of was how badly I wanted him.

He reluctantly pulled away, appearing to battle

with himself the whole time as he did so. We were both shaking with desire as he put his forehead to mine. "You have no idea what you do to me," he admitted softly, and then pulled back out onto the road. We were quiet the rest of the way to his parents' house, but his hand never left mine.

The last road he turned on led us into the forest. Parker's house sat on four acres of land, and the nearest neighbor was over a mile away. We turned the last corner, and I caught my first glimpse of his home. If I didn't know where I was, I would have sworn he had taken me to a wood lodge somewhere.

His house was made of green wood siding and had an extended deck that sat on piers. The roof over the deck was pitched in a perfect triangle, with wood beams forming a V at the front. The adjacent wall to the house had two large triangular windows that mirrored one another, and the effect was beautiful. The house itself was small and quaint, but considerably warm and inviting.

"I love it," I exclaimed as I took it all in.

"I knew you would see it."

I shot him a questioning look, and he explained, "It's a pretty simple place, Avery, in the middle of the forest. Very few people would find it beautiful, but I knew you would, because you see things others miss. It's one of the things I like most about you."

I smiled back at him and then leaned over to kiss his cheek before we made it to the end of the driveway.

His mom and dad walked out of the front door as soon as we pulled up, and each gave Parker a warm hug. Watching them, you could see the closeness and love the family shared.

"You must be Avery!" his mom said as she embraced me. I tried not to show how awkward I felt as I hugged her back. They were obviously as affectionate as Parker was. His dad must have sensed my unease, because he shook my hand, instead, when he welcomed me.

Parker wrapped his arm around me and led me into the house. He fit this place and seemed more at ease than I had ever seen him. The smell of a home cooked meal hit my senses as soon as we walked in the door, and I suddenly felt my stomach growl. Parker had eaten all our loot from the trip, and it hit me how hungry I was.

"You two haven't eaten, have you?" his mom asked as she took pans out of the oven.

"Are you kidding? I'm starved!" Parker answered and planted a light kiss on her cheek. I excused myself to the bathroom, partially to freshen up and partially to get calmed down. As ridiculous as it sounds, I felt overwhelmed by the love in this place. It was real and honest, and I had never experienced anything like it.

They were already around the table when I came out of the bathroom and tried to quietly join them, but my chair scraped across the floor as I did. Parker quickly stood up to help me get settled. He reached for my hand and then took his father's. Next thing I knew, we were all holding hands to say grace, but it was more than just blessing our food. They thanked God for multiple things, even my being there with them. It was authentic, and despite my lack of experience regarding this sort of thing, I felt good when they finished.

We said, "amen" and started passing the food. I started to mentally brace myself for the onslaught of questions that always seemed to follow, but they didn't come this time. Instead, Parker's dad told stories about campers in the woods, and they talked about the missionary work Parker's older brother and family was doing overseas. I found myself slowly starting to relax, enjoying their easy mannerisms as they shared their life with one another. I even found myself laughing and asking questions, as if I had known them for years. It was the first time, since I could remember, that I didn't notice what others were eating or how they were eating it. I didn't even really register my food, only the company, and the freedom in that felt so amazing I wanted to cry.

We were finishing up when his dad leaned back in his chair and said, "Well, Avery, this is the part where we go around and tell each other a high and low for the day. Think you can come up with one?"

I shot a concerned look to Parker, unsure exactly what they were asking me.

"It's easy," his mom said, reassuring me. "I'll go first. My high today was when you and Parker pulled in the drive. And my low was burning my finger on the pan. Frank, you're next," she said, looking at her husband.

"My high will come later when I beat this knucklehead in a game of darts," he teased as he lightly punched Parker in the shoulder. "My low is going to be the dishes I'm sure I'll have to do after dinner." He shot his wife a sad face and she promptly responded, "You're darn right!"

Parker geared up for his turn, but shot me a mischievous look as if to convey his actual high was not going to be mentioned. I blushed as I recalled the heat we generated in the car.

"My high is this wonderful meal. Thank you, Mom. And my low is knowing in two days we have to leave this place, and I won't see Avery for a whole week."

I felt embarrassed by his verbal affection and looked down at my plate.

"We all did ours," Parker said nudging me.

I smiled, enjoying this game more than I was letting on. "Well, I know exactly what my low is. Parker beating me in the last round of Gas Station Scavenger Hunt."

The entire table erupted with laughter as his mom asked, "Did you really make her play that game with you? Avery, Parker used to make us play that every road trip we took from the time he was five years old." She was shaking her head as if reliving a warm, wonderful memory.

Parker's dad continued on, "And the worst part

was, he always won, so we were forced to listen to terrible music the entire trip!"

I looked at Parker, confused, and he explained that the price for winning when he was a kid was control over the radio.

"You're kidding!" I scoffed, hitting his arm. "That would have been way easier than all your questions."

The table erupted in laughter again as Parker raised his hands in surrender. The laughter died down and attention was once again on me, as I was to give my high for the day. There were so many, it was hard to pick. But my mind thought back to the morning and how dark it had felt.

"My high was when Parker picked me up this afternoon," I said confidently.

Parker's mom got a sappy look on her face, and I watched as his dad squeezed her shoulder. There was nothing especially striking about either one of them. His mom was average height and weight. Her hair and clothes were plain and even a little dated. His dad looked very rugged and wrinkled, like someone who had worked outside all his life. Watching them, however, with their warm smiles and kind spirits, I soon started to feel like they were two of the most beautiful people I'd ever met. I totally understood how Parker was such a man of character; he had been surrounded by it all his life.

We got up and brought our dishes from the table. I offered to help clean up, but Parker's parents practically kicked us out of the kitchen.

Parker led me into their small den that housed an old leather couch with multiple patches and an oversized chair and ottoman just big enough for both of us to sit on. The small TV sat in a corner nook of built in shelves, and old wood paneling covered each wall. I imagined Parker in this room when he was a kid and had no doubt it looked exactly the same.

We sat together in the chair, and he lifted my legs so they rested on his and leaned in to kiss me. Parker was exactly the same with me in front of his parents as he was when we were alone, which I loved and admired.

I looked at him and smiled. "You're right, they're amazing."

He reached out and stroked my face with his hand, capturing my eyes with his. "You're amazing."

It was the first time I actually thought that one day I might be able to believe him.

"Lord, deliver her from those would harm her, whose mouths are full of lies. Show her that Your hand will guide her…"

17. GOING HOME

I was cuddled up next to Parker on the drive home, with my head resting on his shoulder. It had been a glorious two days with his family, and part of me never wanted to leave. Between snowball fights and long walks in the woods, I felt more bonded to Parker than I ever had before. I even went to church with him and his family and enjoyed it much more than I thought I would. His world was safe and free, and most of all honest.

I peeked down at my purse and saw the small Bible Parker's mom had given me before we left. Her sweet voice assured me that reading it could solve all of life's mysteries. She also promised me that if I ever needed direction in my life, it would surely guide me. I smiled at the gesture. No one had ever given me a Bible before.

Looking back out the window, I could see the vast darkness as we made our way back to campus; it seemed to match my feelings that something ominous was waiting for me when I got home. I shuddered and tried to push the thought out of my head.

"You cold?" Parker asked, turning up the heat.

"No, I'm fine. Just not looking forward to returning to reality just yet."

"Well, if you want to escape reality again, I have a proposition for you." I perked up, eager to do anything that meant we were together. "You know I go each month to Charlotte for training, right?" I nodded. "Well, along with that requirement, they have a ball each year they put on, and it's mandatory that we attend. This year, in their genius, they scheduled it on New Year's." He sounded frustrated with the prospect. I'm guessing these balls weren't that much fun. "It's a lot of pomp and ceremony during the dinner, but afterwards there is a dance. Anyway, I wanted to see if you would go with me."

He sounded like a nervous teenager, and I had to hold in the laughter. "Of course, I'll go. Why wouldn't I?" I asked.

He seemed surprised and then excited. "I don't know. You were so hesitant to go to my parent's house; I kind of feared this would be completely out of your comfort zone. I already had my convincing speech all ready to go."

I thought about it for a moment and realized that he was right; one month ago I would have shuddered at the thought, but Parker was changing me. Through his eyes, I was beginning to see myself differently, which in turn made events like that one much less daunting.

"No convincing necessary. I'd love to go with you," I assured him and resumed my place on his shoulder. He reached up with his hand and caressed my face. We drove in silence the rest of the way, enjoying the moonlight against the dark roads, until we pulled into the parking lot of my apartment.

I leaned in to give him a kiss goodbye, but he insisted on walking me to the apartment. I wasn't looking forward to the loneliness of it or the prospect of driving nine hours in the morning.

I clicked open the door and was thrilled to see Issy on the couch, randomly flipping through channels at such a speed I didn't know how she could even register what was on.

"Oh, thank goodness you're home!" Issy screamed when we walked in. "This place is a ghost town, and I was seriously about to give in and drive to my mom's house."

I laughed and gave her a hug. Issy hated to be alone almost as much as I hated to be in a crowd of strangers, and even a few of hours of it made her start to go stir crazy. I turned to tell Parker goodbye and that I was going to miss him. He gave me a long, lingering kiss and said to call him when I got on the road in the morning.

Issy piped up from the living room, her eyes remaining fixed on the television screen. "Oh, aren't you two cute! Now get out of here before I puke."

I gave Parker one last goodbye kiss and shut the door, joining Issy on the couch. "That wasn't very nice," I scolded.

"I don't want to hear it. Here I am, all alone, roommateless and cousinless and you're shamefully kissing boys right in front of me." She put on her best pout, and I rolled my eyes.

"Fine. I'm sorry." I reached in my bag to pull out her Christmas present. "Peace offering?"

She took the gift like a three-year-old on Christmas morning and practically jumped to her knees on the couch as she opened it. I wasn't sure what she'd think of the gift. I mean, what does one get the girl who can buy anything she wants and whose only real hobby was partying?

I ended up going with a small silver flask with intricate detailing that ran up the sides. I had them engrave her name in the center and put the quote, "To thine own self be true" on the bottom. She handled it gingerly, running her fingers over each detail. She lingered on the quote for a while and then almost knocked me over with her hug.

"I love it!" she said excitedly, and I was thrilled. The best thing about Issy was that I always knew where I stood. She wouldn't have said it if she didn't mean it.

She ran to her room and came back holding a beautifully wrapped box with a large gold bow. "Your turn."

I smiled as I opened the package, feeling almost guilty for disturbing the perfect wrapping. Inside was a beautiful silver shawl that had just a slight sparkle when it hit the light. It was made of high-end cashmere and felt so good to the touch that I immediately wrapped it around my shoulders. "Issy, this is so beautiful. Thank you so much!"

She seemed uncomfortable with my gratitude and dismissed it saying, "Well, I know how you love your homey sweaters. I figured this way at least you'd look good all covered up." I gave her a look that said I didn't believe her. Deep down she was much softer than she'd ever want anyone to know. I felt lucky to know her and to have gotten her as a roommate.

We spent the rest of the night catching up on what we'd been doing the last few days. I told her about Parker's family and about the ball on New Year's. She became so absorbed in talking about what kind of dress I would wear that I didn't have the heart to tell her I would be shopping at my hometown thrift store for something that would work.

I asked what she had been doing, gingerly trying to stay off the topic of Jake, but it was no use. Issy always said what was on her mind.

"You totally ruined him, you know," she stated nonchalantly after giving me intricate details on the last party they went to.

"What's that supposed to mean?"

"He's all sad and brooding, and worse, becoming a total bore. I can't decide which I like least, obsessive, controlling Jake who I could at least get to have fun some of the time, or this one, who sits and sulks the whole time we're out."

I was sure she was talking about a different Jake. That behavior was so out of character that it was laughable. Despite my doubts, though, I felt my heart pick up pace at the memory of our goodbye, but quickly pushed it out of my mind.

"Maybe it has more to do with Christmas and his mom than me. You seem to forget that he is still dealing with his grief."

Issy raised her eyebrows and sat back on the couch. "Believe what you want, Avery, but things between you and Jake are definitely not over… at least on his end. And by the way you are twisting that pillow apart, I'd say they're not so over on your end as well." Her eyes didn't judge, but I felt guilty all the same.

The next morning came too quickly, after a fitful night of sleep. My mind wouldn't stop working, turning her words over and over in my head. The long drive to my parent's house didn't help either. I oscillated between feeling drawn to Jake, remembering all the good moments we had, to feeling angry and frustrated that I still couldn't seem to break free of him. I hadn't seen him in days, yet his presence felt stifling.

I needed a distraction and decided to hit one of my favorite malls that happened to be just off the interstate. The parking lot was packed, as expected this time of year, but I didn't mind it. I loved walking around the stores at Christmas just window shopping. My mom and sister were big shoppers, so I had lots of practice in these places.

I found a pair of earrings for my sister, completing the last gift I had to buy, and walked to the counter to pay for it. As I reached in my wallet to grab my debit card, I found a small envelope with my name on it. Inside was the gift card Issy's dad had given her and a small note.

Avery,

I know I don't always show you how much I appreciate your friendship, but I do. You are the only person I've ever known that didn't want something from me, either status or money or even Jake. I want you to take this card and buy a beautiful gown for the ball. You should look as perfect on the outside as you are on the inside.

Your friend, Issy

P.S. If you ever mention this to me, I will deny it!

I couldn't stop the tears and excused myself, telling the lady I had changed my mind, and went to find the closest restroom. I pulled myself together and then texted Issy, "Thank you."

She replied, "For what?" and I had to smile. I never would have guessed that two people so opposite from each other could end up being great friends but we were.

Excitement flooded my stomach as I headed

towards Casey's, a store I rarely shopped in due to the outrageous prices of their clothes. They had a large selection of dresses, but most were cut well shorter than I was comfortable with. I finally found a sales rack that displayed some longer dresses—I guess to clear the inventory for spring. It took me only a second to spot the perfect one.

It was a strapless, icy-blue silk dress that fell all the way to my ankles. The color was mystifying because it looked white or blue, depending on how exactly the light hit it. Empire cut, the bodice looked almost like a swimsuit top as the material flowed from the back, to over the breast, culminating in a bunching at the cleavage that released a flow of mild ruffles down the front. The effect was breathtaking and made the front of the gown appear layered, while the back still looked sleek and sexy. I cringed, knowing I had to have this dress, but also that it would probably cost a small fortune. I found the tag and slowly turned it over, keeping one eye closed as I looked. It was on sale for $299. My breath caught and I almost let out an audible scream. It was perfect!

The purchase of my dress changed the entire mood of my long drive home. Instead of thinking about Jake, I sang at the top of my lungs like Issy and just enjoyed every song I heard.

Parker called when I had two hours left, and we chatted the rest of the way. He was already back at his parents' house and made me blush when he said that it was the first time in his life it felt a little empty, all because I wasn't there. He told me that his parents adored me and couldn't wait to have me come visit again. It made me feel so good that people as wonderful as Frank and Amy would enjoy my being there.

However, despite the wonderful conversation and the gold mine I found at the mall, my stomach knotted tighter and tighter as I got closer to my hometown.

I pulled into my driveway, feeling a sense of dread as I looked up at my childhood home. Everything about it screamed middle class, from the one story brick façade that matched every other house on the block, to the SUV parked in the driveway. I never minded that our family was average in every sense of the word, but I knew it always bothered my mom, and she had spent years and years trying to "keep up with the Jones'."

I took a deep breath before getting out of the car. The moment I hated most was about to come. My mom would give me a big hug, look me up and down, and would do one of two things. She would either comment that I had lost weight or would not say anything at all and give me a sad look. It was like she had a weight radar. If she thought I had gained weight, she would quickly mention how she and my sister were exercising in the morning and I should go with them.

I weighed this morning, just to prepare myself for what was coming. I was three pounds heavier than the last time I was at my parents' house, which normally would have put me in a shame spiral right to the kitchen, but, to my good fortune, Issy was still home, and I had managed to get out of the apartment without an episode.

I grabbed my suitcase and walked in the front door with a smile plastered on my face. "Happy" was really the only emotion allowed in this place.

My small cocker spaniel was the first to greet me at the door. She wagged her tail and waited for me to give her all the attention she was craving. My mom was next. She came in for a big hug and then held me back so she could check me out. I cringed as she stepped back, making room for my dad, not saying a word.

My dad gave me his usual stiff hug and patted me on the back. He was relatively uncomfortable with affection, and that was really all he could manage. It was no question whom I favored. I not only looked like my dad, but had so many of his personality traits that my mom would often joke that she was simply a vessel.

My dad took my bag and put it in my room. It still looked the same as it did in high school—cream-colored walls with purple curtains. My double bed had a purple comforter with soft cream flowers on it, and while it felt familiar, it struck me how much my taste had changed in such a short period of time. I also couldn't help but think of Issy's reaction if she saw my room. The teasing would never cease!

I joined my parents in the kitchen and went to the refrigerator to get a drink. I opted for a coke over the bottled water and immediately noticed my mother's disapproving stare as I drank it. I hated it when she monitored what I ate and drank. It was like she scrutinized every piece of food that went in my mouth. I could feel the anxiety start to hit my stomach, and I silently did breathing exercises to get it under control.

"Melissa and I are going to do a Zumba class in the morning tomorrow. You should come with us. She's been so excited to see you," my mom said as pleasantly as she could, trying to hide the deeper meaning in her words. It reminded me of junior high when she would force me to run with her every morning, promising it would help get the weight off. My being overweight bothered her much more than it ever bothered me at that point, but I went anyway, wanting nothing more than to please my mother.

"Sure," I answered nonchalantly. "Sounds fun."

"Melissa is really doing well at her new job. She just got promoted to office manager, and her boss never misses the opportunity to rave about how well she is doing."

In my head I screamed, *Neither do you*, but instead, I just smiled and managed, "That's wonderful." My sister had gone to a local community college after school and got an associates in business. She'd been working for a small sports retailer in our town, and I guess had been doing a lot to improve their sales. We had never really been close. My parents had fostered a spirit of competition between us that ruined any chance of a real relationship.

"How is school going?" she continued while cleaning the already perfect kitchen.

I wrinkled my nose, not wanting to answer, but figured I should go ahead and get it over with now since I was going to have to ask them for money anyway.

"Well, Mom, it was kind of a rough semester. I'm going to have to retake a class."

My dad suddenly became part of the conversation and put down the paper he had been reading. "Does it affect your scholarship?"

Leave it to my dad to get right to the point. "No, I'll still be on scholarship next semester, but I will have to pay for this class. It's not a big deal. I've got money saved from this summer, and I'm going to see if I can pick up some shifts over Christmas. I may need to borrow $500 or less, but I will pay you back, I promise." As soon as the words were finished, I was relieved to have them out of me. I knew I disappointed them, but at least I could deal with it all now and be done with it.

My mom immediately excused herself, saying my father would take care of all of that. I watched her leave, wondering why she even asked when she so obviously only wanted one answer.

My father gave a long sigh and said, "Avery, that money was for your living expenses. How are you planning to eat next year without any spending money?"

"I'll be fine, Dad. It doesn't take much for me to live on. I've really worked it all out, I promise." I tried to sound reassuring, not wanting to cause any more stress than I already had.

"Well, just let me know what you are short. We'll take care of it."

"Thanks. I'm really sorry." Regret was more than apparent in my voice.

"Me too. I expected more from you than this, Avery. You're supposed to be my smart one." He went back to the paper, signifying the end of our conversation. I felt about two inches high. My parents had always put me and my sister into two categories, the smart one and the pretty one. I guess I wasn't holding up my end. I held in the tears until I got to my room and then lay on my bed, letting them flow freely. I hated being a failure. Hated disappointing everyone.

I started to feel trapped in the room that I had called home for eighteen years and decided to go visit Cara. We hadn't spoken in months, and I was dying to see her. I walked down the street to her mom's house. Her parents had divorced when we were in the fifth grade, but her mom never remarried.

I knocked on the door, nervous and excited at the same time to reconnect with her and was joyfully greeted by her mom, who welcomed me in. "Avery, it's so good to see you, dear! It's been way too long,"

237

"Hi, Ms. Andrews. It's good to see you, too. Is Cara back yet?" I asked, looking around.

"Oh no, dear. Cara isn't coming home this year. She and her fiancé are going to his parents' house for the holiday."

I stood in stunned silence. Cara was engaged? She never even told me she was dating anyone. "Wow, I didn't realize she was engaged. Did it happen recently?"

"He did it at Thanksgiving. They came here to spend it with me, and he asked her in front of all of us. It was the sweetest thing I'd ever seen."

I couldn't believe it. Had we really grown that far apart? I said my goodbyes to Cara's mom and slowly walked home.

Telling her my secret had changed everything. She tried to be there for me, and I obviously couldn't handle her knowing. I had succeeded in pushing her away, the one person who ever held me accountable for my actions. I felt the weight of the loss on my shoulders—knowing deep down it was all my fault.

I got back to my house, and it was as if the school conversation had never even come up. My mom was back to being pleasant, and my dad was fully engaged in his paper. I put a smile on my face to match and pretended right alongside them for the rest of the week.

"Lord, Your Word holds truth as does Your promise to always be near us and guide us, even when we aren't able to see the light in front of us..."

18. JUST ONE NIGHT

I saw the sign to Winsor and could almost feel the tension start to ease in my body. I had never been so happy to be back. Six days at my parents' house was about five days too long, I decided, even though I spent most of that time working at the diner or exercising with my mom. I wanted to just get somewhere where I could let my defenses down for one minute and relax.

The sun was setting, and my eyes were starting to feel the effects of the exhausting drive. The only positive of it all was that I could crawl into bed, go to sleep, and Parker would be back in the morning. I smiled as I thought of him; he was the only thing about my week that was good. He called every night, and we talked for hours before drifting off to sleep. In fact, I had managed to survive my parent's house all week without an episode, and I knew he was the reason. My stomach fluttered as I thought of seeing him in less than twenty-four hours.

I lugged my suitcase up the stairs and then ran

back down to the car to get my new dress. I felt the silky fabric under my fingers and smiled. Carefully putting it back under the protective cover, I headed back up the stairs. When I got there, I noticed my suitcase was gone and the door to my apartment was open. I peeked in and saw Issy and Jake dressed and ready for a night out.

They had put my suitcase in my room, and Issy practically tackled me when I got in the door. I pushed her aside, trying to protect my dress, and put it carefully in my closet. I didn't make eye contact with Jake and basically sidestepped him when he came in for a hug.

It just seemed ridiculous that after all this time he could still make me swoon with just one smile, and I was just too physically and mentally tired from being with my parents all week to deal with him. I took a stabilizing breath and returned to the living room, convincing myself that I only had to pretend for one more hour and they would be gone.

I found a spot on the lip loveseat, the furthest point from where Jake was seated and asked how their Christmas was.

"Fabulous!" Issy beamed. "I got everything on my list, including a new BMW from my dad." Jake rolled his eyes, and I tried to keep my jaw from dropping.

"That's great," I said, trying my best to sound as excited as she was.

"We're going out tonight to celebrate, and I will not take no for an answer," Issy stated, her eyes daring me to argue.

"Issy, I'm exhausted. I just drove nine hours, and all I want is a shower and my bed," I insisted, determined not to give in no matter how much she begged.

Jake didn't say a word, just sat there overtly staring at me. It was getting harder and harder to avoid his eyes, and I shifted uncomfortably. Issy dropped on the sofa and folded her arms, pouting.

"I haven't seen you in a week, and you're telling me you can't take two hours to come to a party with me. I'm hurt," Issy whined, knowing guilt was always my Achilles heel.

"But that's just it, Issy, it's never two hours with you. It's more like five or six, and I know I can't make it that long tonight."

Jake finally said something, but of course it wasn't in my favor. "I'll bring you home in two hours, even if I have to go back to get her, I promise." He was still staring at me, and I was forced to look at him to answer. His eyes were mesmerizing just like I remembered, so perfectly green that it appeared unnatural. He was more relaxed tonight than I had seen him in a while, wearing jeans and a tight fitting t-shirt. He looked calm and confident and, worse, believable.

"It's settled then. Avery, go get dressed. We're leaving in an hour," Issy directed as she bounced off to her room.

I ran my fingers through my hair, feeling trapped

and exasperated, and got up to go to my room. Standing in the path to my door was Jake, and I stopped to stare at him for a second as if to say, *Excuse me*.

Instead of moving, he grabbed me by the waist and pulled me toward him so that my torso was touching his belt buckle. I could feel his breath on my hair and tried to stop the trembles I felt coming on.

"You can't avoid me forever," he whispered in my ear as I struggled to get out of his hold. Jake had called and texted several times over the break, but I had ignored all of them. I wanted to be over him, to let him go once and for all.

"Jake, please," I begged when I realized his grip was impenetrable.

"I know you still feel it," he continued as he moved his hand to my wrist, checking my pulse in the process. "Why do you fight it?" His words were soft and soothing as he released the full measure of his charm on me. I closed my eyes. His scent was starting to get to me, as were his words that I knew were true, despite how hard I wanted to believe they weren't.

"Give me one night. That's all I'm asking," he pressed, moving his hand to stroke my face. "If it's not there, I'll leave you alone. I know I screwed up, Avery, and you have no idea how badly I wish I could take it back."

I felt too tired to fight him. He was starting to break me down—to get behind the wall I had put up just to protect myself from him.

"Jake, I'm with someone else now, and I care about him," I pleaded, hoping my honesty would make him leave and allow me to breathe once again.

"I know that, and I'll totally respect it. No inappropriate touching whatsoever. I promise." He was grinning mischievously now, and I raised my eyebrows at him and then looked down at his arm that still encircled my waist. He quickly let go, as if to validate his words, and I couldn't help the smile that appeared even as I scurried past him.

"Okay, I'll go," I resigned. I turned to look as I shut my door. His eyes had the sparkle I hadn't seen in weeks, and his smile melted the last of my defenses. I pushed down the guilt that started to rise up in my chest. It was just one night. How bad could it be?

The party Issy brought us to was much more than just your average college get together. It was at one of the houses around the campus lake, which easily could have fit in her dad's neighborhood. I had run by it a million times, but never realized how beautiful it was until we pulled in the drive. Issy's new BMW fit right in with the others in the driveway, and I mentally prepared myself for the nightmare that I was about to embark on. If this party was anything like Ben's, it would be a very long two hours.

The house was beautifully decorated, with white lights following every turn on the roof and stairs, as well as covering at least five trees in the yard.

Jake wrapped his arm around me as we got out of

the car, looking as awed as I was. "It's beautiful, isn't it?"

I looked up at him, examining his face in the soft glow of the light. He was a different person tonight, and I didn't quite know how to process it. He was waiting for a response, so I finally answered, "It really is. Who lives here?"

Issy piped in before Jake could respond. "My dad has a business partner whose son goes to Winsor, too. They bought this house so they could come and visit him whenever they wanted. Luckily, they are happily at home, and Branson has the whole place to himself. He's got a little crush." I had no doubt it was true. Most men got crushes on Issy.

"Who else is coming?" I asked, as there were only five cars in the driveway.

"It's invite only, so probably no one we know all that well. It's free liquor, though, and Caesar's will be dead until school starts up, so you take what you can get!" She spun around and bounced up the stairs. She looked especially pretty tonight. She had kept the coloring to only a small blond streak by her face and was wearing tight black leggings with knee length boots and a flowing cashmere sweater. Her only punk item was the multicolored rhinestone belt around her waist, and honestly, it made the outfit.

Jake still had his arm around me as we walked towards the door. My conscience told me to move away from him, but I pushed it aside. Branson was there waiting and politely invited us in. You could tell

244

he definitely wasn't someone in Issy's normal circle. He seemed nervous and awkward. In fact, he reminded me a lot of the guys in my study group. He had on khakis and a nice sweater, but wore pretty old fashioned glasses, and his hair looked as if his mother had parted it before we got there.

"There's drinks in the kitchen, and we have music going out back," he explained shyly, barely making eye contact with Issy.

"Wonderful!" Issy said, planting a kiss on his cheek before she headed that direction. I had to hold in my laughter as I watched him stare after her in awe.

We followed her to the kitchen and got ourselves drinks. Jake offered me a glass of wine, but I declined. No need to cloud my judgment any more than it already was.

The back of the house was even more beautiful than the front. There was a long porch with large hanging lanterns around it. The stairs led down to a walkway that ended in a covered pier overlooking the lake. The pier was lit with white Christmas lights and had two beautiful wood rocking chairs that I imagined made for breathtaking sunrises. I was naturally drawn to it and started heading that way.

I leaned on the rail, just watching the black water beneath me. It seemed to captivate me as I stared at it. I started to wonder what I was doing here, and why I always seem to allow myself to be put in situations I didn't want to be in. Why couldn't I just say no? Jake's arms were suddenly wrapped around me, and I immediately felt my heart start to race. It felt too familiar. He didn't say a word, just held me tightly as we watched the water. I thought of Parker and how unfair this was to him. I needed to end this thing with Jake once and for all; I knew I did.

"I want to know why," I said softly. He didn't say anything, just sighed.

I moved his arms from around me and turned to look at him. "I want to know why now, and how you went from being a guy who wanted to just have fun to being this guy? What was the turning point for you? Because it seems you only want me until you have me." My hands trembled. I'd never once confronted Jake on any of his actions and wasn't sure how I had the confidence to do it now.

Jake sat down on one of the rocking chairs, and I followed suit. "The answer is so cliché, I almost hate to say it," he started. "When I first saw you, I was immediately attracted to you. You were bouncing around in your pajamas, without a care in the world. I wish I could say it was more, but honestly, you were just another cute girl who had piqued my interest. But something happened as I got to know you. You did everything different than any girl I had been with. It wasn't just different, but it was right, like you knew exactly what I needed to make my world stop spinning. It would amaze me. I would put you in situations and you came through them beautifully, with such grace and strength that I couldn't get you out of my mind."

"But you broke up with me," I reminded him.

"Because it scared the hell out of me, the feelings I was having. I'd felt nothing for months, and all the sudden, with you, I felt everything." He turned to stare at me, and my eyes filled with tears.

I was not expecting this answer from him, and it seemed to do nothing but muddy my already delicate resolve. He responded by standing and bringing me up to him, staring so lovingly in my eyes that I was sure I would faint.

"That night together…" He trailed off as he caressed my face.

The tears were spilling over my eyes now as I felt all the hurt that night had brought me. He wiped them away with his thumb and drew me into a tight hug. I could hear the music from the house and watched as the lights danced across the lake. "I'm so sorry I hurt you."

"We should get back," I whispered, knowing that if I stayed in his arms too much longer, I would do something cruel to the one person in my life who didn't deserve it. Thinking of Parker made my stomach turn. He deserved better than this from me.

Jake kissed me longingly on my forehead and then let go so we could head back to the house. My mind was spinning from his confession, and I decided to have that glass of wine after all, hoping it would somehow clear my head.

The party was in full swing when we returned to the house, with Issy naturally at the center of it. She squealed when she saw me and pulled me on the makeshift dance floor with her. I tried my best to get lost in the moment and put the confusion and chaos out of my mind, but Jake's eyes were relentless as he watched me dance, and I soon felt insecure under the scrutiny. I told Issy I was done, and her eyes knowingly glanced in Jake's direction.

"No problem," she said and put her arm through mine. She lead me to multiple groups of people, who surprisingly turned out to be really interesting. Most of them were actually in college to learn something and could hold a conversation without slurring their words. I especially liked Branson. He was kindhearted and so sweet to Issy. She was miles out of his league, but she allowed him to dote anyway.

True to their word, Issy and Jake left at the two-hour mark. Issy wasn't too drunk, which was a nice change from the norm and was actually a lot of fun tonight.

"I had a great time," I announced as we walked in the apartment. The wine had gotten to my head, making me more relaxed than usual.

"Of course you did, silly. You were with me," Issy responded, heading to the kitchen to rummage through the pantry. I shot her a look, and Jake laughed. It was a beautiful sound, and one I hadn't heard from him in a long time.

"I'm going to bed," I said.

"No! It's too early! Stay and watch a movie with us. It's my turn to pick and we can totally watch a chic flick." Issy had already put the popcorn in the microwave and was getting us all drinks. I had to admit it sounded fun. After a week of walking on eggshells with my parents, it felt good to be around Issy and her carefree honesty.

I went to my room and put on my favorite pajamas. I knew I should check my phone to see if Parker called, but for some reason I didn't. Instead, I shut the door and joined Issy and Jake on the sofa. I started by sitting with my legs crossed in the middle of them, but somehow throughout the evening I ended up cuddled next to Jake, and that's where I was when I woke up at two in the morning.

He was on his back asleep, and I was curled up on his chest just like we had done so many times before. His arms were locked tightly around me, and I could hear his rhythmic breathing as he slept.

I quietly wrangled out of his grip and stepped off the couch. Issy must have gone to her bed because she was no longer on the sofa. I softly shut my door and checked my phone.

Parker had called twice, once at 10:00 p.m. and again at midnight. I felt a little pang in my chest as I realized how selfish I had been last night. I didn't even tell him I got home safely. I knew deep down that I didn't call because I didn't want something to stop me from doing what I knew was wrong. I didn't want the accountability. I curled up in my bed, feeling horribly guilty. Last night had been a mistake—one I wouldn't let happen again.

"I pray, Lord, that she knows she has a Savior who is able to sympathize with her weakness, and that she knows she can find grace in her time of need..."

19. TELLING SECRETS

The morning seemed to come too quickly for me as I dragged myself out of bed. It wasn't early, but I still seemed to lack any energy. Parker was coming home today, and the thought of seeing him made me nervous. Two days ago, I had been so sure, convinced that I had put Jake out of my life for good. But last night, he was broken and honest, all the things I loved so much about him when we first met.

I needed to run, to clear my foggy head. I got dressed and opened my door—sure Jake would be long gone. He always seemed to disappear when things got too intimate, and last night was well beyond the limit for him.

But, he wasn't. Instead, he was sitting on the couch in his undershirt and boxers watching Sportscenter. He looked disheveled and ridiculously sexy, and I immediately blushed when I felt myself daydream of us together.

He looked up and saw me, flashing me his signature grin that always made my heart stop. I had to snap out of it. It was unhealthy how easily I could get sucked back in.

"I thought you'd be gone already," I said, walking towards the kitchen. His eyes followed me as I moved, making me feel self-conscious about how I was dressed.

"I thought we might go do something today. You got plans?" He was standing up to stretch, and I could see his muscles bulge through his shirt. I looked down, embarrassed, but he was quick to catch me staring.

He walked to the kitchen, grinning and kept putting himself in my way so I would naturally bump into him.

I was getting frustrated and it only made the sparks between us that much more intense. I finally was about to say something when Issy walked out of her room. She looked like her hair had spun in the dryer for two days, and I couldn't hold in the laughter when I saw her.

"Ha ha. We can't all look like a running goddess in the morning," she snapped and then noticed Jake standing right behind me, his hand resting on my hipbone. "What are you still doing here?"

"Lovely to see you too, sleeping beauty," Jake replied as he walked past her, ruffling her already crazy hair. He settled back in on the couch, but shot me a seductive look before he did. Before I could even get my hands to stop shaking, there was a knock at the door.

"You expecting anyone?" I asked Issy as she drank her coffee at the bar. She shook her head like I was crazy to even think she'd have someone here this early. They knocked again, and I realized that no one else was moving to get it.

The minute I unlocked the door and cracked it open, Parker was inside the room, cupping my face and kissing me with full abandonment. I hardly had any time to react before he stopped and looked lovingly at me.

"I have been wanting to do that for days," he whispered as he leaned in to kiss me again. I pulled back before he could, gesturing to the others in the room.

"Morning, Parker," Issy called from the bar, enjoyment apparent in her voice.

Parker didn't take his eyes off Jake, who sat comfortably watching TV as if he owned the place. "Good morning," Parker finally said back to her.

The tension in the room was palpable, and the longer the silence hovered, the more severe it became. Jake never took his eyes off the screen, but I could see a slight hint of a smile on his lips. I grabbed Parker's arm and motioned to my room. He followed stiffly, never fully taking his eyes off Jake. We got in the room, and as soon as I shut the door he asked, "What's he doing here, Avery?"

I could tell he was upset. "He's Issy's cousin. They are pretty close to inseparable," I explained, trying to downplay the situation.

"He sleeps here?"

"Um, yeah, most of the time. He has a key. Sometimes they crash at his place too. It just depends. He comes and goes at will."

Parker seemed even more irritated at that piece of information, and I knew I needed to distract him before he started reading too much into it. "I don't want to talk about that, though," I said, walking up to him and putting my arms around his neck. "I missed you."

He took the bait and leaned down, capturing my mouth in his. I kissed him back this time and he seemed to relax.

"I was worried when I didn't hear from you last night," he said softly, running his hands through my hair as he looked over my face like he was taking in all of me.

"I know. I'm sorry. Issy got me right as I walked in the door and dragged me to her friend's party. We got back so late, I didn't want to bother you." It wasn't totally a lie, although my heart was racing as the guilt started to eat at it.

"Avery, it's never too late to call me, okay? I always want to know you're safe."

I nodded, frustrated at myself for thinking about Jake for even one second when I had such a wonderful man.

"So, I've come to kidnap you," he said with a sparkle in his eye.

"Really, where are you taking me?"

"It's a surprise, but I can tell you that you need to wear jeans and hiking shoes."

"What, my running attire is not acceptable?" I gave a little curtsy.

He looked me up and down, and his eyes got a sultry look to them that made my stomach do a somersault.

"They're something alright." He turned away to look at other things around the room. "I have to admit, Avery, it bothers me that he's here, especially knowing you look like this in the morning."

I knew I was being forward, but I didn't care. I walked up to his back, wrapped my arms around him and started moving my hands across his chest, running my fingers along each of his muscles, while I slowly kissed his shoulders. I could feel his body tensing, but I just continued to persist. I wanted to feel close to him, wanted something that would finally break through all the confusion.

He turned around and captured me in his arms, kissing me with such ferocity that heat started to consume my body. We fell on the bed, and I continued to be bold, pulling him closer and closer. I put my hands under his shirt, rubbing them all over his back and chest. He started to do the same and then froze, pulling his head away, trying to catch his breath. I continued to tug at him, searching for his lips, but he was moving off me with determination.

I sat breathless on the bed, while he stood gripping the desk. "You're making it very hard for me to stick to my convictions. I think your room is now officially off limits." His voice wasn't harsh, just labored, as I knew he was fighting to regain control. He looked up at me, and we stared at each other in silence before he moved to the door. "I'll wait for you in the car while you change." He headed out my door and the apartment without saying another word. I felt stupid and insecure for pushing him when he had made his feelings on it so clear.

I saw Jake looking in my room at me. He had a smug look on his face, and I was sure he misread Parker's quick exit. I got up and shut my door. He was the last person I wanted to see.

It took me less than fifteen minutes to get ready to go, opting to pile my hair on top of my head with a clip versus trying to do something with it. I locked my door and turned to see Jake leaning against the sofa with his arms folded. He had showered and changed and looked like he was waiting on me.

"Trouble in paradise?" he asked, looking disturbingly pleased with himself.

"No, not that it's any of your business."

He stepped towards me and grabbed my arm so hard it scared me. Our faces were close to touching and his eyes looked dark. Dangerous. "He's never going to be enough for you," he seethed. "We belong together. And no matter how much you deny it, I can see it every time you look at me." His voice got softer and his grip lighter, but I still felt frozen by his words.

We stared at each other defiantly for a long time

until he finally walked out the door, shutting it far harder than was necessary.

Issy was still at the bar and put up her hands in surrender when my eyes searched her for some explanation.

"Don't look at me; I told you he was complicated," she said flatly and went off to her room. The worst of it was that I had caused this. I had let Jake see that he could still get to me—that I hadn't fully let him go. I sat on the couch, trying to get my pounding heart to settle before I met Parker at the car.

He was leaning on the car hood, messing with his phone, when I finally came down the stairs. My walk was tentative, as I felt I owed him an apology. I wrapped my arms around his waist and pressed my cheek to his hard chest. "I'm sorry."

He kissed my head and hugged me back. "Don't apologize; it's not your fault. I know better than to put myself in situations where I can lose control." He tenderly lifted my chin and kissed me as if to confirm he wasn't upset, then opened my door so I could get inside the car.

"So now can you tell me where we're going?" I asked after he had pulled off campus. "The suspense is starting to get to me."

"Okay, my impatient girl. I have a friend whose parents own a cabin just a half hour from here. It sits right next to Pisgah National Forest and has unbelievable hiking trails. Anyway, I called in a favor, and it's ours for the day," he shared, grinning.

I reached over and kissed his cheek, thinking this was exactly what I needed today.

The cabin sat four miles from the Blue Ridge Parkway, where Mount Pisgah could be seen in all its glory. The cabin itself was small and very rustic, with a mix of horizontal logs and stone for its façade. The gray stone fireplace must have been added on later, because it jutted out of the house, offering character and charm to the small cabin.

Inside, most of the walls continued to be made up of large horizontal logs, and those that weren't were covered in rich wood paneling. A large oval rug lay on the wood floor in the living room, where there was only one oversized red couch and a brown leather recliner. The homey feel continued in the kitchen, where bar stools were covered in a southwestern pattern of reds and oranges. I noticed one bedroom with a bathroom that sat just off the living room, but no other doors except the one to the back of the house where a large deck was overlooking the amazing views.

Parker didn't say a word as I absorbed the space and the atmosphere but looked pleased that I could appreciate it. I walked out back to enjoy the fresh mountain air and felt invigorated by its beauty.

"This is unbelievable."

"I knew you'd love it," he said affectionately as he wrapped his arms around me. Every time I was in his presence, I felt safe and loved, and each time I was without it, I'd forget how amazing it made me feel. Just last night Jake had tried to hold me the same way, and while familiar with him, Parker's arms felt stronger and right. So right. I leaned back into his chest, absorbed in how perfect this moment was.

"The trail starts over there, and it's a six mile hike round trip. It may take us a few hours, so we should probably get going so we get back before dark."

"Sounds great!" I exclaimed, excited to go, but secretly disappointed when he let go of me.

He gathered all we needed in his backpack and took the lead up the trail. At first the path was pretty easy, just basic forest bedding and a few stray branches. However, a mile into the hike, the elevation picked up and we navigated through large boulders and steep cliffs. It was physically challenging, but I was never scared because Parker was at my side with each step, helping me through any obstacle that came my way.

It took us two hours to complete the three mile ascent, but the beauty that awaited us at the top was totally worth it. We stood on a stone ledge and overlooked the mountain range; I had never seen anything so beautiful in all my life.

A few feet away was a large waterfall that fell to at least one hundred feet below us. The sound of the rushing water made my pulse quicken as I thought about the power behind such a wonder of nature.

We found a safe place to rest and sat in silence, enjoying the view and the light mist that came up from the falls. I reflected on the journey I'd taken with Parker, how he found me so devastated and broken, yet now I sat at the top of a mountain ridge, with the world awaiting me. The tears hit me with such a force that I couldn't hold them back, and Parker quickly came to my aid, asking what was wrong.

"Nothing's wrong," I assured him, smiling through my tears. "I just feel free, like genuinely, fully free, and it's a little overwhelming is all. A month ago, I didn't know how I was going to get out of bed, and now…"

He wrapped his arms around me and held me while I cried. He was so good, so honest and perfect, that I knew in that moment I had to tell him. My heart started pounding as I searched for the words, my mind trying to convince me not to do it. But I wanted him to know, even if it meant he'd never look at me the same. Somehow, being up there gave me the strength to open up fully to him. I felt I owed it to him, to be completely honest about who I was, when he had given me so much.

"I have to tell you something," I said, turning my body so that we were facing each other. He looked concerned, almost nervous, as if I was about to drop a huge bomb on our relationship.

I put my hand on his cheek softly to reassure him and began telling him my story. I could feel my hands shaking, and every part of me screamed to stop for self-preservation. I almost changed my mind, but one look in his genuine eyes, and I knew it was time.

"Parker, there is a lot people don't know about me. I'm kind of a closed book in a lot of ways. But you are always somehow finding ways to read me and break through the barriers I set up to keep people away. It scared me at first, but now I feel like I can tell you something I've only told one other person in my life. It's something that I never share because I know that if I ever told the truth, people would look at me differently, see me as the fraud that I am." My voice caught as I said the last word, and Parker grabbed my hand, encouraging me to go on.

"The reason this matters is because feeling in control is vitally important to me. My family were pros at avoiding conflict, so whenever there was one, nobody seemed to know what to do. I learned very quickly that feelings were best left to myself, and that's what I did every time I felt anything. I would swallow it and put on a smile, determined to be as strong as I appeared.

"But I wasn't strong, and I found at an early age that I could find solace in eating. That it would calm my nerves or ease my pain if I needed it to. It was something I could control when nothing else was going right. The end result was that in junior high I got really heavy. And while it didn't bother me that much, it just about killed my mom. She started putting me on diets and making me exercise with her, all trying to get my weight under control.

"Eventually, kids started teasing me at school and

soon it became very easy to believe the things they said, which were that I was ugly and fat. Between my mom's need to change me and the teasing at school, my self-worth revolved around my appearance. Worse, every time I looked in the mirror, I hated what I saw."

Parker reacted to that admission and moved closer to me, taking just a moment to caress my cheek while he listened.

"A few years later, my body changed, and I lost a lot of the baby fat and developed in a way that made boys notice me. It was the first time in years that I felt good about myself, and I started to obsessively diet and exercise to ensure that the weight would never come back.

"Unfortunately, since I had already wrapped so much emotion into eating, I found it really difficult to eat in a healthy manner. I would sneak food when my mom wasn't looking to get the comfort I needed. But the weight started to come back, so I thought I'd try something I had heard people do, which is to make yourself throw up so you wouldn't gain weight." I stared down at my hands, not wanting to go on, but Parker lifted my chin, letting me know he wanted to hear more.

"It worked for a while. I would diet for days or weeks, depending on my will power, and then when it got to be too much, I would go on a binge and afterwards throw it up. I had convinced myself that it was the perfect weight maintenance plan and never realized how much it consumed me. I had convinced myself that I was controlling it, not the other way around.

"When I got to college, I thought it would go away. I believed that being here would somehow heal me. I stopped, but only for about four weeks. When I looked in the mirror, I could only see the flaws, and somehow throwing up would make me feel better about it, and then worse again, creating this vicious cycle.

"Soon, it would make me feel better about a lot of things, a bad grade, a hurt feeling, a bad conversation with my mom. You name it, it became my coping mechanism, and I realized that I couldn't stop. It was starting to control my life.

"I never told anyone. It was my secret, and I knew as long as no one knew, I could continue to do it, but I started to see how it was affecting the rest of my life. One, I spent most of my freshmen year in isolation, not participating in events or with other students, because I felt so insecure about how I looked. I was constantly comparing my body to other women and always came up short.

"It was overtaking my life, and I wanted it to stop. So, I told my best friend, and she was great about it. She would call and check up on me and would be there for me when I was struggling. This summer, I hit a milestone. I had gone two months without throwing up until the day I stepped back on campus, and then the stress and pressure hit me like a ton of bricks.

"That night in the quad wasn't just about Jake or my failure at school, but it was also about this. I was in a shame spiral and had just spent weeks indulging in it every day…for hours at a time. I got to the point where I couldn't even look in the mirror without crying, because I hated what I saw so fiercely."

I took his hand and stared up at him, wanting to convey all the emotion I felt towards him. "And then I met you, and somehow it got better. Somehow, I started to believe in how *you* saw me more than how *I* saw myself. I still mess up, but for the first time in a long time, I feel like there's hope for healing, and I know you're a part of that. You always say no secrets, so I'm telling you this, because I wanted you to know I trust you."

My heart beat so hard it was hurting my chest, and I kept my eyes away as he processed all the information I had just thrown on him. This was always the moment I dreaded, the one that had previously kept me from sharing my secret. The moment when they would look at me for the first time, and despite how hard they tried not to… they would see me differently. I tried to mentally prepare myself for it, for the loss of adoration.

His hand cupped my face. My eyes were glassy, and I knew I was seconds from breaking down.

His stare was like a caress. "I love you, Avery. And not despite this or because of this; I love you because you're you. That will never change."

264

I felt myself exhale as I lost all composure and cried in his arms. I believed him, and I wanted so badly to say it back, but I never found the words. Instead I held him close, hoping in some way he knew how precious he was to me.

When I had calmed and wiped my eyes, Parker took my hand and squeezed it. "Avery, I know I've failed when it comes to talking with you about what I believe, but I think now, more than ever, I need to explain why my faith is so important to me. You see, Christ is the one who has shown me how to love, because He loves us even though we constantly mess up. It's important you understand this, because I know that I can only offer you a small glimpse into the unconditional love Christ has for you."

Parker's eyes light up with passion and intensity. I knew he fully believed what he was telling me. I wanted to believe it too, but it felt too easy. If there was a God, He certainly wouldn't find me worthy of His love.

I didn't want to talk about it any more, so I just smiled at Parker and said, "Thank you." As usual, he sensed the conversation was over.

We made our way back down the mountain and enjoyed the sunset together out on the deck. Parker told me all his stories from Christmas, and I spent most of the time laughing so hard my stomach hurt. His brother and family were in the States for the holiday, and their three-year-old son was quite the showboat, always looking for new ways to get everyone's attention. It sounded like an amazing time, and I couldn't help but hope one day I would get to meet them.

Parker grilled us a wonderful meal, and it honestly felt like I had stepped into a perfect world I never wanted to leave. He didn't even watch me while I ate, which I was sure would happen once he knew my secret. In fact, the knowledge of it didn't seem to change us at all. It almost made me wonder why I had kept it hidden for so long.

We started a fire and then stretched out on pillows and blankets that Parker put on the floor for us. The fire was crackling, and I could hear Parker breathing as my head rested quietly on his chest.

"Can I ask you a question about it?" Parker asked hesitantly after a few minutes of silence.

"I guess that's fair after dropping it on you like that." I was trying to make light of it, but deep down I was nervous.

"When is the last time you did it?"

"Finals week, and before that it was the night we walked along the river," I answered honestly. "I've gotten to the point where it's not a daily struggle anymore, but I seem to get just shy of that one month point, and then something triggers it. It's like this elusive goal I can't seem to reach."

"You'll reach it. I know that without question," he said confidently. "And what about your friend? Is she still there for you to talk to?"

My heart tugged a little as I thought of the

estranged relationship between Cara and me. "No, our friendship wasn't able to handle her knowing," I answered with regret. "It wasn't her fault. It was all me."

He seemed to hold me tighter, and I wondered if he was questioning like I was, if ours, too, would fail this test.

I suddenly felt nervous and wanted reassurance that we were still close, that he still wanted me like he used to. I rolled over and started kissing him, moving my body to where it was completely on top of his. He responded, as I'd hoped and kissed me back with all the passion and desire he once had. I felt desperate to be closer to him, like I wanted his body to completely envelope me into it. I straddled his waist and started kissing his neck and his ear. I could feel his rapid breath and the more passionately he kissed me, the bolder I became.

He sat up and pulled me close to him, our torsos touching. I had never wanted him so badly and pulled his shirt off with such force that my body was shaking. He grabbed the back of my head and brought our lips together. Every one of my senses awakened.

But, like always, he slowly put the brakes on and left me panting, needing so much more.

"Don't you want me?" I asked, breathless, staring at him.

"Of course I want you, Avery. You have no idea how badly, but we're not ready for this," he said, his face as flushed as mine.

I got off his lap and turned away. I could hear him put back on his shirt and come sit next me as I faced the fire.

"If we do this now, it will confuse everything."

"What if it doesn't? What if it makes it better?" I felt rejected and desperate.

"It won't."

"You don't know that, Parker."

"Yes, I do," he stated softly. "Avery, we aren't there yet. I know you don't fully understand my convictions, but I pray one day you will. I believe that sex is meant for marriage, when two people are promised for a lifetime. If we cross that boundary now, we can't go back, and it will give us a sense of closeness to each other that we aren't emotionally ready for."

I put my head in my hands, not wanting to hear what he was saying. How was it possible that I was trying to convince a twenty-one year old man to have sex with me? It seemed laughable.

"Avery, part of what's so special in our relationship is the journey, and I don't want to take any step for granted." He moved a piece of hair off my face and looked pleadingly at me, trying to get me to understand.

"So you've never been tempted?"

"Tempted? Yes, all the time, especially since I met you," he answered honestly. "But I've never acted on it, and I try my best to stay out of compromising situations."

I turned my head away, ashamed I couldn't give the same answer.

He was quiet for a long time and then asked, "Have you?"

I didn't say a word, just stared at him with all the shame and hurt consuming me.

He let out a long sigh and lay back on the floor with his hands over his head. "Jake," he said, his contempt apparent. "Is there anything that guy didn't take from you?" He wasn't really talking to me anymore—just seemed to be asking the air.

I felt the tears start to come and wanted to crawl into the deepest hole I could find. He was too good for me, and he deserved better. I knew it, and it was only a matter of time before he realized it, too.

After he seemed to have time to process the new information, he sat back up and wrapped his arms around me. I immediately relaxed into him, wanting to enjoy the last few moments I had before it was all taken from me.

"It doesn't change anything for me," he whispered softly.

"How can it not?" I asked through my tears.

"I won't lie, I hate it. I hate it so much that it makes my stomach turn when I think of you with him. I don't think I'd be human if that weren't true." He moved my hair so he could kiss my shoulder. "You have to understand, though, when I look at you, I just see you. Nothing else. And I'm in love with you.

I don't care about your past. I see who you are becoming." His voice was soft, and I felt like his words caressed every inch of my soul.

That day with Parker had been the most amazing of my life, and even though I felt physically drained when he walked me to my door, I was more emotionally sure than I had ever been in my life. He kissed me goodbye with all the tenderness I had come to love about him, and I shut the door.

Jake was on the couch, sleeping, and I looked at him resting peacefully. He still looked strangely confident and vulnerable at the same time, but different tonight, less enchanting somehow. I could see him clearly, without blinders, for the first time. I stepped quietly into my room. There was no confusion tonight.

"Lord, I pray that she will soar like the eagle's wings and that You will enable her to stand on the heights..."

20. NEW YEAR'S

The day of the ball was finally here, and I felt as giddy as a school girl. Issy was in her own frenzy, getting the apartment ready for the "epic" party she had planned for tonight. I helped her by vacuuming and cleaning the kitchen, although I couldn't understand why she cared when her friends were just going to trash the place within fifteen minutes of getting there.

"Are you sure you want to do this, Issy? New Year's parties have a bad habit of getting out of control," I asked as we cleaned.

She gave me a disapproving look and scolded, "Avery, you are way too practical. I am the queen of party hosting; I practically do it all the time at other people's apartments. This time I won't have to go anywhere. Besides, it's all apartment folks, so they will totally go home when it's over."

"Did you invite Danny and Aaron?" I asked hesitantly. Issy and I hadn't discussed him in a while, but I'd run with him the other day and he seemed to be doing better.

Issy rolled her eyes and grabbed her phone. "You don't want to go there. I'm still trying to decide how you are going to make this one up to me." She handed me her phone and pressed play on the voicemail. The sound of Danny's voice was heartbreaking. He was obviously drunk and slurring his words, and he went from yelling at her to telling her how much he cared about her.

I looked at Issy who had her eyebrow raised and was tapping her finger on the countertop. "That little message got him put right on the blocked caller's list," she said flatly. It amazed me that she could have no compassion for him at all. I shook my head and handed the phone back to her.

Minutes later, Jake was hauling in kegs with a dolly, and I cringed when I saw there were three of them. I felt grateful Issy's family was wealthy, because I had a bad feeling that this place was going to need some serious work in the morning.

I pulled off the latex gloves I was wearing, the fumes from the cleaning products starting to make me dizzy, and went to my room to go change. I needed to get a run in before Parker came to pick me up. It was a two and a half hour drive to the ball, and we were leaving at three-thirty to give us plenty of time to get there. Parker tried to explain all the military jargon and expectations to me, but they were way over my head. It all seemed to boil down to the fact that we couldn't be late.

Jake looked up as I walked past him and shot me his signature smile. No butterflies came. "You're going to be here, right? It's only fitting that you would toast in the New Year with us."

"Um, no, I have plans tonight with Parker. We are going to a military ball."

"Sounds horribly boring," he replied, raising his eyebrows as if I felt the same way. If he was trying to be charming, he was failing miserably.

I shot him a dirty look and turned away. "No, it doesn't."

"So, are you two going to get all shacked up in a sleazy hotel tonight and finally consummate this relationship?" Issy asked from the kitchen in her usual playful tone.

"Issy!" Jake and I yelled in unison.

"Why don't you two worry about your party and not what I'm doing," I retorted, frustrated with their implications. "I'll be back tonight, but it will be well past midnight, and my clothes will have stayed on."

Jake rested his arm on the bar and smiled mischievously at me. "I'll be here when you get back."

I rolled my eyes and slammed my door. He frustrated me so much. Their comments did nothing but cheapen the relationship I had with Parker, one that went well beyond parties or lust. It was real and honest, and I refused to let them ruin what I knew would be a perfect evening.

Hours later, I stood staring at myself in the

mirror. I was ready to go, wearing the most beautiful gown I had ever owned. I piled my hair up on my head and just let multiple ringlets hang down around my face and down my back. The exquisite shawl Issy had given me hung around my shoulders, and I chose long silver earrings as my only accessory. I examined every inch of my body and face, and it looked different tonight. My reflection wasn't perfect, but I was okay with it. I could even see the beauty in it.

The clock said 3:20 p.m., and I knew Parker would be here soon. I stepped out of my room, making sure to lock the door. Jake was standing near Issy's room, talking to her as she got ready. He glanced my way, and I saw his face change. It was a look I'd never seen before, but so intense that I had to look away.

I heard a knock on the door and Jake yelled, "Come in," without once taking his heated eyes off me. I started to feel insecure, wondering what he was thinking, until I saw Parker step through the door. He looked breathtakingly handsome in his military uniform. It looked much like a tuxedo, complete with a bow tie, but had metals on the front and rank on the shoulders. The uniform fit him perfectly and showed off how incredibly fit he was.

He walked right up to me without saying a word, and I immediately felt good again. I looked in his eyes, realizing how lucky I was and how absolutely special this man was to me. He was gentle and loving and made me feel like a princess.

"You're a vision," he said softly.

I smiled playfully and looked him up and down. "You're pretty dashing yourself, soldier." I felt his fingers lightly touch my face as he leaned down for a soft kiss, not wanting to mess up my masterpiece.

We said our goodbyes, and Issy was over the moon about how we looked. She doted and cheered and of course made inappropriate comments, but she was sweet, and I couldn't help but hug her before I left. She had made all this possible. Jake didn't say a word, but I didn't expect him to, nor did I need him to. Tonight wasn't about him.

We got to the car, and Parker stopped me before I opened the door.

"I have something for you," he said as he pulled out a long, white jewelry box. "I know we already did Christmas, but I saw this and it reminded me so much of you that I had to get it."

I opened the box and pulled out a delicate silver necklace that had an intricately carved silver rose in the center of it. It was finest piece I'd ever seen, and the detailing was so precise, there was even one small thorn on the side of the stem.

"It's beautiful," I exclaimed.

He put the necklace on me and stared lovingly into my eyes. "It's a gift for when you reach the one month point. You can look at it every day and know you accomplished the impossible."

Tears immediately hit my eyes as I reflected on what an incredibly insightful gift it was. He believed in me. "Why the rose?" I asked as I ran my fingers over the delicate metal.

"It's the perfect balance of softness and strength. Just like you."

I reached up and hugged him tightly, not caring if I wrinkled him or me. No words would express what I was feeling, and I just hoped that my touch could. He hugged me back, reciprocating all I felt and then kissed me softly before opening my door.

The drive to Charlotte went by quickly as Parker explained all the ceremonial things I needed to know for the dinner. There were rules on standing and toasting and even what type of dinner conversation was acceptable. I started to worry, but he assured me that all the rules were for the cadets and not for their dates.

We pulled up to the hotel and a valet took Parker's car. It was a beautiful building that had to be at least one hundred years old. Inside, a large entryway with an enormous staircase went up one level and then split into two smaller staircases going in opposite directions. The entire hotel was decorated for Christmas and had three large Christmas trees, each artfully decorated in creams and reds, and rich greenery laced through the railing along the stairs.

We ascended the stairs to the second floor, where a large banquet room was full of round tables, with one long table at the front of the room. No one was sitting yet, and Parker led us to a reception area where all the other couples were mingling and getting drinks from the bar. The men all looked the same in their uniforms, but Parker was by far the most handsome one there, and I felt proud to be next to him.

He introduced me to his friends and to his commanders, who were all very polite and complimentary. Even the women were friendly and seemed genuinely happy to be there. Anytime I started to feel nervous or overwhelmed with all the new people, Parker would subtly rub my back or squeeze my hand, and I would immediately calm down. He seemed to be completely in tune to me and to what I was feeling at any given moment. I had no idea how he always knew.

I heard a bell ring, and Parker indicated it was time to get seated. We entered into the vast dining area and found our table, our names delicately etched on a piece of parchment above our place setting. We stood until the head table arrived, and then Parker pulled out my chair, indicating we could now take our places.

The dinner actually turned out to be pretty fun. In front of the head table, there was a toilet bowl full of edible things, like orange juice, Dr Pepper, marshmallows, and gummy bears, just to name a few. They were mixed together to create something that could only be described as disgusting. Each time one of the cadets would do something to break "the rules" Parker had told me about, they would have to report to the head table, salute and take a drink from the bowl. Even Parker ended up taking two trips. He was so charming and gracious about it that I joined in with the laughter of the group. It was obvious the cadets thought as highly of him as I did.

The dinner bell chimed for a second time, which signified the end of dinner, and each table stood while the head table departed first. When it was our turn, Parker led us back to the reception area where they had opened several large doors that lead to a breathtaking ballroom, complete with wood floors and stunning chandeliers. The ornate windows were all stained glass, giving the atmosphere one of historical charm. The band on stage welcomed us in and started the evening with a perfect rendition of Frank Sinatra's "Fly me to the Moon."

Parker glanced toward the dance floor, a smile creeping across his broad lips. "Would you like to dance, my lady?" he asked with a slight bow.

I blushed and took his hand, already swept off my feet. Parker was incredibly light on his feet and boldly took the lead as we danced, circling us all around the dance floor. The music seemed to jump off the walls and touch every inch of my being as Parker mouthed the words, "I love you" with the song. It was magical, better than any dream I could have ever conjured up, and I wanted to pinch myself just to believe it was really my life. I felt like Cinderella at the ball, only I wouldn't lose my handsome prince at midnight.

The music continued all night, ranging from current hits to timeless classics. Parker and I danced the night away, getting lost more than once in each other's arms. When it was nearing midnight, waiters came around passing out champagne to every person. The whole room started the count down, and with each number, I felt the weight of the year start to fall off my shoulders. I had done it. At midnight, it will have been one month, and there was nothing but promise in the New Year.

We clicked our glasses together as we cheered, "Happy New Year!" Parker gathered me in his arms and kissed me with all the joy and promise that encapsulated the room. Others came by to hug us or kiss our cheeks, but I was always acutely aware of Parker's presence, making eye contact every chance I got.

The high we got from the evening remained as we drove home, the hum of the car engine matching the peace and comfort we felt with one another. I was tired, but was willing myself to stay awake and talk to Parker for the duration of the drive, not wanting him to get drowsy himself. He seemed alert and perfectly comfortable behind the wheel, allowing me to doze off for just a few minutes.

The sound of gravel under the tires brought me back to consciousness, and I sat up startled, unsure where we were.

"Shh. It's okay, we just got home," Parker said softly, rubbing his hand on my back.

"I slept the whole way?" I asked horrified. "I'm so sorry."

"Why? I loved watching you sleep," he assured

me with a smile.

The lights were on when I looked up towards my apartment and I dreaded the scene I was going to walk into.

Parker opened my door and walked me upstairs. It was almost three o'clock in the morning, and I knew he was tired. I tried to get him to go home, but, as usual, he first insisted on seeing me safely to my door. It was cracked open when we got to it, and I pushed it a little to see how many people were still there. Surprisingly, it was quiet.

I walked in with Parker not far behind and was struck by the disaster that had once been my apartment. Red disposable cups lined the floor. One of the kegs was laying on its side while the other two still had beer dripping from the nozzle. Liquor bottles covered the bar, and a thick, red substance was dripping to the linoleum floor in the kitchen. Around the blender, you could see droplets of thick goo, where someone had obviously forgotten to put the lid on when they turned it on.

Jake was passed out on the couch, fully clothed, but with a half-full glass of beer sitting on the coffee table. I walked towards Issy's room, careful to step over the cups along the way and noticed a large hole in the wall right by her room. Her door was slightly open, and I pushed it a little, feeling my stomach turn with uneasiness.

She was lying face down on the bed with her arm hanging over the side. Right below her fingertips sat the silver flask I had given her for Christmas. The delicate bottle was turned over on the floor and sat in a puddle of liquid. The room was dark, but the light from the living room was casting a glow over her.

My heat pounded against my chest. There was something about her color that didn't seem right. She was always pale, but tonight her face looked sallow…almost blue. I inched closer.

"Issy?" I whispered, hoping to get some response. She was laying eerily still and didn't move even when I said her name two more times. I approached the bed and realized her head was lying in a puddle of vomit. I started to panic and shook her fiercely, with no response. Her hands were cold, and I could tell she wasn't breathing.

"PARKER!" I screamed as adrenalin rushed through every part of my body.

Parker was there in an instant, taking in the sight that had me so shaken. He tried unsuccessfully to wake her, too, and looked up at me. He was completely calm, a stark contrast to my panicked state. "She probably has alcohol poisoning. You need to call 911 right now." He had moved her off the bed and was starting CPR as I rushed to the living room to get my phone.

My hands shook uncontrollably as I dialed the number.

"911, what's your emergency?" the voice on the other line asked.

"My roommate isn't breathing. She was drinking

and I don't know what happened, I just got here. Please, she's not breathing, you need to get here right away!"

"What's your location?"

"We're in University Apartments, building 1, room 204. Please hurry." Fear was starting to consume me as tears racked my body.

"Ma'am, we've got an ambulance on the way. I need you to calm down. Is someone there with your friend?"

"Yes, my boyfriend is doing CPR…" My voice trailed off as I looked up and saw Parker still frantically trying to revive her. I set down the phone and ran over to Jake, shaking him with all the force I still had left in me.

"Jake, you have to wake up. Issy's in trouble. Wake up!"

He wrapped his arms around me and pulled me in so tight I could hardly breath. He wasn't fully conscious and was still slurring his words. "My sweet Avery, you came back to me. I knew you'd come back to me."

I struggled against his strength, pushing hard on his chest to wake him.

"Jake, you have to wake up!"

He jolted up so quickly that I was thrown hard against the coffee table. The searing pain I felt in my back only lasted a second as the adrenalin took over again.

Jake stared at me, disoriented, as if he was in the

middle of some strange dream.

"It's Issy, Jake. She's not breathing," I said again, trying to get him to understand.

My words finally registered, and he jumped off the couch and ran over to her room. Parker was still doing CPR, but Issy's color wasn't improving. Jake stood there in cold silence, frozen by fear.

I heard the ambulance outside and ran to the stairs, waving at them to let them know where to find us. They rushed in with speed and professionalism and had Issy hooked up on a stretcher faster than I could even believe. Jake got in the ambulance with her, and Parker and I followed along in his car.

The shock had started to wear off, and my tears came in uncontrollable waves. Even Parker's reassuring hand did nothing to stop the fear that was gripping me.

We waited in the emergency room for what felt like a lifetime, until Jake finally appeared to give us an update on her. I could tell by his demeanor that things weren't good.

I stood, gripping the chair, unwilling to accept anything but news that she would be alright.

Jake stopped right in front of me, virtually ignoring Parker as he spoke. His eyes were hollow and vacant, the emptiness so apparent that my stomach turned.

"She's stable, but not out of the woods yet. They have her in a coma and are moving her up to ICU now. I put you down as her sister so you can visit her whenever you want. There are no set hours for family." His voice was flat and hardened. "You should probably go home and get some sleep. There won't be any change tonight." I reached out to hug him, but he stiffened underneath it, refusing to hug me back.

"I'm going to get back up there," he stated after I let him go. Before he left, he turned to Parker, his face still devoid of any emotion. "I suppose I should thank you." It wasn't a question, but more a resigned statement.

"Nah, man, no need," Parker said graciously.

Jake just nodded his head and turned to leave. My heart wept for him and what he must be going through, watching Issy lie there just as helpless as his mom had for so many years.

Parker put his arm around me and led me to the car. I was silent the entire way home, still unable to process the events from the night. I walked in a daze to my apartment, where the scene hadn't changed from the mess that was there before, but now there hung a darkness that gripped my soul the minute I walked in.

"Let me stay with you tonight," Parker offered, pulling me in for a hug. I pushed him away, not wanting anything that would make me break down again.

"I'm fine. I'm just going to clean up a little and go to bed, so I can get back to the hospital tomorrow." My voice was as vacant as my heart felt.

"Avery, you don't have to go through this alone. I'm here for you," Parker insisted, once again trying to draw me in.

I put my hands up to stop him again, not wanting to be touched. "I'm fine, Parker, really. I just want to be alone for a little while."

He seemed frustrated at what I was saying, but at a loss as to how to reach me.

"Please, Parker. Just let me be alone for a while. I promise I'll call you tomorrow."

He finally agreed and kissed me on the cheek before he left, glancing back at me one more time, hoping I'd change my mind. I shut and locked the door and went to my room to put on sweats and take down my hair. What had begun as the perfect night, turned into the worst of my life.

I grabbed a trash bag from the kitchen and started desperately filling it with all the bottles and cups that were strewn around the apartment. After I had filled three bags, I pulled out the kitchen cleaner and scrubbed each counter with all my might, hoping with each brush I could erase the horror that had happened here.

I grabbed another bag, went into Issy's room and pulled off the sheets that were stained in vomit and alcohol. I threw them resentfully in the bag and felt the tears start to streak down my face. I wanted to scream how unfair it was to take her right when things were going so good. Then I felt something against my foot as I threw the bag out of the room. It was her flask, the one I had given her that obviously held the last drop of alcohol she drank before passing out.

I was suddenly slammed with a weight of guilt so heavy it pushed me to the floor. It was my fault. Surely, Jake would never let her drink so much. She must have kept it hidden, and I had provided her the means to do so. Sobs racked my body as I felt desperately incapable of calming down. It was me. I did this.

I stood, shaking, trying to get my anxiety under control. I ran to my bathroom and leaned over the toilet, holding back the necklace Parker had given me so that it wouldn't fall in my face. I suddenly felt nothing but contempt for it and took it off violently, throwing it on my bed where I wouldn't have to look at it. *What a farce!* I thought angrily. *I'm not strong. I'm nothing.*

I put my fingers down my throat and allowed all the pain and fear and guilt I was feeling to be washed away. The numbness was short lived, as usual, and I slowly got up off the floor, feeling just as terrible and defeated as I had before, only more exhausted.

I walked back into Issy's room, determined to finish my task, and was jarred once again by the emptiness of it. I walked by her bed and saw a little stuffed bear on the floor. It was weathered and old, as if it had been used for years. I picked it up, bringing the soft fur to my nose to take in the scent. It smelled like her perfume, rich and expensive, with a mix of exotic fruits and rich floral.

I immediately knew I had to bring it to her. I grabbed a bag out of her closet and quickly packed it with essentials she would want if she woke up. I shook my head. When she woke up. Her little bear and favorite pajamas sat on the top as I zipped the bag.

I was surprised by how alert I felt driving to Asheville, even though the sun was rising and I had only slept for a couple of hours in the car. The nursing staff didn't give me any hassle, just as Jake had promised, when I came in and led me right to her room. The blinds were drawn and the room was fairly dark, making the lights and sounds from the respirator even more distressing.

Jake was asleep in the recliner with his arms folded and his head lowered as if he had fought sleep as long as he could. Issy looked frightfully pale and fragile under all the tubes that surrounded her face, and I delicately brushed away a piece of her dark hair that had fallen over her eye. I set her bag down as quietly as I could and pulled out her bear, setting it carefully in the fold of her arm. I held her hand and sat on the chair that had been pulled up next to the bed, feeling the tears start to fall again.

"I'm sorry," I whispered, hoping that somehow she could hear me.

I heard a rustling noise behind me and turned to see that Jake had woken back up and was sitting with his head in his hands. He looked wrecked and completely exhausted. I walked over to him gingerly and sat on the ottoman in front of him. I put my hands on his wrist and kissed the top of his head, trying to bring any comfort I could. He looked up at me, his eyes no longer vacant, but full of all the pain and fear I knew he was facing.

"She's going to get better," I assured him softly. "There's no way Issy's going out like this. She's way too bullheaded." I tried to flash him a smile and offer up strength that neither one of us had.

Jake slowly shook his head and whispered, "I'm not so sure."

I let go of his wrist and put my hands in my lap. Jake quickly grabbed them back and stared at me.

"Jake, what happened?" I asked, wanting so badly to hear it wasn't my fault.

He stayed deafly quiet and then reached up to caress my face. "You have this look you get. Did you know that?"

I was taken aback by his switch of topic. "What do you mean?"

"There's a look you have that betrays everything you are feeling. It's a mix of adoration, respect and love, all rolled into one." He spoke softly with a slight rasp in his voice. My stomach knotted a little, not knowing where he was going with the conversation, but I didn't say a word, just let him go on.

"I was actually surprised at how quickly I earned that look from you, and it kind of freaked me out at first. No one had ever looked at me like that, and I felt this expectation to be great, to be better than I knew I was. My mom would give me a similar feeling. Towards the end, she couldn't do much more than hold my hand, but her message was still loud and clear. She believed in me."

He stopped for a moment and ran his fingers through his hair before he looked at me and continued, "After she died, it all went away, and I just slowly disappeared. Then there you were, looking at me like that, seeing only the best in me, and it made me mad. Made me feel all this grief all over again. So I'd do something horrible to push you away, to get rid of that look when you saw me. But then I'd miss it. Sometimes it would take me a while, but I would always get it back, reassuring me that I hadn't lost you.

"At Christmas, I knew I wanted you back, and that I was finally ready for you. I knew about your guy, believe me, Issy made sure of it. But I wasn't worried about him, because I saw how you always responded to me, even if you had just been with him. I just had to convince you to trust me again."

He stopped talking and let me take a moment to hear all he had told me. Everything seemed to make more sense, as if seeing things from his perspective changed the reality in my head. I was just about to say something when I heard him start back up again.

"Last night, I was so irritated you weren't staying with us. Irritated that you were still with that joker when I knew we were meant to be together. Then you walked out of your room, looking like an angel, and I knew I wasn't going to let you walk out of there with him. I was ready to grab you and pull you away, sure I could take him out with one good punch. But then I saw it, that look, full of love, admiration and esteem, everything I had longed to see. Everything I *needed* to see. Only... it wasn't for me. It was for him. And everything just went black," he finally said, his eyes glossy as he rubbed his right knuckle.

It was the first time I noticed how bruised and cut up it was, and I immediately remembered the hole in the wall outside of Issy's room. It was right where he had been standing when we left for the ball.

My breath caught as I put my hand over my mouth. "Jake..." I didn't know what to say, just felt helpless sitting there.

"I was mad at her," he explained, the tears spilling over now. "Mad at her for rubbing it in my face when you left. Mad at her for saying everything that I knew was true. I didn't check on her all night..." He couldn't continue, and I held on to him and let him cry it out, running my fingers through his hair as I had so many times before.

A knock on the door startled us, and I stood up abruptly as a nurse came in to check Issy's vital signs. Jake had pulled himself together and was immediately in caretaker mode, asking a series of questions about things I had no background on. The nurse finished her chart and then left the room as quickly as she had entered it.

290

"What does all of that mean?" I asked, walking to the other side of her bed.

"It means nothing's changed. It also means I'm going to have to make a very difficult phone call to her mom this morning." He fell back down in the recliner, taking the same seated position he had been in all morning. "Avery, I know I was a jerk, and I deserved to lose you. But I don't think I could get through this if you weren't here with me. Even if it is just as friends."

I walked back up to him, taking his hand in mine. "Of course. I'll always be here for you. You know that."

He flashed me an appreciative smile and squeezed me hand. I closed my eyes for just a second.

The butterflies were back.

"Lord, I pray she will always know that Your power is made perfect in her weakness. I pray she knows You will not only share in her suffering, but also in her comfort…"

21. THE AFTERMATH

I spent three more hours with Issy and Jake in her hospital room, until exhaustion finally took over. I must have fallen asleep while talking to her, because next thing I knew, Jake was rubbing my back to wake me up.

"Why don't you go home and get some rest? I'll call you if there's any change."

I nodded and grabbed my things. On my way out, I held Issy's hand one more time and scolded her, "Now, if you don't wake up before I get back, I'm not doing any more late night movie nights. You hear me?" Her response was a steady beep from the heart monitor, and I turned away sadly.

Jake caught me before I got to the door and pulled me to him. We held on to each other as if our sanity depended on it, each using the other to give us strength. I pulled away and left the room quickly before I had a meltdown.

I was halfway through the parking lot when I heard my phone start buzzing from my purse as a flood of messages finally downloaded to the phone. There were three missed calls from Parker this morning and a text asking me if I was okay. I knew I should have felt grateful, but I only felt irritated by them. I called him back anyway, and he immediately picked up.

"Hey, are you okay?" he asked, his voice full of concern.

"Yes, I'm fine. I've just been with Issy this morning, and I guess my phone doesn't have any service in there. I'm just about to go home now and get some sleep."

"Are you at the hospital now?"

"Well, if you count the parking lot, I am," I teased, trying to get him to stop worrying.

"Avery, why don't you just come to my place? You can rest here and then head back to see her after you've had some sleep."

"Doesn't that break one of your rules?"

Parker had set his place as off limits after things got too heated on his couch one night.

"These are extenuating circumstances. I think we can control ourselves." I could hear him starting to relax, and I had to admit the idea of only driving five minutes, versus thirty, was appealing.

"Okay, I'm heading your way now."

Parker was waiting outside his door when I pulled in the parking lot. He was in sweats and a t-shirt, and I could tell he hadn't shaved yet this morning. He took my bag out of my hands when I walked up and pulled me in for a hug. I hugged him back, but he still seemed disappointed.

"Is Randy here?" I asked when I realized his apartment was empty.

"No, he's gone until Sunday. He didn't want to come back until right before classes started again." I looked up at him, remembering that class started in only a couple of days. That meant the syllabi were already posted, and I was probably already getting behind again.

"Don't look so panicked. We'll pull up your classes tonight and make sure you're on track."

He was always taking care of me, and I felt my heart warm to him again. "You're too good to me," I stated, knowing more than he did how true those words were.

He responded with a satisfied smile and led me back to his room. I had never been in there before but wasn't surprised when I walked in. It reminded me of his parent's house, with rich browns and creams, and I could feel him all around me as his scent tickled my nose. His bed was made neatly and his desk was covered in papers and books, as if he had been studying all morning.

"Still working your system?" I asked playfully, nodding towards his messy desk before I leaned down to take off my tennis shoes.

"Still a hater, I see," he bantered back, pulling back the covers for me so I could get in his bed. While our conversation was light, I knew something

294

was off. The natural comfort that we always had was missing, and everything this morning felt forced. I pushed the thought out of my head, chalking it up to fatigue and stress, and laid my head on his soft pillow.

He started to leave, but I looked up at him and asked if he would lie with me for just a little while. He sat on the bed, staying above the covers, and ran his fingers through my hair as I closed my eyes.

"I noticed you weren't wearing your necklace," he said softly after we sat a moment in silence.

"Oh, yeah, I took it off to shower, and was in such a rush I just forgot to put it back on." It was a bold faced lie, the first I had ever told him, and while he seemed to believe me, I knew something was changing. I was doing it again, pushing away the one person who knew my secret.

He continued to rub my head, making me relax as I felt my eyes start to get heavy. Parker telling me I wasn't alone and that he was here for me were the last words I heard before I let sleep fully encompass me.

A buzz from my phone woke me out of my slumber, and I answered it groggily as I tried to get my eyes to focus. "Hello?"

"Hey, babe, it's Jake. I just wanted to give you an update on Issy." His voice was soft, but he sounded a little excited, which immediately got me to focus.

"Did she wake up?" I asked, sitting upright in bed.

"No, not yet, but the doctor thinks she will soon. They were able to take her off the respirator, and she even moved her fingers a little."

"Oh, Jake, that's wonderful! I'm going to head back there now."

"Great. I'll see you when you get here."

I hung up the phone and felt my heart skip a beat. Issy might be safe. My body immediately relaxed as I felt the best I had since we'd found her. It was two in the afternoon, and I had slept for four hours, further adding to my renewed vigor. I made Parker's bed and grabbed my bag. I didn't see him when I walked out of the room, but then noticed his feet on the edge of the couch.

He was lying on his back with a book on his chest, indicating he fell asleep while reading.

I walked up to him and knelt down, watching him as he slept. He looked so strong and handsome, and he exhibited a peace I'd never experienced.

Feeling more drawn to him than I had since the ball, I leaned over and kissed him lightly on the lips. His eyes fluttered open, and he shot me his smile that once again made everything seem possible.

Touching my face, he pulled me in for a much deeper kiss, and this time I was able to give him back all he was giving to me. The more I responded, the tighter he held me and more fiercely he continued to kiss me. Desire rolled in my stomach, and I pulled back, knowing that he would any minute if I didn't.

He looked at me lovingly and said, "I could definitely get used to being woken up like that."

I smiled and then looked down at my fidgeting

hands, feeling a little embarrassed. "I wanted to tell you goodbye before I headed back. Issy's made some progress, so I wanted to go see her."

"Just give me ten minutes, and I'll go with you," he offered, sitting up and stretching.

"Oh, you don't have to," I stammered, not sure why I didn't want him there.

"Avery, I want to go," he assured me, stroking my cheek before he stood up. "Ten minutes, I promise. Hey, you can print out your syllabus while you wait."

He headed off to the bathroom and I didn't argue, knowing I really didn't have a good reason for not wanting him to go anyway.

I looked at his computer and scowled. I didn't want to think about school. I just wanted everything to be back to how it was on Christmas break. I looked up my classes anyway and was pleased to see Thermo was the only one that had anything posted. I had a different professor this semester, and I could already tell the class load would be lighter.

Relief flooded me as I noted that I was still well ahead of the class. I had already done the reading assignment and problem set due the first week and felt pretty comfortable with the material. My "back to the basics" strategy from last semester was definitely going to pay off.

Work-study started up again next week as well, and Dr. Davis' grad student had actually requested me by name to work the final phase of his thesis. I should have been glad, but the idea of another hundred and fifty hours in the lab made me kind of want to scream. Oh well, it was better than being known as the class flake.

I heard Parker's door shut and looked up to see him walking my way. He looked more like himself, clean shaven with jeans and a black t-shirt.

He noticed me at the computer and raised his eyebrows. "Everything okay?"

"Yep," I said, standing. "So far, so good. Hopefully I can keep it that way."

"Are you kidding me?" He wrapped his arms around me. "You've got me this semester, and you know what a good study partner I am."

I laughed as I thought about how distracting he was in the library, but he was right. I always did better with him than without him, in every sense. I gave him a big hug, feeling the comfort return. He really was the best thing that had ever happened to me.

Parker and I reached Issy's floor and could hear the shouting before we even got off the elevator. My stomach dropped as I immediately thought the worse. Parker grabbed my hand for reassurance as we walked toward the chaos.

The scene was like something out of a movie. Issy's dad shouted demands to nurses and doctors, while Jake stood toe to toe with him, arguing about everything he was saying. Issy's dad was the most intimidating person I had ever met, and even though

Jake was only a couple inches shorter, I still felt as if her dad significantly had the upper hand.

"Mr. Summers," Jake stated adamantly. "Moving her now is ridiculous. She's already made great progress in the last twelve hours, and all of her friends are here. I'm here."

Issy's dad ignored him as he barked at the nurse to get the transfer paperwork going. She practically ran out of the room, and finally he turned and acknowledged Jake. His voice was calm, but cold and condescending, and the undertone of hatred was enough to give me chills.

"Friends? Really? The same friends who put her in this place to begin with? And you? Where were you when all this was happening, huh?"

I could tell his comment got to Jake because his face immediately became stiff and vacant.

"Don't you dare lecture me about being there for her." Jake's tone matched that of Issy's dad but with more volume. "If you weren't such a colossal failure of a father to begin with, Issy wouldn't feel the need to drown herself in alcohol. Who do you think has been there the last four years picking up the pieces of the broken lives you left behind?"

I realized I was holding my breath. The tension in the room was so electric that, at any moment, I felt it could burst into flames. Issy's dad was looking venomously at Jake, who stared defiantly back at him.

Before they could say another word or do worse, I heard Parker clear his throat to alert them to our presence. They both looked over and showed equal contempt when they saw us in the doorway. I knew Jake's wasn't towards me, but it didn't stop me from shivering anyway.

"You have no business being here, young lady. Issy's done nothing but go downhill since you moved in that apartment with her," he stated authoritatively.

My heart stopped as I stood in stunned silence. I felt Parker tense and then position himself in front of me as he addressed her father.

"Sir, I understand that you are upset and frustrated, but there is no reason to talk to her like that. Avery wasn't even at that party, and if she hadn't thought to check on her when she got home, we'd be at a funeral right now instead of a hospital. She saved her life." Parker's tone was compassionate but stern, and there was no indication that he felt intimidated by Issy's overbearing father.

The mood in the room changed as Issy's dad turned away and sat down in the chair nearest to his daughter. It was the first time I saw him as a worried father and not a dictator ordering people around. I felt sorry for him. I turned to Parker, who failed to even mention his part in all of this. He was the real hero, not me.

Jake, on the other hand, was still shaking and walked right past us, out of the room, not failing to shoot Parker a stare of pure hatred as he left. I turned to look at him, and he held my gaze for just a second before turning away.

I felt torn in half, wanting to run after Jake and comfort him, yet wanting to stay next to Parker's calm demeanor and trust that everything was going to be okay.

My thoughts were interrupted by the nurse coming back in to inform us that the transfer was complete, and they would be airlifting her to Duke University Medical Center in two hours. Everyone in North Carolina knew that hospital was superior, and even nationally recognized, so part of me was glad Issy was going to have the best medical care possible.

Parker guided me towards Issy's bed despite my hesitation, and I stood opposite her dad as I took her hand. I couldn't stop the tears as my heart feared it could be the last time I ever saw her alive.

Issy's dad was massaging his temples and then started talking. This time his tone was resigned and broken. "The doctor said that the CPR she received on site was critical to her having any chance of recovering, and if it had been even ten minutes later, she wouldn't have survived."

My heart skipped a beat as the "what if" scenarios started running through my mind.

"I'm sorry I yelled at you," he continued. "I just don't understand how it got this bad."

I just nodded, unable to say anything else for fear I'd totally lose it. Parker grabbed a piece of paper and wrote down my name and phone number on it. He handed it to Issy's dad who reluctantly took it.

"We'd like to stay in the loop if you don't mind

keeping us updated on how she is doing. We really do care about her and can do anything you need on this end to help."

Issy's dad nodded his head and put the phone number in his wallet. He stood up, looking more vulnerable than I'd ever seen him, shook Parker's hand and then walked out the door. Parker immediately enfolded me in his arms, and I cried until I felt I had no more tears left. He didn't say a word—just allowed me to access all of his strength, so I could get through it. He was more than Issy's hero. He was mine, too.

When I had finally calmed down, I kissed Issy's forehead and told her I expected to hear from her real soon. Parker kept his arm around me all the way to the car and quietly drove us back to his place. I spent the evening with him, not wanting to leave and go back to the empty apartment waiting for me. We were curled together on the couch, watching a movie, and I felt so grateful to have him. I looked up at him, not trying to hide any of the emotion I felt, and kissed him with everything I had.

He kissed me back and then looked in my eyes, a smile slowly appearing on his face. "There you are," he said softly.

I looked at him questioningly and sat up a little.

"You've just been distant since last night, but it's nice to have you back," he explained, stroking my cheek.

Settling my head back on his solid chest, I turned

my attention to the movie. It scared me how well he knew me, as if he could read my mind and sense the minute I felt nervous or afraid or even confused. He didn't hold anything back from me and wanted nothing more than for me to do the same. I once again felt torn, unsure if I could ever fully meet that expectation.

It was midnight before I finally drove home, and I made sure to text Parker as soon as I got there. I flipped on the light to the apartment and immediately felt grateful that I had done so much cleaning the night before. Everything looked normal, despite the glaring reality that it wasn't. I looked over towards Issy's room and noticed the hole in the wall had been fixed and now just needed a coat of paint. It registered at the same time that the trash bags I had filled were gone as well, as were the beer kegs. It was almost as if the events from the last twenty-four hours had never happened.

I sighed and walked in my room, eager to finally shower and crawl into bed. The water was like a life force through me and seemed to rejuvenate every part of my body. I put on my pajamas and got ready for bed, stopping in the kitchen to grab a bottle of water. I heard the door lock turn and felt my stomach drop. I hadn't realized how eerie it was to be in here knowing Issy was gone and not coming back any time soon.

Jake saw my startled face as he opened the door and apologized for scaring me.

"I didn't think I'd see you back tonight," he said as he walked over to the wall near Issy's room. He was carrying a small can of paint and a paintbrush with him.

"Thanks for cleaning up, Jake. It was nice to have it gone when I got home," I said softly, walking over to him. I felt nervous being alone with him.

"I didn't do much. You had most of it done when I got here. I'm sorry you had to do anything at all. It was our mess." He still hadn't really looked at me, just kept focused on painting over the patch in the wall.

"It's fine," I assured him. "It was actually a good distraction."

He nodded his head and continued to work. The silence felt awkward, and I started towards my room, unwilling to stay in it any longer.

"I'm going to bed. Are you staying here tonight?" I asked tentatively, realizing it was a dumb question as soon as I did. Why would he stay without Issy?

He finally looked up at me, his eyes still dark and broken. "Do you want me to?" he asked softly.

I felt nervous and flustered and had no idea what to say. Of course, I wanted him there for comfort and security, but at the same time, I knew saying so would imply other things that were well beyond what I could cope with at that moment.

He set down the paintbrush and walked over to me, lightly caressing my face and hair. "I'll stay. You don't have to ask me to. I know what you're feeling," he whispered as he pulled me in for a hug.

I allowed him to be there for me, to hold me up and give me the strength I desperately wanted.

He stood firm, continuing to caress me as I buried my face in his chest. "I'm here, Avery. Always."

"Lord, I pray that You are faithful and will not let her be tempted beyond what she can bear, but when she is tempted, I pray that You will provide a way out so that she can stand up under it…"

22. GUILT

It was four days later when we got the call that Issy had woken up. Jake had faithfully come over every night around midnight and stayed on the couch until I left for my run in the morning. Neither one of us went near Issy's room as we waited and hoped we'd hear something soon.

Earlier that night, Parker and I had gone out to dinner and a movie to enjoy our last night of freedom, and while it felt good and normal to be there, I found myself thinking about Jake and wondering if he was going to come by again tonight.

"Is everything okay?" Parker asked as he was driving me home. It was a question that came regularly now, as he could sense I was pulling away from him.

"Yeah, fine. Why?" I asked, squeezing his hand and offering him a smile.

He smiled back but was uneasy. "I just can tell something is up with you. Any word from Issy's dad?"

I let out a long sigh and shook my head. The waiting was unbearable. To make matters worse, I had done some research on comas and learned that after a certain number of days, the chance of the patient recovering was slim to none. Issy was at the halfway point.

Parker squeezed my hand back, trying to reassure me, and then thankfully changed the subject. "Are you ready for tomorrow?" he asked brightly, knowing full well I wasn't.

"Yeah, I guess so. I'm supposed to be in the lab at ten to meet with Russell and get the plan for his final phase of work. Just the thought of the lab makes me want to scream. Worse, I have Thermo at noon and Dynamics at two. My Mondays, Wednesdays and Fridays are going to stink!" I whined as I laid my head back on the headrest in his car.

Parker let out a chuckle and then shot me a warm smile. "Let's meet in the quad after class. I want to hear all about it."

I turned to him, feeling guilty for the millionth time that night. I hadn't told him that Jake had been staying over even though Issy was no longer around. I tried to convince myself it wasn't a lie if he didn't ask. "What about you?"

"I've got three booked back to back starting at nine. I like to get them out of the way early."

"Wow, 9:00 a.m., me and that class would not do so well," I teased, knowing full well that running was the only thing I was willing to wake up early for.

He smiled again but didn't say anything. We sat in the uncomfortable silence that seemed to hound us a lot the last couple of days, until he finally pulled into my parking lot.

"You don't have to walk me up," I insisted as I leaned over to give him a kiss goodnight.

"Avery, you know I'm going to," he replied as he put the car in park.

We both got out, and he wrapped his arm around me as we went up the stairs. I put mine around his waist, but again it felt forced, almost unnatural. I didn't know what was wrong with me, why I was all of a sudden so distant from him. We stopped at the door, and he pulled me to him, looking deep in my eyes, searching me. I felt embarrassed and guilty and could hardly stand to look at him.

"You have to talk to me. I can feel you slipping away, and I don't know how to stop it." He held my face in his hands, desperately trying to get me to open up to him.

"I'm not," I tried to assure him and leaned in to give him a quick kiss.

He tightened his grip and kissed me passionately, trying to evoke any emotion he could from me. I did my best to respond equally, but it was no use. He knew me too well and slowly let me go, resting his head on mine for just a moment before he said goodbye.

I could feel my heart cry as he walked down the steps, but I felt helpless as to how to close the gap that seemed to grow wider between us each day.

I walked into the apartment, and to my surprise Jake was already there, working on his laptop at the bar. My heart skipped a beat as I thought of how awkward it would have been if I had opened the door with Parker standing next to me.

"You're here early," I said as I set my keys down, noting it was only ten o'clock.

He looked up from his laptop and shot me a breathtaking smile. Next thing I knew he had lifted me off the ground in an explosive hug while telling me Issy was awake. I stood stunned as it registered what he as saying and then jumped back in his arms with a squeal.

"Is she okay? Any long term damage?" I asked when we finally calmed down.

Jake gave me another big smile, his emerald eyes sparkling with joy. "None. She was a firecracker the minute she opened her eyes. She had no idea where she was. As far as she was concerned, it was New Year's Day. Can you believe it?"

I shook my head, still feeling numb at the news. She was okay. A huge load of bricks tumbled from my shoulders, and I felt happy and lighthearted for the first time in days.

"So…" Jake said mischievously as he walked back to the kitchen. "I've brought us something to celebrate with!" He came around the corner with a large bottle of champagne and two glasses.

"Jake, I have class tomorrow. Hard classes," I

replied, shaking my head as I headed to my room.

"So. Just one glass, Avery, come on. This is huge! Please?" His words were as charming as ever, and I knew immediately that I would have at least one glass. I had no resolve with him. He knew exactly how to push my buttons.

"Fine. Just let me get comfortable first." I went in my room and threw on some sweats, brushed out my hair and clipped it up. For some reason, dressing down made me feel less guilty about hanging out with Jake. We were just friends, right? And friends could have a drink together. I pushed the guilt away once more and met Jake on the couch. He already had our glasses full and light music playing in the background.

I sat on the couch hesitantly, and he handed me the glass.

"Here's to Issy and her stubbornness, without which, I doubt we'd have anything to celebrate." Jake looked happier than I had seen him in months, and I couldn't help but smile too.

"To Issy," I cheered as I brought my glass to his and took a sip.

We continued to talk well past midnight, and before I knew it, I had drunk three glasses and was starting to feel a little lightheaded. Jake was keeping step as well, and it seemed that the more we drank, the funnier and more relaxed both of us became, even broaching subjects that might otherwise be forbidden.

"So, what do you like about this guy, anyway?" Jake asked as he poured the last of the bottle into our two glasses.

"Parker?"

"Yeah, who else?"

"Honestly, Jake, it'd probably be a shorter list to ask me what I don't like about him."

His jaw clenching told me he didn't especially like my comment. "Okay fine, what *don't* you like about him?"

"Nothing really. He's pretty much perfect." I paused for a second, thinking about it. "Maybe just how insightful he is, I guess. I don't feel like there can be any boundaries with us, and it makes me nervous. He wants too much from me," I explained honestly, even surprising myself with the answer.

"That would drive me crazy," Jake said, settling back in his seat. "If I were you, I would feel like he was judging me all the time, trying to make me perfect too. I guess I tend to want someone with flaws, just like me."

"Why?" I asked curiously.

"Because, what happens when they finally realize that you are never going to be good enough? They are either going to stay with you out of pity and be miserable, or they are going to cut their loses and move on. Either way, it's got disaster written all over it."

I thought about it for a minute and didn't want to admit how much his words got to me. It was always my biggest fear that Parker would one day see me for the flawed person I really was. I shook my head, hoping to empty it. I smiled up at Jake and teased, knowing it would change the subject. "So you are saying I wasn't perfect?"

Jake looked over at me and gave me a devilish grin. "Perfect for me… yes. But perfect… no. At least I would never expect you to be."

I sighed and turned to lay my head on the armrest of the couch. Jake pulled my legs on his lap and started massaging my feet. I closed my eyes and enjoyed how good it felt. I had drunk too much, and the room was starting to sway.

"You like that?" he asked softly, and I nodded my head, keeping my eyes closed. I felt him let go, and then the couch shifted as Jake moved his body over mine. He began kissing my neck, and I felt him take the clip out of my hair and the waves tumbled down the side of the couch.

"What about this?" Kiss. "And this?" More kisses moving up my jawline.

My heart raced and my stomach filled with butterflies. I knew what we were doing was wrong, but as much as my head said to stop it, I felt paralyzed by my body and how each kiss torched my skin and reminded me of old times. Freer times.

I opened my eyes and looked right into his. He was moving forward, and I knew it was a point of no return. If I let Jake kiss me, it meant the end for me and Parker.

Parker. The guy who was too good for me. The guy who challenged me to be more. Who forced me to face fears and trials I didn't have the strength to face. The guy who would leave me the minute he realized how broken I really was.

Jake caressed my face and smiled. "Baby, it's always been you and me." he whispered as he moved forward.

I closed my eyes, waiting, and right when I felt his breath on my face, my phone rang.

We both froze and Jake whispered, "Ignore it," as he continued to move closer.

I turned my head right as he touched me and moved underneath him to grab the phone. It was Issy. I jumped off the couch and answered it, watching Jake put his head on the armrest in frustration.

"Hi!" I practically yelled into the phone when I answered it. "How are you?"

"Wow, Avery, you're like breathing heavy. What did I interrupt?" Issy asked playfully. She was absolutely her old self. I immediately blushed as guilt hit me hard in the gut.

"Nothing! Jake and I were just celebrating your waking up!" I knew my voice was louder than usual, and even I didn't recognize the tone of it.

"Have you been drinking?" she asked with a laugh. "And with Jake of all people?"

"Just a couple of glasses of champagne, nothing big," I answered, trying to justify it. For some reason it sounded worse when Issy said it.

"Avery, champagne is the worst. No wonder you

are slurring your words. What happened to Parker?"

Issy's usual straightforwardness annoyed me. "Nothing. Jake and I are just friends."

Issy sat quiet for a moment and then got really serious. "Avery, I love Jake, you know that. But he cannot be trusted with you. He's not there out of friendship. You didn't see him last night. I did. I mean New Year's, whatever. Anyway, Parker is a good guy, and I've seen the way you are with him. You need to really think this through."

I felt my heart race again. I couldn't believe Issy was lecturing me not even six hours after waking up from a coma. I didn't want to think about this now; my head was swimming with all the emotions of the night.

"It's good to see you are back to your old, opinionated self," I replied, trying to find some humor in my voice.

"Would you expect anything less? Hey, since he's there, will you let me talk to him for a minute? I can't seem to get ahold of my mom. I'm guessing my dad verbally accosted her pretty well."

"Yeah, he's pretty efficient at that," I agreed without thinking.

"You too? Man, he's a piece of work. Every nurse on my floor shakes when he's around!" I could almost see Issy shaking her head as she spoke, and the depth of how much I missed her hit me, reducing me to tears before I could control it.

"Avery, what's wrong? Are you crying?" she

asked, stopping her rant.

"Maybe," I sniffled. "I'm just so glad you're better. I don't know what I would have done if anything happened to you." I knew Issy hated this kind of stuff, verbal affirmation was not something she was comfortable with at all, but I couldn't help myself.

"Avery, this here is why you stay away from champagne. Give me Jake," she scolded.

I handed the phone to Jake and excused myself to my room to cry it out. It was the first time I had let the tears flow since the accident, and now I wondered if I would ever get them to stop. I had buried so much of my anxiety and fear, and now it all came out with nothing to hold it back. I wanted someone to hold me, and ironically, it wasn't Jake.

I missed Parker. Missed his strength and compassion. I wanted to call him, but it felt wrong. How could I ever turn to him now after what had almost happened tonight? It was shameful.

I could hear Jake yelling at Issy from the other room. "Like hell she is!" he screamed into the phone. "He's just the rebound guy!"

I didn't want to hear anymore and went to the bathroom to pull myself together. I came out as Jake was getting off the phone.

"Wow, did I get an earful. I'd be totally annoyed if I wasn't so thrilled she's back," he said, laughing as he walked in the door. He took one look at my face and stopped smiling, walking over to pull me into a big hug. His arms felt good, but I felt empty.

After a few seconds he asked, "Are you okay?"

I simply nodded my head and continued to rest against his chest. He put his hands on my face and lifted it up to have me look at him.

"Now, where were we?" he asked softly, hunger more than apparent in his green eyes.

I stepped back and pulled his hands from my face, still holding them as I spoke. "I should probably call it a night. I have to be up early tomorrow."

He seemed to understand, but his body was stiff as he ran his hands through his hair in frustration. He pulled me close and kissed me softly on my forehead, as he was accustomed to doing lately, and left the room.

My sleep was more than fitful that night, and I didn't even notice I had turned my alarm off when it went off at 8:00 a.m. I finally woke when the light from outside my window was too much to ignore.

My head pounded with such force I could barely open my eyes. I turned to my alarm, wondering how early it was, and practically jumped out of bed when I saw it said 9:45. I ran around my room in a frenzy, throwing on jeans and a sweatshirt. I rushed to the bathroom to brush my teeth and recoiled when I saw my reflection in the mirror. I looked terrible and more than obviously hung over. I pulled my hair into a tight ponytail and tried to use makeup to hide the black circles under my eyes.

After ten minutes, I at least looked presentable,

but I knew without question I would be late to meet Dr. Davis' grad student.

I ran to my phone and sent him a quick text that I was on my way and grabbed my backpack, which I had thankfully prepared the day before. Jake was still asleep on the couch when I left. I checked his alarm to make sure he hadn't missed it, and when I saw that he had set it for ten, I left quietly before it went off. I didn't want to talk to him this morning.

Russell was less than thrilled with me when I ran in the lab, ten minutes later than agreed upon.

"Avery, I need to know right now if you are going to flake out on me again this semester?" he asked exasperated. "Precision is an absolute must for this phase, and even ten minutes late matters."

I pushed down my frustration as I tried to see his point of view. "Russell, I promise, this is a one-time thing. I got some news yesterday about my friend who had been in a coma, and I stayed up a little too late celebrating. It won't happen again."

The sympathy card seemed to work as he simply huffed and then went on to explain the new phase of work. He was right, precision was essential, and it looked like I would be taking samples all five days during the week. The positive was that it meant only two hours at a time in the lab, but every day felt like a daunting task.

After an hour with him showing and reshowing me the steps, I started to feel nauseous and excused myself to the restroom, hoping cold water on my

317

neck would calm my stomach. One of the worst side effects from years of throwing up was that my body immediately reacted the second my stomach felt even a little queasy. Today was no different, and within minutes I was re-tasting the champagne from the night before.

When I was finished, I tried to rinse my mouth out with water and then chewed on a mint. It didn't matter though, even I could smell the alcohol. Great, what a way to make a good first impression on my new professors.

I bought a bottle of water from the vending machine in the hall and headed back to the lab, determined to get through the morning.

I finished up with Russell and made my way to my Thermo class. It felt different than last year, mostly because I didn't recognize any of the students in there. My group had all advanced to Thermo II. I sighed and took out my book, ready to learn what seemed impossible last semester.

I had survived my first day, barely, and was on my way to meet Parker in the quad. My stomach had been in knots all day just thinking about seeing him after last night. I knew my behavior was unacceptable, and he deserved so much better than me. Jake had been right. I was far too flawed for a relationship of this magnitude, and if last night proved anything, it was that I would never be able to fully give my heart to Parker the way he expected me to. I felt frustrated by my own weakness and saddened at the idea of losing someone so special.

I neared our spot and quickly spotted him lying on the grass with his head propped up on his backpack. My stomach clenched and my heart started racing. I felt the dread run through my body as I began to question if I would be able to do this.

His eyes were shut as I approached him as quietly as I could. I set my backpack down and lay next to him. His hand immediately found mine, and I felt my eyes well up with tears. He rolled over on top of me and gave me a long lingering kiss. I kissed him back with everything I had, wondering if it would be the last time I ever felt his touch again.

He sensed my urgency and kissed me with even more passion, taking in every inch of my mouth while he stroked my face. The quad was packed with students, but I didn't care. I never wanted to let him go.

He finally pulled away but hovered just an inch above my face. "I missed you," he said softly.

My tears could not be contained, and his face quickly became concerned. "What happened?"

I forced a smile, not wanting to have *the conversation* yet. "Issy woke up."

He sat up quickly and pulled me up as well. "When?" he asked enthusiastically.

"Last night. I even got to talk to her, and she sounded exactly the same. It was amazing." The tears were still flowing as I spoke, only they weren't tears of joy like Parker thought.

"Oh, baby, that's wonderful!" Parker cradled me in his arms. "Why didn't you call me?"

"It was late," I lied. It was becoming all too easy to do lately.

"It's never too late, babe, you know that," he said softly as he ran his finger up and down my back.

I took a deep breath, trying to settle my frazzled nerves. It was now or never, and if I waited any longer, I knew I wouldn't do it.

"Parker, I think maybe we should press pause for a little while." I said it so softly, I wasn't even sure if he had heard me until I felt his body tense and him move my face up to look at him.

His eyes showed hurt but also determination as he spoke. "Don't do this. You've been pushing me away for days now and there is no reason to."

"I just think it's for the best," I choked out, pulling away just enough to get him to let go of my face.

"For the best? Are you kidding me? Avery, baby, just last week we were kissing on New Year's, totally optimistic for what this year would bring. There is no way things have changed this drastically in days. It doesn't make sense." He pleaded with me now, and I knew I had to say something fast or my resolve would be gone. I was hurting him and it broke my heart.

"I'm just no good for you, Parker. How do you not see that?" I asked as I grabbed at the necklace he bought me. "See this, I don't even deserve it. I threw up the night of Issy's accident and never told you. I'm a fraud, Parker, while you're… well, you're perfect." I could feel my voice getting louder and I tried to quiet myself when others around us took notice.

Parker pulled me to him again, despite my attempts to push him away. "I'm not perfect, Avery, although I'm flattered you think so. So you made a mistake, who cares, all you can do is move on and learn from it. I'm not going to judge you for it."

"But you will," I whispered. "Maybe not today, but one day you are going to see just how flawed and damaged I really am. When that happens, you aren't going to look at me like this anymore. And you're going to regret that you ever did."

Parker flinched as if I had stunned him and then looked at me skeptically. "Where is this coming from? It doesn't sound like you at all."

I didn't answer but continued to look at him sadly. He sighed and then started talking again, "Sweetheart, I already see you, and I love everything about you. What I can't figure out is why you can't accept this from me."

"Because it doesn't make sense…" I'm scarred, damaged, used, broken. "There's nothing here worth loving."

He pulled me to himself, shaking his head the whole time. He began to kiss my forehead and moved on to kiss both my cheeks and finally my lips before sternly saying, "I don't ever want to hear you say that again. And a pause is out of the question. You're not getting rid of me without a fight." He held me tighter, and I stopped fighting him, allowing myself to return his hold. I was so selfish and weak. I knew I needed to release him, to let him have a life free of me and my self-destructive behavior, but I just couldn't do it.

Finally, he stood up and pulled me up with him. We grabbed our things and started walking toward the library.

"I don't want to study there today. I just don't feel like it. Could we study at your place and then just hang out for a while?" I asked, giving him a pleading look. I would have offered mine, but I was not taking any chances with Jake still having a key.

"Sure," he said, laughing, but I could tell there was still sadness in his eyes. Our talk had affected him more than I thought it would, and it became more and more apparent as the night went on.

He kept his hand on me at all times, like he was reassuring himself that I was still there. The most distance we got was when we were studying. I had convinced him to let us go to his room since his roommate, Randy, was watching TV, and I couldn't concentrate.

I had sat on his bed with my study system fully set up, and he was shuffling papers on his desk. I finished all my work in forty-five minutes and just lingered there smiling as I watched him try to be quiet and concentrate.

He looked especially handsome tonight, and I

couldn't help but watch as his muscles tensed through his t-shirt. Without thinking, I walked over to him and rubbed the back of his head as I sat on his lap facing him. I started kissing him before he could protest, and it didn't take much before he reciprocated with all the emotion we had both felt earlier in the day.

I slid my sweatshirt off, which left only my tank top underneath. I wasn't wearing a bra, and the impact on Parker was even more significant than I thought it would be. He kissed my neck and even trailed down to the neckline of my tank. I felt him tense as he whispered, "Avery, we can't..."

"Shhh, just a little longer," I pleaded, taking his mouth in mine again. I needed this tonight, needed this closeness to help make sense of everything I was feeling.

His willpower waned some more as he lifted me on to the bed. His body covered mine, and I took the opportunity to explore every inch of his muscled back until he grabbed my hand and held it in his as he continued to kiss me.

Slowly, the kisses became less hungry and more tender as he once again regained control of the situation. He pulled me up to the sitting position, still tenderly kissing my lips, and helped me put my sweatshirt back on.

I sighed when he suggested we go watch some TV and followed him out of the room. He continued to keep me close the rest of the night and didn't say a word about our study session until he walked me to the car.

I unlocked the door and turned to say goodbye when I felt his hungry lips capture mine. He backed me against the car, and my whole body caught on fire. After just a minute, he pulled back, but the look of desire in his eyes was startling.

"I'm not perfect, Avery, so don't think that wasn't the hardest thing I've ever had to do in my life. But… you're worth waiting for. And today, especially, it just felt wrong," he said softly with a rasp in his voice.

I knew he was right. I was trying to avoid the emotional intimacy I was still unwilling to give him. It wasn't fair to either one of us.

"You're right," I agreed as I kissed him one last time before getting in my car. He watched until I was out of sight, and then I took advantage of the next stop sign to text Jake to let him know I didn't need him to stay over anymore now that Issy was awake. He replied with a sad face and an "okay."

I felt relieved as I drove home, but the feeling was short-lived because Jake was already situated on the couch when I walked in my apartment. He stood up defensively when he saw the look on my face and explained, "I was already here when I got your text, so I just wanted to see you before I left."

I set my backpack on the table, trying my best to avoid eye contact with him. "Jake, what happened the other night can't…"

"Can't happen again. I understand," he said

quickly, interrupting me mid-sentence. "We both had a little too much to drink, and it crossed the line, I know. Just friends. I haven't forgotten."

I walked into the kitchen to get a drink, and he leaned on the counter to ask about my day. I filled him in on the mad dash to the lab that morning and made fun of both of my engineering professors.

He shared his day with me, too, and it was nice to just relax and laugh with him without all the usual tension between us. He made Issy's absence seem less staggering, and by the time he left I was actually grateful he had come by.

The next day I made sure to be five minutes early to the lab, and Russell was there again, mostly to check up on me, I think. He seemed pleased by my punctuality and didn't stay too long. My three classes for the day were easy enough, and I didn't even feel tired when I found Parker in the library that afternoon.

"Hey!" he said with a smile when I sat down. He leaned across the table and gave me a kiss hello. "How was your day?"

"It was good. Nothing really to report." I hadn't told him that I was late to the lab on Monday, so it seemed stupid to mention that I was on time today. "My Technical Writing class is going to be a breeze. What about you?"

"Ugh, and that doesn't even begin to describe it. My Tuesday, Thursday classes are miserable this semester. What's worse, they both include one-hour labs." He wrinkled his nose. He seemed to be a little more relaxed with me today, which was good.

"Well, you know how much I love lab work. Sounds fun." The sarcasm was dripping from my voice, and he laughed, knowing my hatred for it.

When he stopped, he finally noticed I hadn't pulled out any of my books. "Aren't you going to study?"

"Not really. I got everything done in the lab this morning. I just wanted to come by and say hi."

He seemed disappointed and surprised. Last semester I always stayed with him, even if I was finished for the day. For some reason today, though, I just wanted to get home.

"Is everything okay?" he asked with a weary voice.

"Of course," I assured him. "You just haven't seen me in school without being covered head to toe in stress."

His long sigh said a million things I didn't want to hear. "Can I come by when I'm finished?"

I hesitated. "I'm going into Asheville to do some shopping today, so why don't you just call me when you're done and we can meet up." I threw it out there a little too quickly and it didn't sound convincing, even to me.

"You're doing it again." His hurt was palpable.

"Please don't read into this. We spent so much time in the library last semester. I'm just a little tired of constantly studying. I know you have to, and that's fine. I'll just meet you later." I stood and grabbed my backpack. He stood too and walked around the table to take my hand.

"How is it possible that I'm looking right at you but still miss you so much?" he questioned in a resigned tone. I couldn't figure out why he was so hurt. I just didn't want to study, that's all. He was making me frustrated and irritable.

"I don't know why you are getting so upset about this."

He took my other hand in his and looked at me the way he always did, making me feel loved, yet this time I felt guilty all at the same time.

"You're not here with me, Avery. I can sense it. You're holding back again, and honestly, I'm still a little haunted by our conversation yesterday. I just want to spend time with you."

I sighed and touched his face. "And we'll see each other tonight. I promise." I gave him a quick peck on the lips and turned to leave. I saw his head drop as he sat back down to study.

My stomach turned, knowing I was the cause of his pain, but it wasn't enough to make me turn around and stay. I pushed through the big library doors and sucked cool air into my lungs. The feeling of suffocation was finally starting to leave my body, and I turned to go home, keeping my eyes averted from the spot that Parker and I usually shared.

Halfway across campus, I heard my name being called behind me. I turned around to see Jake jogging to catch up.

"Hey," he panted with his hands on his knees. "Wow, that was harder than I thought it would be. Whatcha up to?"

"I'm just going to get my car and head into Asheville. I'm feeling the need to get off campus for a little while," I explained, watching him pant. It was mildly amusing.

"Want some company?"

"Sure," I agreed a little too eagerly. I then remembered that Parker was going to meet me later. "I can only hang out for a little while. Parker's supposed to meet me when he's done."

"Sounds good. Come on, I'm parked at your place anyway," he said with a grin. Somehow he had managed to get his hands on a housing parking pass. I didn't ask how.

"So, did you make it to the lab this morning without my bad influence?" he asked as we walked, taking the opportunity to nudge me with his shoulder. I started laughing and nodded, telling him about Russell still checking up on me. I went on to tell him all about my other classes and was surprised how much I had to say when just minutes ago I had felt blank with Parker.

All the lines were blurring, and nothing made sense anymore. I used to feel nothing but comfort and peace around Parker, and now I just felt so guilty every time I saw him that all I wanted was to run away. With Jake, I could just pretend that every thing was fine and not have to deal with all the drama. He wasn't asking me every five minutes to open up to him, and it felt nice to have all my emotions safely tucked away in my head.

I looked up at him while we walked, and he shot me his signature smile, making me turn away blushing. Somehow he had done it, made me forget all the heartache and pain I used to feel whenever he was around.

Lord, I pray that You will bring to light what is hidden in the darkness and expose the motives of the heart. I pray that she sees You have set her free so that she can stand firm and never again be burdened with the yoke of slavery..."

23. CAUGHT

Parker met me at the coffee shop by the river just after eight and apologized profusely for it taking him so long. I assured him it was no problem and began rubbing his back as he sat down. He still seemed stressed and tense, and I felt for him.

"Your classes are that hard, huh?" I asked sympathetically as I tried to rub out the knots in his shoulders.

"Yeah, they are, but that I can handle. Feeling this distant from you is about to kill me," he replied honestly, looking strained as he glanced at me.

The guilt tore at my insides. "I'm right here, silly," I teased, continuing to rub his shoulders and shake them a little. He shot me a forced smile and put his hand on mine.

"To make matters worse, I have to leave this weekend for my monthly training. The timing just feels all wrong."

"When are you leaving?"

"As soon as I get out of class on Friday. Hopefully Sunday will be a short training day and I'll be back around dinnertime." He put his hand on my leg and rubbed it a little. "I'm coming straight to see you, so don't make any plans!"

I smiled up at him and put my head on his shoulder. He was right. The timing was all wrong, everything felt wrong. I wanted more than anything to click my heels together and go back to New Year's. It felt like a lifetime ago.

"You eaten yet?" he asked, looking toward the counter.

"Nope, I was waiting on you. I'm starved."

He leaned over and gave me a kiss, pinching my chin at the same time. "You know I love you, right?"

I nodded and kissed him again before we got up to make our order. I sighed as I held on to him in line; I wished so much I could love him back the way he deserved.

The next few days flew by as I eased back into the school schedule. I would run, then hit the lab, go to class and then meet Parker in the quad. Jake would still come by at night but only stayed for an hour or so just to talk and catch up.

I started to believe my own lies that I wasn't doing anything wrong and that it was perfectly fine for Jake and I to be friends. The guilt was less and less biting, and while still strained, things did seem to be getting better with Parker, or at least I thought so. He continued to press me on a regular basis to talk to him, but I kept insisting there was nothing to talk about.

He left on Friday right after class, but not before meeting me outside my Dynamics class to say goodbye. I felt a little awkward with my study group staring blatantly at us, but I kissed him anyway and told him I would miss him.

"If there was any way I could get out of this, you know I would."

"Parker, it's just a couple of days." His worry seemed excessive.

"I know. I just don't feel like I should leave you alone right now."

Heat stretched up my neck. He thought I was going to have another episode. It all made more sense now. I shook my head, realizing it was going to be exactly like it was with Cara.

"I'm not going to do anything," I said defensively, pulling away from him. "You could just ask me about it instead of insinuating what a horrible failure you expect me to be."

Parker looked stunned and then confused. "What are you talking about?"

"What are you talking about?" I answered, now wondering if I had jumped to conclusions.

"I am just worried because Issy is still gone and you've been so cold this week. Eventually those emotions are going to hit you, Avery, and I don't want you to be alone when they do."

I sighed as I realized what he was saying and immediately felt wretched because I knew I had already felt all those emotions… with Jake, not him. I could barely look him in the eye when I hugged him one more time and assured him I would be fine.

He kissed me softly and then turned to leave.

"Be careful!" I yelled out before he hit the exit doors and turned to give me a heart-stopping smile.

I slumped in my chair and put my face in my hands. I was such a jerk.

"Is that your boyfriend?" a girl next to me asked.

"Yes."

"Wow, he's really cute."

"Yeah, he is, and about the greatest guy you'll ever meet," I admitted, no longer really talking to her.

She smiled at me and then sat back in her chair because the professor had gotten there. I had no idea how I was going to concentrate in class.

"Get dressed! We are going out tonight," Jake ordered as he walked in the door. "We've done enough homebody stuff for one weekend."

Jake had come over on Friday and wouldn't leave when he found out Parker was gone for the weekend. He talked me into watching a movie he had rented and stayed until after I had fallen asleep.

Parker was able to call this morning and talk for about fifteen minutes. He asked me what I did last night, and while I was honest about watching a movie and turning in early, I didn't mention the company that had come over. I knew Parker would never understand that Jake and I had become really good friends.

"Jake, are you trying to be a male version of Issy, because I swear you sounded just like her right then."

He bounced on the couch next to me and then shoved me off. "Get dressed!"

I rolled my eyes but did as he said and got ready to go. I picked jeans and a silk top, trying to keep from looking too much like I was on a date. Knowing it was going to be hot at the bar, I opted to braid two chunks of hair on each side of my face and pull them together in the back.

Jake stood up when I walked out of the room and shot me an appreciative smile. "You look great!" he exclaimed, kissing my cheek as I approached him. I noticed he was becoming more and more affectionate as time went on, and since he had yet to cross the line again like he had the champagne night, I didn't bother to stop it. He grabbed my hand and led me out the door, letting it go for only a moment to lock the door behind us.

Since Caesars was so close, we just walked there, not wanting to bother with a car or designated drivers. I felt weird at first holding his hand, but he squeezed tighter when I tried to let go, so I didn't say anything.

The bar was packed when we got there, a testament to it being the first weekend school was back. I ran into at least twenty people I knew and would have easily gotten separated from Jake if his arm hadn't been firmly around my waist the whole time.

"Want a drink?" Jake asked when we finally made it to the bar.

"No, I'm good."

"Come on, Avery, it's just one drink," he coaxed, giving me a sad face.

"That's what you said last time," I reminded him, and he didn't press the issue, instead just ordered a beer for himself.

We were surrounded by people everywhere and fielded a million questions about where Issy was. Jake and I had decided before we came to stay cryptic on the details and just told everyone she was going to school in her hometown for the semester. Issy had told me about her father's ultimatum earlier in the week, and she was pretty devastated she was going to be held captive in her dad's house, taking classes at Western Carolina. I reminded her it was a small price to pay to get to return to Winsor in the fall.

My thoughts were interrupted by one of the guys from my apartment complex asking me if I wanted to dance. Jake glared at him and put his arm around me. He left before I had a chance to decline.

"What was that about?" I asked after the guy had run off.

"What? I'm watching Parker's back. I wouldn't want some random guy dancing with my girl," he answered playfully and then pulled me out to the dance floor himself.

I looked at him in disbelief as he pulled me close

to him. "I'm not some random guy," he whispered in my ear and winked at me. I felt my stomach fill with a million butterflies from both the feeling of Jake's breath on my ear and the reminder that I was still Parker's girl.

We danced for hours, only stopping to get drinks when we got too hot. I was really having a good time, and it felt invigorating to just escape from reality for a little while. We hit the bar again, and my face was flushed and hair damp from all the dancing. Jake moved to get the bartender's attention while I waited on a stool for my water.

"Avery!" I looked up when I heard my name and saw my friend from Dynamics waving as she walked over to me. "Wow, I never see you out anymore."

"Yeah," I agreed. "It's been a while."

"You look so pretty tonight. Have you lost weight?" she asked sweetly.

I knew she meant to ask that as a compliment. Most women liked that kind of thing, but I detested it. I hated any indication that people were noticing my weight whether positive or negative. It made me self-conscious and insecure. But, there was no need to dump all my baggage on her, so I just gave her the same response I did everyone when asked that question. "Nope. I pretty much stay the same size."

"Well, you look great. In fact, is that another boyfriend?" she asked with a snicker as she looked over to Jake at the bar.

I was horrified by her implication and knew my

face said as much. "No! We're just friends. He's my roommate's cousin."

She laughed and shook her head. "That's not what it looked like on the dance floor. But, hey, I'm not one to judge. I say more power to ya. He's hot too." She gave a little wave goodbye and a wink when Jake returned with our drinks.

"Who's that?" he asked as she retreated.

"No one," I said scowling, still shocked at what she had said. "I think I'm ready to go home."

"Did something happen?" He continued to look in her direction.

"No," I lied. "I'm just getting tired."

He quickly downed his beer and then led us out the door. I wouldn't hold his hand on the way home, and he looked at me questioningly, but didn't say anything.

He opened the door to the apartment and immediately fell on the couch. "Man, that was fun. I can't remember the last time I had so much fun at Caesars."

I didn't want to admit it, but I felt the same way.

"You know what it reminded me of?" he continued with a wink. "That night we all went to the Varsity, and I kissed you for the first time."

I threw my purse down on the love seat and sat down in a huff.

"Jake, why do you keep saying stuff like that? Just when I think we've finally got this friend thing down, you go and blur all the lines again." I felt torn and guilty and frustrated all at the same time.

"Maybe my lines have never stopped being blurry," he said, looking at me in a way that definitely did not scream friendship.

"I have a boyfriend!" I yelled, jumping to my feet, not sure who I was madder at, him or me. "An honest, good, and *faithful* boyfriend, which is more than I could say when I was dating you!"

Jake stood up angrily and got within an inch of me. "Don't do that! Don't put this back on me. I told you why I did the things I did and we got past it. But since you brought it up, have you ever stopped to wonder why you are still with him when you spend every night with me?"

My fury and the tension that always existed when Jake was around were too much to bear, and I lost all resolve. "Yes, I wonder!" I yelled back, the tears now running down my cheeks. "And I hate myself for it every day." I turned around, unable to face him.

He wrapped his arms around me tightly and nuzzled his face in my hair. "Then stop fighting it and come back to me," he whispered. "I miss you so much."

I stood there and cried, feeling the pit gripping at my feet, the darkness trying to make its way back up my body. Jake was holding me tighter and tighter as he ran his hands seductively up and down my arms. He began kissing my neck, and I suddenly felt an overwhelming need to flee. I rushed to my bedroom, locking the door behind me.

I heard Jake as he put his head to the door. "Avery, I'm sorry. Don't run away from me. It's just the alcohol talking, I promise."

I lay on my bed, still sobbing as I felt my heart breaking. Once again, it was my fault. I let it get to this point, and once again I had become a person I had no respect for. I shuddered as I thought of the quad that fateful day, and how familiar that feeling was becoming again. However, this time, I feared there would be no Parker to pull me out of it.

With the morning sun came some clarity and the feeling that I may have overreacted the night before. I had let a comment from someone I didn't even know that well make me feel cheap and guilty, and now I was starting to wonder why.

Jake was gone when I went for my morning run, but I wasn't surprised as I had heard him calling around for a ride last night. I ran by his car in the parking lot and shook my head. I was going to have to decide what I wanted, and soon, before I lost both of them, or worse, lost myself once again.

I felt my phone start to vibrate to signify an incoming text. It was from Jake.

"Please don't be mad at me," he wrote and added a sad face at the end.

I chuckled to myself and slowed to a walk so I could text him back. "I'm not. May have overreacted a bit."

"Good! Want to do dinner tonight?"

"Can't. Have plans with Parker."

He sent another sad face and then, "Okay, I'll call you Monday. I'm sorry."

"Me too," I texted back and put up my phone, returning back to my run pace. While I felt better about Jake, my stomach turned a little as I thought of Parker's homecoming tonight. Something in my gut told me things were never going to be the same.

I paced the living room as I waited for Parker's call. It was getting close to eight, and I still hadn't heard from him. Finally, the phone rang and I grabbed it after one ring.

"Hey! Are you home?" I asked a little too enthusiastically.

"No, babe, I so wish that was true. We just finished training and still have to go clean all our weapons before leaving. I don't think I'm going to be back for at least three more hours."

My heart sank, but I didn't want him to feel worse than he already did. "That's okay," I assured him. "You sound tired."

"Completely wiped out," he admitted. "We've been up since four in the morning with this exercise, and I can barely keep my eyes open. It's going to take a lot of coffee to get me home tonight."

"Parker?"

"Yeah?"

"What's an exercise?"

He laughed on the other end, but it felt empty as his exhaustion was apparent through the phone. "It's when we play like we're at war."

"Are you sure it's safe for you to drive tonight? You sound like you might fall over right now."

"I admit, I've thought about staying. Most of the guys here are," he acknowledged, sighing. "But I want to see you so bad, it seems worth it."

"Don't come back just for me! That's crazy, and I'll die of worry. Go get some sleep, and I'll see you after class on Monday. We can spend the whole night together."

"I feel like such a bad boyfriend."

"Don't say another word. I'll be fine. I'm going to find a good chick flick and do my nails. You just take care of yourself for once."

"Okay Avery, I think I may just do that. You're the best, you know that?"

I shook my head and felt my eyes tear up. I was absolutely not the best, not even close. "Go get some sleep."

We said our goodbyes and hung up the phone. I looked down at the outfit I had agonized over all day and started to pull it off. If I was going to watch a movie, it was going to be in my pajamas.

I finished getting comfortable and then went to put in the movie when I realized that it was still in my car. Throwing on some flip flops, I walked out the door, immediately feeling the chill of the wind. I hugged myself tightly and ran as fast as I could to my car, shivering the entire way.

Within minutes I was back on my couch with a blanket, trying to get warm again. I heard my phone buzz and ran to get it, thinking it might be Parker again. It wasn't.

"Why are you in your pajamas? I thought you had a date with Parker tonight." I stared at the text, wondering how he knew.

"Jake, are you stalking me?" I texted back.

"Lol. No. I came to pick up my car and saw your mad dash. What's the story?"

"Still out of town. Rescheduled for tomorrow."

I had barely put the phone back down when I heard my door open and saw Jake with a big grin on his face. He shut it behind him and fell on the couch next to me, resting his hand on my thigh. "So what are we doing tonight?"

I looked at him with my mouth open in disbelief. "I'm watching a movie," I said sternly. "You are going home."

He put his hand across his heart as if I had wounded him and then got up to grab a Coke out of the fridge. "Seriously, what movie is it?"

"Jake, I am being serious. We need a little space."

"Ah, come on, you said you overreacted last night."

"Yeah, so?"

"So, what's the big deal? I've always watched movies with y'all on Sunday nights."

"Jake, in case you haven't noticed, Issy doesn't live here anymore, and people are starting to get the wrong impression about us."

"Technically, Issy does still live here. But, fine, I'll just stay for an hour, I promise."

I rolled my eyes and then warned him if he said a word about my movie choice, he was immediately evicted. He agreed whole-heartedly and joined me back on the couch.

Almost two hours into the movie, I felt my stomach growl loud enough that even Jake heard it. "Skip dinner tonight?" he asked with his eyebrows raised.

"Yeah, I did. Want some pizza?" I asked as I grabbed my phone to make the order.

"Of course. I never turn down pizza."

I placed the order and then scowled when they said it would be at least forty-five minutes until they got there.

Jake looked up at me as I rejoined him on the couch. "I have to admit, this is a pretty good movie. I was worried when I saw how long it was," he said with a grin.

"It is, isn't it? I know how to pick'em," I beamed, feeling proud of myself. He shook his head and laughed, pressing play on the DVD player again. He leaned back on the couch and pulled me toward him. I started to resist, but he insisted it was more comfortable that way.

Twenty minutes later, there was a knock at the

door and we both jumped.

"That was fast," I said, rushing to my room. "Get the door, and I'll grab my wallet."

It took me a while before I found where I had set my purse, and I felt guilty knowing the guy was standing out there in the cold. I finally spotted it and started towards the door, pulling out the money as I spoke. "Sorry it took me so long, I couldn't find my pur…" I looked up and my heart stopped. Standing in front of my closed front door was a stunned Parker and Jake, who seemed almost amused.

"It wasn't the pizza," Jake said matter-of-factly.

I couldn't move, and immediately my heart raced so fast that I thought I might pass out.

Parker took one more look at Jake and then walked past me into my bedroom, glancing my way in the process. His face showed a combination of shock, hurt and anger. What I didn't see was the usual adoration that I had grown so accustomed to, and I felt a shiver go down my spine. I turned and watched him disappear and then slowly walked towards Jake.

"You should probably go," I whispered, my body still trembling from the shock.

"I'm not leaving you alone with him," Jake said sternly, glancing into my bedroom.

"Please, Jake, Parker would never hurt me. Just go. I begging you, please, go."

He must have seen the desperation in my eyes, because he grabbed his keys and started for the door. Before leaving, he turned back around and pulled me towards him, planting a kiss on my forehead. I cringed as he lingered there, his eyes never leaving the door of my bedroom. He finally let go and walked out the door, leaving me to wonder if Parker had just witnessed that scene, which appeared far more intimate than it actually was.

I took a deep breath and walked towards my bedroom, my heart pounding harder with each step. When I finally got there, Parker had his back towards me and was staring at the wall with his hands on his head. I could see that every muscle in his body was tense, and it was more than apparent he was fighting for control.

"Parker, it's not what you're thinking." I closed my eyes as I heard myself speak, remembering how painful those same words had been when Jake said them to me.

Parker didn't move from his stance, just asked two simple words. "How long?"

I started to get nervous, as I knew he was jumping to the wrong conclusion. "It's not like that. There's nothing going on," I pleaded.

Parker turned around, and his face showed an emotion I had never seen before. He was mad. Really mad. "How long?" he asked again, his voice louder.

When I didn't answer, he clarified, "How long has it *not* been what I'm thinking? Huh, Avery? How long have you *not* been hanging out with him ALONE in your apartment, watching movies together in your pajamas and doing God knows what else?" His voice raised each time I deflected the question, and I felt my hands start to shake as I realized this was a much bigger deal to Parker than I thought it would be.

"We're just frien--"

"HOW LONG?" I jumped when he yelled and answered before I even had the time register what I was saying.

"Since Issy's accident," I whispered.

Parker's face changed as he processed the information. I watched as he relived every conversation, every touch we had had since that night, and the magnitude of the betrayal hit me as I watched it hit him. He fell back, sitting on my bed for support. I felt sick to my stomach as I watched the pain on his face.

"I knew something was wrong," he whispered, his voice quivering a little. "My instincts were screaming at me, but I never imagined it was him."

His heavy sigh hung in the room, and the silence felt crippling. Finally he spoke under his breath, but I had to strain to even hear his voice. "Do not be yoked together with unbelievers."

I had no idea what he meant but felt the words must have been significant because he put his head in his hands when he said them. His resigned tone stung at my heart, and I reached for his hand, begging, "Parker, please."

He jumped away from me as if my hand seared him and walked to the other side of the room. I could see his body shaking, and I felt real panic for the first time that I was going to lose him.

"Why? It just doesn't make sense after how much he hurt you. Two months ago you couldn't even be in the same room with him without shaking." His body was still rigid and his voice still hard, but I could sense the hurt was starting to replace the anger.

"When Issy was in the hospital, we were there for each other, and the past just seemed to disappear."

He didn't like my answer; I could see that right away.

"I wanted to be there for you... tried to be there for you a million times. You pushed me away, wouldn't talk to me and completely shut me out." His exasperation resonated across the room.

"I didn't mean to shut you out. I just didn't know how to let you in. Jake offered friendship, and I took it."

Parker let out a stunned laugh, as if I had lost my mind. "Avery, you can't be friends with him! And if you believe you can, you're lying to yourself as much as you are to me. He's your first love; the only guy you've ever had a sexual relationship with." We both flinched as he said those last words, hurting him almost as much as they did me.

He closed his eyes as he fought to regain control again. "Did you even wait five minutes before inviting him over after I said I wasn't coming back tonight?"

"I didn't even know he was coming over. He just showed up."

"Are you sleeping with him?" His voice was cold

and harsh, matching the look in his eyes.

"No!" I yelled, feeling angry at him for the first time.

"It's a fair question."

"No, it's not, and it hurts me that you would even ask me that."

Parker just shook his head in disgust. "You have no idea," he scoffed, looking away from me again. "Did you kiss him?"

"No. I told you, it wasn't like that," I argued, my voice shaking now.

"Well, he obviously feels comfortable kissing you, so what am I supposed to think?" he retorted, matching the volume in my voice. It was just as I feared. He had seen Jake kiss me goodbye. I had nothing I could say to that. We stood staring at each other for what felt like an eternity before Parker sat back down on my bed and put his head in his hands.

I walked over to him and kneeled down in front of his legs, careful not to touch him this time. He looked up and his eyes were glassy. The anger seemed to be gone, and all that registered was hurt and pain.

"I won't share you," he whispered, his eyes piercing me.

"You're not," I pleaded, once again, trying to make him understand.

"You don't get it. Every moment you give to him is a moment that is ripped away from us. I am the one you should turn to when you're hurting. Not him. And the idea that I only get half of you because you've given the other half to him makes me sick. Can't you see that?" The anger was returning. He paused but didn't take his eyes off of me. "You can't sit on the fence. I won't take less than all of you. I won't move forward until I know we're on the same page."

He said what I always knew to be true and what I feared one day he would ask for. I hung my head, not knowing how to respond. I felt his hand on my chin as he tilted my head up to look at him.

"Why can't you let him go?" he asked painfully, his voice catching when he did.

I felt the tears flow freely as I whispered back, "I don't know."

He let go of my chin and stood. Before I even realized what was happening, I saw him grab his keys and head for the door.

"Wait, you're not leaving are you?" I asked, feeling a panic so severe it almost paralyzed me.

He opened the door to the apartment right as the pizza guy was about to knock. I saw his body go stiff and then he turned around to me, his mannerisms so cold and distant that I almost didn't recognized him. "I guess your pizza's here."

Seconds later he was gone, and my body was crushed with an emptiness exceeding any I had ever felt before.

"Lord, I pray You draw her to You. I pray that she may have the power to grasp how wide and long and high and deep is Your love for her…"

24. TRUTH

I couldn't seem to move from the bed as I replayed our conversation over and over in my head, reliving every word, every image and every touch. He was gone, and I had no one to blame but myself. I had once again succeeded in pushing another person away who demanded more from me than I was willing to give.

The smell of the pizza consumed the apartment, and I felt my stomach growl. I was still hungry but knew without question that if I took even one bite I wouldn't stop until I had purged all of it, hoping the emotion would go with it. As much as it appealed to me, I knew it wouldn't help. This ache was impossible to comfort.

I thought back to the first time I ever decided to try throwing up and shook my head. How naive I had been. It was a regional cross country meet, and we were all staying in a hotel the night before. They had a big buffet for us with lots of pastas and carbs for us to load up on. I ate what the other girls ate but kept hearing my mom's voice in my head telling me how bad pasta was for me. Almost out of spite, I ate more than I needed and felt uncomfortably full.

While the rest of the team was still in the lobby flirting with the boys, I snuck up to the room I had been assigned. I tried lying on my bed to ease the fullness, but it didn't help. I had recently read an article in Food Magazine that gave statistics on how many girls suffered from eating disorders. While the numbers were concerning, I still wondered if it really worked. There had to be a reason so many girls did it.

I shook my head, remembering clearly the minute I decided that I was going to try it. I wish someone had told me what I was getting into. I wish the article had said, "Stop, this is bondage!" I wish I knew then what I know now—that choosing this path would be the biggest regret of my life.

I heard my phone buzz and quickly reached for it, hoping for the best. I felt my chest heave in disappointment when I saw it was Jake.

"Are you okay?" he texted.

"I'm fine."

"Can I come over?"

"No."

I didn't give any more information, even when he asked please. I just told him I would see him tomorrow. I felt numb and had no ability to deal with another confrontation, especially one with Jake, because he always seemed to jumble my good sense. I stood up, suddenly feeling the need to pace, as unease hit me again. The smell of the pizza was getting overwhelming, and I could feel the temptation start to surface.

I decided I would take a shower; it always helped to ease the panic, but I stopped when I passed my desk and saw a large manila envelop on it. I slowly picked it up, trying to recall where it came from. I vaguely remembered seeing Parker with something in his hand at the door but dismissed it as soon as I saw his face.

I turned it over and opened the clasp, pulling out an eight by ten photograph. It had been printed on a hard backing, and my breath caught the minute I looked at it. The background was pitch black at the bottom, and starting from the top was a close up of rose petals, at least four layers of them. The petals were crisp white but showed signs of wear and tear as small lines encroached across their delicate surface. On each one, sat multiple water droplets, each a perfect circle, catching the light beautifully and making each petal more vibrant than I had ever seen before.

I slowly reached for the rose pendant around my neck and knew he found this picture just for me. I turned it over to see if the photographer was listed, but instead found a note on the back, written in Parker's masculine handwriting.

Avery,

I found this picture the other day after our talk and knew I had to get it for you. I know sometimes you wonder why I feel the way I do about you, when you are still learning to love yourself. You said you were flawed and damaged, but, my love, we all are. The storms in your life don't make you less than perfect; they make you beautiful and full of character, with the ability to use all you've learned to impact the rest of the world. I've been wishing for months there was a way you could see yourself through my eyes. Well, here it is. This is how I see you, and the rain has only made you more breathtaking.

All my love,
Parker

I stared at the note and read it again and again, unable to pull my eyes from his words. Devastation gripped me as I crumpled to the floor, still holding the last remnant of Parker's unconditional love for me. I had taken it all for granted, treated it with so little respect, when, in reality, it had been my life force.

I eyed the pizza box again and could almost feel it drawing me toward it. Suddenly, I was consumed by emotion and instantly felt nothing but contempt for the square box. It fueled me with unrecognized determination as I grabbed it fiercely, storming through the front door and out to the dumpster. It was as if I could physically feel the chains falling away from me as I moved.

Fury enveloped my body like a blanket, and I took out all the rage I'd buried on both the pizza box and the metal dumpster.

The sounds of my fists echoed through the night as I cursed myself for being such a coward. But it was more than myself I was angry at, and rage gripped me as I cursed my mom for every "helpful" comment she had ever made, cursed my father for making me feel that my sister was the pretty one and all I could offer was a sharp mind, cursed Issy for drinking so much and never caring about the impact it had on all of us, cursed Jake for how he hurt and betrayed me, yet refused to go away so I could get on with my life, and finally, I cursed Parker for always demanding so much more than I wanted to give, and for making me see life differently, which meant the status quo no longer satisfied me.

I kicked and slammed at the dumpster until exhaustion took hold and every emotion I had ever pretended didn't exist was left exposed on the concrete. I kicked it one more time for good measure and stalked back to my apartment, feeling somehow vindicated.

Several people had come out of their apartment, no doubt to ascertain the source of the pounding I had just given the dumpster. I didn't care and didn't offer an explanation as I walked past them to my apartment. I was done caring what everyone else thought. Done being the "Avery" everyone else wanted me to be. I walked by my mirror on the way back to my room. I looked different, even with the tear-streaked face, red nose and cheeks from the cold, and wild hair that went everywhere.

I smiled at my appearance, finding the humor in my madness and knew it was true… I was going to decide what I wanted for MY life, no one else.

The morning came with a renewed sense of determination as I hurried through getting ready for the day. I texted Russell that I would be in to take the morning sample but was only staying long enough to do so. I also informed him that I would continue to help until Dr. Davis could reassign me to the structures department for work-study but that he should start to look for a replacement.

"I knew you'd flake out on me again," he responded. "Don't worry about this morning, I've got it." It was a text message, but I could still hear the judgment in his words.

Where I would normally feel guilty or bad about myself, I just felt relieved. Now I could take care of what was really important.

I got in my car and headed north towards the Pisgah National Forest, feeling more and more conviction with each mile. My phone started buzzing, but I turned it off without even looking to see who the call was from.

The building looked exactly the same as it had when Jake took me here months ago, but I realized as

I drove up how different I had become since that day. I had been lonely and scared, and Jake offered all that I wanted in one beautiful smile. I parked my car and headed to the entrance. This was where I fell in love with him, and I knew it the minute my foot stepped off the platform that day.

The guys behind the counter shot me a smile when I entered the small building and asked if they could help me.

"I was wondering if I could go on a couple of the lines. Maybe go out for an hour or so?" I asked, getting my purse ready to pay for the adventure.

"I remember you, now. You're Jake's girl. Sure, I'll take you myself," he beamed, and I smiled back, thinking the irony of those words were almost too much.

"Thanks, um, how much do I owe you?" I asked, still holding my wallet.

"Oh, please, your money is no good here. Come on."

He was around the counter in a flash and pulling off harnesses for both of us. My stomach knotted in anticipation of doing this on my own, but I willed myself to continue. I needed to know I could do it.

The one mile walk felt different today, partly because I spent more time looking at the scenery, where as last time I was either staring at Jake or at my feet. The woods were amazing in a different way. They were stripped of their fall colors but still were a commanding presence that exuded strength and resilience. I marveled at the idea that being stripped down to nothing could offer more healing than simply living a life full of color. It certainly had for me.

We reached the first platform and my stomach lurched again as I looked down at the depths. It appeared farther this time without the leaves to block the view.

"You ready?" he asked after hooking me up to the line. I nodded and he stepped back, waiting for me to take the plunge. I took a deep breath and jumped, allowing the speed and adrenalin to make my body shiver in excitement. I kept my grip loose to get the full effect of the speed this time. The fear was gone.

My guide hit the platform seconds after I did and whistled after he got his footing. "Wow, you were way faster this time. You been practicing or something?" he asked, not hiding his admiration.

"No, just came in with a different frame of mind," I explained, smiling back. "I think I'm done, though."

"What? You just got started?"

"I know, but I have something else I need to do today." Part of me wanted to stay and do more lines, but I knew my next stop would take a while, and I had already accomplished what I wanted to by coming here.

He shrugged his shoulders and led me back to the trail that would get us back to my car. He asked how Jake was doing, and I told him all good things, not feeling the need to explain our relationship. With a quick goodbye, I was back in my car and heading west towards Mount Pisgah and the cabin that Parker had taken me to after Christmas. Feeling thankful I had gotten the address, in order to send a "thank you" card to the owner, I followed the winding road through the forest until the small cabin appeared through the trees.

Thoughts of Parker brought tears to my eyes as I thought of our horrible fight the night before. I looked towards my phone and wondered if he had called. With the strength of a thousand horses, I somehow managed not to check and got out of my car. I tried knocking on the cabin door, but no one was home. Just as well. My purpose for this trip was the trail anyway.

Grabbing my backpack with food and water, I followed the trail Parker had shown me. It was harder to navigate on my own, but I managed, scraping my palms and elbows in the process. After three and a half hours, and a body that ached with fatigue, I was finally at the top of the ridge, looking once again at the waterfall that consumed the view.

It seemed more powerful today, fuller, as if nature had directed all its fury into one place. I stared at it in awe as I watched it roll over the side of the mountain and onto the rocks below. Rocks so beaten by the ferocity of the water that it made you question their strength, but yet I knew that with one slip, those same rocks could take my life in second.

I walked over to the place where Parker and I had rested, and where I had shared my deepest secret with him. I could almost still feel his touch as I remembered his words to me that day. They were words of unconditional love, the likes of which I had yet to ever experience in my life. I knew I loved him too that day. I had been lost and broken, and with one word, Parker had given me everything I needed.

I sighed as I looked at my watch. It was getting late, and I had a long trip back down the mountain. I turned to look at the view one more time before my descent and nodded. Like the zip line, I had gotten what I needed by coming here.

It was approaching five in the afternoon by the time I reached my car again, grateful that the dropping temperatures had dried the sweat accumulating on my face.

I headed back to the road and backtracked to find the crossroad that would take me to the highway. Just as I approached the turn, I saw a huge meadow situated behind one row of trees. The sun was low in the sky, which cast a perfect golden glow over the dried grass.

I pulled off the road and climbed through the old log fence surrounding the property. There was no one around for miles, so I didn't think anything of it when I walked to the center and sat down. The grass was hard and crunchy, the effects of the cold winter apparent wherever you looked. I lay back and stared at the sky, soaking in the last warmth the setting sun had to offer. There was something else I had to do, and it couldn't wait any longer.

I turned on my phone for the first time since the morning and searched out her number.

"Hello?" my mom answered in her usual tone.

"Hi, Mom."

"Avery! Hey, hun, how are you?" she asked in her equally cheery voice.

My heart started racing, but today had been a day about overcoming fear, and I was not going to let it stop me now. "I need to talk to you. Do you have a minute?" I asked, determination resonating in my tone.

"Sure. Is something wrong?"

"Mom, I need you to know I love you, and I want a relationship with you. I also need you to know that relationship can only happen if we no longer discuss what I weigh, how I eat, how much I eat or how much I exercise. Is that possible?"

There was silence on the other end. "Mom?"

"I'm here," she answered quietly.

"I know you didn't realize what those words did to me, so I'm not angry at you, and I don't blame you," I continued. "I just need you to know now that they have to stop. I have to know you love me even if I'm not perfect."

"Of course I love you, honey. I just wanted the best for you. I didn't want you to end up unhappy with yourself," she explained, and I could tell by her voice she was crying.

"I know, Mom. Let's just find some new common ground and start from there. Okay?" I offered, knowing my mom didn't cope well with confrontation, and it was time to end the conversation.

"Okay, Avery. I can do that."

"I love you, Mom."

"I love you, too," she replied before hanging up the phone.

As I hung up the phone, I felt a surge of emotions fill me. I had spent most of my life hating who I was, constantly trying to be something better. For as long as I could remember, I wanted to be anyone else but me. I looked around the meadow, taking in the landscape that sat just below the picturesque mountain range and marveled at the beauty God had created. I thought back to the words I heard in the quad that horrible night. "Fearfully and wonderfully made," the pastor had said. "Darkness becomes light." Words that were from the Bible, words that Parker said were the very breath of God.

I remembered the Bible Parker's mother had given me, which still sat untouched in my purse. I ran to the car and pulled it out, hoping I could find the answers I so desperately sought.

As I found my place back in the meadow, I began to flip through the pages and noticed a small piece of paper that had fallen in my lap. The letter was from Parker's mom, and its words were like warmth on a snowy day.

Avery,

  Ever since Parker was a baby, I have prayed scripture over him and his future wife. When I met you at Christmas, I finally felt I had a face to go with those prayers. I have prayed that God protects you and guides you in your journey though life. I have prayed for peace in the midst of turmoil and strength in the midst of temptation.

  I have prayed that He let you soar on wings like eagles, but also that He keeps your path straight. I have prayed all these things because I believe that God's word never comes back void. The Bible says that it is by grace we have been saved, through faith in Jesus Christ. Avery, grace means unearned favor. It's in your imperfection that God's glory is revealed. If you want to know Him, all you have to do is accept His perfect gift of love. Don't worry about what to do and how to do it. When the Lord calls to you... you will know."

In His love,
Amy

I felt my heartbeat start to pick up as the need to know Him pulled me with an unexplainable force. I went to my knees and spoke, feeling somewhat insecure, as I had never done this before.

"Jesus," I spoke as I looked around. "I don't really know where to begin or what to say. I never really even knew who You were until I met Parker and his family, but part of me wonders if that was Your doing as well. They tell me You want to know me, and that You love me unconditionally—that You

362

know my thoughts and my actions and still love me. I've never understood unconditional love until I met Parker. Jesus, if that's what You are offering to me, I want it. I know that means You expect all of me, and I'm ready to give it. No more fear, right? I'm so flawed, and I feel lost in darkness almost all of the time. Please come save me from this pit I've let myself sink into. I don't want to be here anymore."

I let out a sigh and let the tears flow down my cheeks without remorse. I welcomed them, welcomed all that they symbolized and all that was being cleansed in me. It was in that meadow that I felt the one thing I never thought possible—I felt the unconditional love of Jesus Christ, and surprisingly, an unexplained love for myself.

"Lord, may Your love give her strength to become the woman I know You want her to be…"

25. CLARITY

My heart felt like it was in overdrive the entire way to Asheville, as I rehearsed my speech to him over and over in my head. Everything was so crystal clear that I wondered how it ever seemed so muddy. I parked the car and boldly walked to his front door. It was finally time to do this.

It took me knocking three different times before Jake finally answered the door. He looked tense and agitated, like he had just spent hours pacing the floors. It took him a second to register that it was me, and then he pulled me into his arms tightly while he shut the door behind us with his foot. He buried his face in my hair as he held on to me.

"Where have you been? I've been going out of my mind! I've called you a million times. I went to your apartment twice. Baby, you can't do that to me," he exclaimed as he pulled back to look at me.

I shrugged and pulled away from his embrace. "I needed to get some things worked out in my head," I explained.

He wasn't satisfied not touching me and reached

out to take my hand in his while he whispered, "And?"

I looked at him clearly, taking in the face that had haunted my dreams since the day we met. I felt every emotion that I had buried, and the anger, the hurt and the love I had once felt for him came rushing back. "You hurt me," I stated with more force than I intended.

He could see the tears in my eyes and pulled me closer to him. "I know," he whispered, his voice full of regret.

"You devastated me," I clarified, my voice a little softer this time.

My words seemed to be physically hurting him as I said them, but he only responded by pulling me closer and running his hand over my cheek. "I know."

I wasn't finished. He had to know how I felt. I was tired of hiding, tired of letting everything pass with a smile. "I gave you everything, trusted you explicitly, and you shattered my heart into a million pieces. And worse, you turned around and tied my hands together so I couldn't even pick them up."

He finally let go and ran his fingers through his hair in exasperation. "Avery, I know!" He came back to me quickly after saying that and took my face in his hands. "I didn't want to love you," he whispered. "But, I couldn't let you go, because I think I always knew, deep down, you were it for me."

I took his hands off my face and held them firmly in mine. "Jake, someone did want to love me, and he meticulously picked up every piece of my shattered heart and put it back together with such care and precision that now it's stronger than it's ever been."

His face looked sad as he pulled me close to him, wrapping my arms around his waist as he started to caress my face once more. "I see that. I see how strong you've become. I see that you and I are exactly where we need to be to make this work. It's the first time in my life I'm looking forward to my future. I promise you, Avery, this time I will handle that heart with so much more care."

Somehow the conversation had turned, and I was standing there in Jake's arms as he leaned in to place a soft kiss on my lips. He pulled back, smiling, thinking he'd won, but I didn't want this. The blinders were off, and I knew without question that his arms were the last place I wanted to be.

"Jake," I said, putting my hands on his chest and stopping him as he came in for a deeper kiss. "I didn't come here to talk about our future. I came to finally say goodbye to the past."

My words took a minute to register, but when they did, he grabbed my wrists and pulled me back to him, pinning my body between himself and the wall. His demeanor had shifted so quickly that I froze in stunned silence as he spoke to me.

"You don't mean it; you're confused and scared, because you don't trust me anymore. I get it. It's all I thought about last night, because I knew he'd manipulate you into making the wrong choice."

His voice sounded desperate as he leaned against me, nuzzling my neck with his lips as he spoke. His body weight was crushing, and my heart started to race as I felt my breathing become labored. He took my reaction as encouragement and started kissing my jawline as he spoke.

"You've just forgotten," he purred. "Forgotten how great we are, how much you love me." He paused for just a second and then continued, "I love you, Avery, you have to know that; I'll never let you down again."

With those last words, he pressed his lips to mine, forcing them open as he imposed his body on mine. When I didn't respond, he got more eager and more aggressive, squeezing my wrists to the point where they throbbed. I moved underneath him, trying to get any space I could. Butterflies surged in my stomach, but not because it felt good or exciting, but because it felt wrong, so wrong that I somehow found the strength to turn my head enough to stop the kiss and mumble, "Jake, stop. You're hurting me."

His body went rigid as he set his forehead on the wall behind us. "And what do you think you're doing to me?" he asked, his voice cracking as he did so.

He slowly loosened his grip, and the blood rushed back to my fingers, bringing relief and pain at the same time. He backed away from me, allowing my lungs to take in a full breath of air, and slumped over to the couch to sit down.

I took a deep breath, calming my pounding heart

and sat down next to him, taking his hand in mine. "I fell in love with him," I said softly, hoping those words would explain it all.

"You used to be in love with me," he stated flatly, looking up at me with his piercing green eyes.

"I was obsessed with you. So much so that I allowed it to infiltrate every aspect of my life. I would have been anything you wanted me to be, done anything you asked of me, just to be with you. Even if it meant losing myself completely."

"Baby, that's what love is."

"I used to think so," I explained, "but now I realize it is so much more. As much as you think you love me now, you don't." He started to interrupt, but I continued, cutting him off. "You don't know me. I'm just starting to get to know the real me."

"And you think he does? Know you, that is," he asked, contempt dripping from his mouth.

"I think it doesn't matter. What matters is that I love myself enough to do what's best for me."

"And what do you *think* that is, Avery?" His words were full of bitterness as he looked at me.

"Letting you go," I stated softly. His face immediately changed as disbelief and anger set in. I made sure he kept eye contact with me as I continued, "And if you care about me as much as you say you do… you'll let me do that."

He stared at me for a long time as if daring my eyes to say what my mouth just did. I held my ground, matching his silence with my own, never taking my eyes from his. He finally shook his head and jumped off the couch to walk away. I didn't turn to look at him and jumped when I heard the bathroom door slam behind him.

I stood up and took a deep breath, feeling relief cover me as I left his apartment. I whispered, "Goodbye, Jake," before closing the door behind me for what I knew would be the very last time.

The tears streaked down my face as I turned out of his parking lot. But I knew, no matter how hard it was to put him behind me, what lay ahead held so much more promise. That was, of course, if I hadn't already lost it.

It was only a ten-minute drive between Jake's and Parker's apartment, but it gave me the time I needed to regroup. I had no idea how Parker would react or if he would even see me at all. None of the messages on my phone had been from him, meaning he wasn't ready to talk, but I prayed he wouldn't refuse me in person.

Unlike at Jake's, his door opened after the first knock, but my heart fell when I saw Randy in front of me.

"Is Parker here?" I asked tentatively.

He scowled at me but stepped out of the way so I could come through the door.

"What did you do to him?" he asked, his tone not hiding its accusation. "I've never seen him so messed up."

I didn't respond, but looked down the hall

towards Parker's room. The door was shut.

Randy followed my eyes and let out a deep sigh. "He's not here. Left before I even woke up, and I haven't seen him all day."

"Do you know where he is?" I asked, trying to keep my voice from pleading like I wanted to.

"I don't know, probably studying. His life isn't going to stop just because you broke his heart," Randy spat, not even trying to hide his disdain for me.

I didn't blame him. I would have felt the same thing for anyone who hurt Parker. I thanked him and turned to walk out the door.

"You're not good enough for him," he shouted before I was able to shut the door.

I stopped in my tracks and opened it back up so I could face him. "Yes, I am. It just took me this long to realize it," I said with a small smile, keeping my eyes directly on his.

He seemed taken aback and didn't say another word as I shut the door. I felt a little nervous. If Randy's reaction had been any indication of what this evening was going to be like, I had a feeling the next person whose heart would be breaking would be my own.

The thirty minutes from Asheville felt like a lifetime, but finally I reached my apartment and parked the car. The sun had almost completely set, but there was still enough light in the sky to quickly make my way to the quad. If he had gone to class today, he would probably be in the library studying.

I walked with determination, eager to get there before he left. The library was the first building that came into to view as I approached the grassy area of the quad. I smiled as I remembered all the time I had spent there with him, laughing and teasing each other while we studied. I looked over to our spot, where he had kissed me for the first time, and felt deflated when I saw it taken by two other students catching a quick nap. Everything I looked at reminded me of him, and I started to wonder how I ever questioned his place in my life.

I turned the corner, my eyes searching for the bench I sat on the night we first met. I wanted to relive that moment with him in my mind and knew sitting there would calm my sizzling nerves.

But it, too, was occupied, only this time it wasn't by a stranger, but by the only man I wanted to see.

Parker had his elbows on his knees and his hands clasped, with his forehead resting on them. He looked defeated, and I started to cry, knowing I had done that to him. He had found me in the same place months ago and lifted me to the heights, and now here he sat, in my place, as broken as I was that day.

I approached him slowly, not wanting to ruin the opportunity I had been given, and knelt in front of him so that I could be face to face with him. There was a single tear running down his cheek, and he looked surprised when our eyes made contact with one another. He didn't recoil like I expected him to, but waited, looking intently at me.

"Hi," I said softly, but he didn't respond. I wasn't surprised. Small talk wasn't what he wanted from me.

I took a deep breath, wondering how I could have forgotten all the words I rehearsed over and over. Instead of panicking, I spoke directly from my heart.

"If I had realized when I met you that you intended to turn my world upside down, I may have tried a little harder to resist all your charm."

He didn't move, but I knew he was listening.

"I know I hurt you and believe me, I don't think anyone on earth is angrier at me than I am. But, in some ways, I'm glad last night happened, because it woke me up and made me face things that I had been denying for years. The biggest one being that I am a complete mess. Half the time I don't know what I want or who I am or even why I'm here at Winsor.

"But you, you never cared if I had all those things figured out. It didn't matter if it was a good day or bad day, or if life had me so messed up I couldn't see straight, because you loved me. It didn't make sense to me, and with each passing day I started to wonder when the ax was going to fall, because I knew at any moment you would wake up and see how wrong you were. But that day never seemed to come, and even when I exposed all my demons, you didn't run away but pursued harder, wanting even more of me. I grew up in a house of pretenders, and you wouldn't let me pretend with you. It terrified me. So much so that I did the only thing I know how to do… run."

I stopped for only a moment so I could catch my

breath as I felt the tears start to find their way down my cheeks. I knew I was about to lay it all on the line, and the fear I had conquered earlier tried to slip back in. I pressed on, though, knowing I had to say it.

"Parker, I love you, and I have for a really long time. I've just been too afraid to admit it, too afraid to be that honest and vulnerable with someone. But, I get it now. I prayed today, for the first time, and finally understand what you've been talking about. I finally see that I am worthy to be loved and that I don't have to be perfect because Christ is perfect.

"I don't know what all that entails, but I know I want to take that journey with you. I know I messed up, and I deserve to lose you, but if there is any way you will let me try and earn your trust again, I am begging for that second chance. I'm going all in, not holding anything back this time, I promise."

He still hadn't moved, and I sat there shaking but kept to my word and didn't pull back. If he was going to reject me, at least I would know that I gave it everything I had. I reached out to touch his cheek and said the words again. "I love you, Parker. Please, please, forgive me for being so blind."

His embrace happened so fast it almost knocked me over. Elation penetrated every part of my being. His arms were strong and safe, and I knew I belonged there for the rest of my life.

He cupped my face and pulled back just enough to look in my eyes. "You're all in?" he questioned, making sure he had heard me right.

I smiled, my eyes conveying all the love and faith I had in him. "I'm all in."

He smiled back, and in his eyes, I saw he had forgiven me. "You never lost me," he said as he wiped the tears from my face. "You just had to finally open your eyes before you could find me."

I hugged him again as tightly as I could. He pulled me back and then kissed me gently, his warm lips sealing what I think I'd always known since the first night his hand held mine, that I would love this man for the rest of my life.

"And, Avery…" he stated after we pulled apart. "We're changing your locks immediately."

I started laughing as I nodded in agreement, embracing him even tighter than before.

It was as if my life had converged to this one moment. Christ had loved me unconditionally, giving Himself to me fully before I was even ready to return it. Through that love, I was able to see in myself a person worth loving, a person who was worth leaving behind destructive people and behaviors to pursue a life of freedom and promise. I no longer was going to find my value in what others thought of me. Parker had shown me my value in Christ; and as we sat there holding on to each other, I could honestly say, for the first time ever, that I believed him.

EPILOGUE

I lay quietly on the grass, soaking up the May sun as I waited for Parker to meet me there after his last final. Mine had been done for days, and to my joy, I had managed to pull the 4.0 GPA required to get off probation. I had also found my second love—structures. I spent the last three months in the structures department helping graduate students work on building multiple things for state-wide competitions. Our latest project was a canoe, and I'm proud to say that ours was one of only ten that actually stayed above water for the entire race. Dr. Davis was thrilled.

It had also been four months since my last episode. I almost expected to never be tempted again once I became a Christian, but that wasn't the case. The temptations were still there. The lies I had believed for so long still lingered, but it no longer felt hopeless, and I knew one day God would deliver me from this. In His timing. More than anything, I knew that secrets were tools the enemy used to keep me in bondage, so I tried my best to tell Parker every time I was tempted. I also promised to tell him if I ever again had an episode. Honesty meant freedom.

Parker had encouraged me to start seeing a counselor on campus, and she was really helping me find alternate means of coping when life started to feel stressful and out of control. I also learned that dieting only exacerbated my problem and found volume control was the best deterrent I had for binging. I chuckled to myself as I thought of the goodbye ceremony I had for my scale. It was my counselor's idea, and I have to say not a day goes by that I'm not thrilled I finally chucked that thing. It had held me captive for way too long.

A shadow crept over my face, and I knew without looking that it was Parker. I pulled him close for a lingering kiss, knowing each day I fell more and more in love with him.

"How was it?" I asked enthusiastically, so glad we were both finally be done and could get the summer started. We had planned a month long road trip that included stops at both of our parents' houses.

"I survived," he said as he pulled me up off the grass. "I kept getting distracted by thoughts of you!"

"Me? Well, I won't complain," I teased as I threw my arms around his neck to kiss him.

He smiled back at me and then looked a little nervous. He pulled me in for one more kiss and then started, "Avery, you know I love you. I have since the first time I saw you. And every day we spend together, I am more and more sure that we are meant to be together forever. You inspire me and make me want to be a better person, not just for myself, but also for you, so I can be the kind of man you will love for a lifetime. The thing is, I'm impatient, and I want that lifetime to start now, so…"

My breath caught as I watched him drop to his knee and pull out a small black box. "Avery Elizabeth Nichols, will you do me the honor of walking through this crazy world with me, allowing me to love and adore you for the rest of our lives?"

I didn't need even a second to respond. "Yes," I answered without hesitation. "Only if you let me love and adore you right back."

He pulled out the ring, a small round diamond on a delicate gold band, and placed it on my finger. The students who had witnessed our display began to clap as Parker swung me around and kissed me, his enthusiasm apparent to everyone around us.

"I love you," he said with a grin, staring deep into my eyes. "With everything I am."

"I love you, too," I whispered back.

A NOTE TO MY WONDERFUL READERS:

I hope you enjoyed Avery and Parker's story. Please take a moment to leave a review on Amazon. Your feedback is critical to us self published authors.

Book 2 in the Winsor series, Shackled Lily, is available on Amazon. See how Issy's life is changed by that fateful New Year's Eve party.

The Winsor Series concludes with Jake's journey in Splintered Oak, also available on Amazon.

And don't miss my Winsor spinoff, Mercy's Fight. Available Now!

I'd love to hear from all of you. Connect with me on Facebook to hear all about my upcoming projects:

https://www.facebook.com/tlgraybooks

Or sign up for updates on promotions and new releases via my newsletter at http://www.tlgray.com

ABOUT THE AUTHOR

Tammy L. Gray is the kindle best selling author of the Winsor series and Mercy's Fight. Her mission is to provide clean, culturally relevant romances that incorporate messages of hope and healing.

When not chasing after her three amazing kids, Tammy can be spotted with her head in a book. Writing has given her a platform to combine her passion with her ministry.

Tammy L. Gray has lots of projects going on. For all the latest info, visit her website at http://tlgray.com

I'd love to hear from all of you! Come join me on Facebook at https://www.facebook.com/tlgraybooks or twitter @tlgraybooks